WITH

Prologue

Winterborn, Kansas 1885

Zoe Bradshaw walked into the sweltering bedroom, dread filling her heart. Addy and her husband lay on the bed, their nightclothes soaked with sweat. "You rang the bell?"

Addy whispered, "John's gone."

Zoe's hand flew to her throat. She stared at the middle-aged man, lying still as death. "I just checked him a few minutes ago. Why didn't you call—"

"He took a long, deep breath and stepped over."

Moving closer, Zoe gently closed the deceased's eyelids, whispering, "Rest in peace, John."

"He's in God's care now."

Zoe still remembered that cold Kansas winter morning when John had accepted God's gift of salvation. She and Addy had been young girls. Kneeling beside her best friend, Zoe held tightly to her hand. Addy was more sister than friend. They had walked to school every morning, carried each other's books and lunch pails, shared their dreams. Addy knew everything about Zoe, and Zoe knew everything about her. The dam burst and tears rolled down Zoe's cheeks. John and Addy only had the fever a few days. How could such a small sickness take John? Addy would be brokenhearted, and her four children devastated. Addy's hand tightened in Zoe's. "You have to do something for me."

"I'll take care of the services, the wake——"

"No. Send for Cade."

The mention of Addy's brother stopped Zoe's tears. She lifted her head. "Don't bring him back here, Addy. Please. I'll take care of everything. I'll look after the children and you." Zoe had finally gotten Addy's brother out of her heart. Six years ago she had married Jim Bradshaw, the mercantile owner. Jim hadn't brought out the same giddy emotions that Cade could, but they had had a good life. A gratifying life. Together they had run the mercantile. When Jim was shot and killed a year ago in a senseless robbery, she had been able to go on. Addy had seen her through the first few months of grief. Zoe had begun to look forward to what each new day had in store, before Addy and John both took ill with the fever.

"I need my brother, Zoe. Cade was young and restless when he rode out of here fifteen years ago. He's a different man now."

Perhaps, but Zoe didn't want him back in her life. Not ever. Stepping to the open window, she called Brody, Addy's oldest son. The boy came running.

"I need you to go into town and get some help——"

"Ma?"

She shook her head. "Just tell Gracie I need help right away. Ask Holly to keep Will and Missy outside until you get back."

The boy left at a run.

Turning back to Addy, Zoe forced a normal tone. "What possible good would it serve to bring Cade back? I'm widowed. Together, you and I can raise the children. They're already like my own."

Addy's feverish hand sought Zoe's. "I want Cade to decide who'll raise my children."

"You're talking nonsense. You're not going to die—John was weaker. You'll be fine soon." Her gaze avoided John's lifeless body lying next to Addy's.

"Tell Cade…" Coughing, Addy sat up and Zoe spoon-fed her drops of cool water. When the spasm subsided, her friend dropped back to the pillow and closed her eyes. "You must do this for me, Zoe."

"Of course." When the crisis passed and Addy felt better, the promise would be moot. "If anything happens, which it won't, I'll send for him." Curiosity made her wonder why Addy would even ask such a thing. Cade was a bounty hunter, a man with no roots and, if you asked Zoe, no heart. Addy's children were like her flesh and blood, and Addy knew Zoe could never have children of her own. The fever must have addled her reasoning.

Zoe sat quietly beside the bed in the airless room. Outside, darkness closed in around the small log house. Gracie, the mayor's wife, would feed the children supper. Winterborn took care of its own. *Please, Lord, don't take Addy. I've made it without Jim, but if I lose Addy too...*

Addy's eyes flew open and fixed on the ceiling. Zoe leaned closer. "A little more water?"

"Cade. Tell him I love him, and I understand why he did what he did to help Ma and Pa."

"Addy, please. You're going to be fine. You can't die. I couldn't live without you." Zoe turned away briefly to wring out a cool cloth, and when she turned back, Addy's eyes were closed.

Stepping back, she straightened, her eyes automatically checking for the slow rise and fall of Addy's breathing. Leaning closer, she frowned. Throwing back the light sheet, she bent her head to Addy's chest and listened for a heartbeat.

The only sound that met her ear was the buzzing noise of the cicadas outside the window.

Chapter One

"Well, if that don't beat all. Cade Kolby, showin' up after fifteen years as if he hadn't been gone a day." Sawyer Gayford shifted in his chair to watch the town's famous prodigal son ride in.

Roy Baker, editor of the *Winterborn News,* elbowed the dust from the front window of the barbershop and craned his neck. "Never saw anything like it. Look at him. You'd swear he didn't know he was the most feared bounty hunter in Kansas."

"There's your headline this week, Roy," Sawyer said. "'*Kolby Shows Up for His Sister and Brother-in-Law's Deaths*', only they been in the ground a week."

Roy snorted. "This *week*? Cade coming home will be news for months to come."

"Kolby left as a boy, but he's coming back a man." Walt Mews motioned for Roy to sit back down in the barber chair. "Looks like he's been rode hard and put away wet."

Sawyer spat tobacco juice in a tin can he carried. "Heard tell he's shot and killed ten men."

"Some say twenty," Roy said.

Walt snipped the final bits of hair around Roy's ear. "More like fifty." Then he shook out the barber cape. Reaching into his pocket, he plucked out a coin and flipped it to Roy. "You win. I bet he wouldn't come."

"I knew he would," Roy said, chuckling as he pocketed the windfall. "Mac and Senda raised him right."

"Humph. He's ornery, if you ask me. Run him off once with a shotgun for tying my cats' tails together," Sawyer complained. "Nearly killed each other afore I got 'em loose."

"He was full of it, all right," Walt agreed, glancing out the front door.

Adolescent boys playing marbles around the hitching post abandoned their shiny agates and shooters and raced to watch the arrival of Winterborn's most notorious citizen.

"He wasn't all that bad as a kid," Walt mused. "When my Edna hurt her back, he showed up to weed her rose garden. Then he sat a spell with her to eat the sugar cookies she baked him. Seems like he was a right thoughtful young'un."

Sawyer grunted. "The boy's made hisself quite a reputation."

"The missus don't hold with all that killin', but I say a man's got to do what he's got to do." Walt closed the shop's door. "A man with a price on his head expects trouble."

Roy snickered. "That little redhead's been in a snit for fifteen years, thinking he wasn't going to show up. The girl's ill-tempered as a hornet. The wife sent me over to the store this morning for flour and oatmeal, and Zoe nearly took my head off."

"Hard to believe she was sweet on Cade at one time."

Sawyer nodded. "Yeah, you'd think she'da had better sense."

Walt straightened the shelf beside the mirror in front of his barber chair, lining up pungent-smelling hair tonics alongside each customer's personalized mug, painted by Edna Mews's questionable artistic hand. "Zoe's daddy, may his soul rest in peace, would've stripped the hide off Cade if he'd known those two were sweet on each other."

Roy got up to stretch. "He knew. He just couldn't do nothin' about it."

"I say it's good Kolby left when he did. Zoe might not have married Jim Bradshaw if he'd stuck around," Walt said.

The men looked toward the front window as Cade's brown-and-white pinto trotted by.

Sawyer shook his head. "Wonder how long he's gonna stay?"

"Just long enough to find his sister's brood a good home, I'll wager." Walt patted his pocket. "I got a silver dollar says he's not planning to raise those kids. Men like Kolby don't stay anywhere long."

"Times are hard. Won't be easy to find a family eager to take on four extra mouths to feed," Sawyer said.

Roy lifted a shoulder. "I heard Zoe wants the kids, but I don't know how she thinks she could take care of 'em. Jim left her a mountain of debts when he died, and she can't keep the wolf from the door as it is."

Walt polished his spectacles with a cloth, his eyes still following the rider. "I heard she's got some real financial woes with the store. That little woman's seen her share of trouble."

Roy scratched his head. "It'll be interestin' to see how she and Cade take to each other after all these years."

Sawyer chuckled as he got up and put on his battered hat. "Yep. Real interestin'."

Chapter Two

A grin played at the corners of Cade's mouth as he rode through town. Winterborn hadn't changed.

Old Man Thompson peeked out the land office window, checking his watch as though he had some place to be. Walt was looking out the barbershop window, making bets on the chances of him showing up. Cade chuckled, thinking about how he and Ben Pointer had often snuck Walt's *Police Gazette* out of the shop and read it behind the livery.

Bet my last silver dollar that same row of mugs with Edna's silly pictures is still on the shelf in front of Walt's chair. His grin widened when he thought of those mugs. Bless her heart, no one thought of Edna as an artist except Edna.

Milly Mason's millinery boutique still sat above the barbershop. Ladies favored the outside entrance to avoid the "unsavory" atmosphere of Walt's shop below. The men's salty language had put a bloom on many a sensitive cheek.

Unless someone had struck gold, very few in town could afford Milly's fancy Eastern hats, and it appeared that fifteen years hadn't changed her clientele.

Nodding, Cade graciously doffed his hat to a couple of well-dressed ladies about to enter the millinery.

The image of his mother ogling Milly's hats weighed heavily on his mind. Senda Kolby wasn't able to afford even the ribbons from one of Milly's bonnets, much less the whole fine creation. But she never complained. As she said, she prayed for the best, expected the worst, and thanked God for what he gave her.

The smile faded. He could afford a hundred bonnets now, but Ma wasn't around to enjoy them. Regret hit him hard. Word of his folks' death had reached him six weeks after their burial. Pa had died from a farm accident; Ma, a month later, from pneumonia. He tried not to think about family. Or settling down to a good life with kids and a wife. He would take care of Addy's business and clear out as quick as possible. Winterborn wasn't home anymore.

The mare picked her way slowly down Main Street, approaching Ben Pointer's blacksmith shop and livery stable. The sign over the door said Ben would shoe horses and oxen, sharpen plows, and repair farm implements.

"Ben Pointer and Sons" registered. Ben was a couple of years older than Cade. Did he have boys big enough to help? A lot could happen in fifteen years.

The jail came into sight. Was Pop Winslow still sheriff? Was he still handing out horehound sticks? Memories gripped Cade, deepening the ache like a branding iron hot in his belly. He'd known coming back wasn't going to be easy.

Up ahead, the old swing he and his sister, Addy, had played on still hung next to the windmill. Worn and frayed, the rope swayed loosely in the late summer breeze.

Memories rushed back, and he blinked hard to clear the mist from his eyes. Him and Addy playing at the jail as youngsters or diving into the swimming hole. But now Addy was dead. Only thirty-two years old, and she was gone. Distance and years had failed to dim the closeness they shared. He might not have come back home as often as he should have, but he'd always known she was there. Each night as he'd gone to sleep in a cold bedroll before a waning campfire, he'd taken comfort in the thought that he had people who cared: Ma, Pa, and

Addy—a family waiting for him, when or if he came back. Somehow it had made the days and nights more tolerable.

Now Ma and Pa were gone. Addy was gone.

The corner of his eye caught a glimpse of a redheaded woman entering the drugstore. His quickening heartbeat caught him off guard. For a moment he thought it was Zoe. It wasn't. He settled back in the saddle, his grin resurfacing. Zoe Bradshaw. Now there was a woman not easily forgotten. Visions of a cloud of red hair, damp and tangled after an afternoon swim in the river, caused a twinge. Fifteen years, and he still hadn't met a woman to match her.

Her message the previous week had been curt. "Get your worthless hide to Winterborn. Now."

Worthless was a little harsh; he wasn't *worthless*. Some would even say he was doing a civic duty by bringing in a ruthless killer, but in Zoe's eyes he wasn't a man of his word. The thought still stung, but he supposed he'd earned her disrespect. When he'd ridden out all those years ago, he'd promised to come straight back. "Straight back" turned out to be fifteen years.

He'd meant to come back, eventually, but after so many years passed, with as many outlaws looking for him as he was for them, he'd figured it was better to keep going for a while. Next thing he knew, Addy had written and said the redhead was marrying Jim Bradshaw. Zoe and Bradshaw? Now that provoked him. She hadn't waited for him—she'd gone and got herself a bridegroom. So who was fickle? He'd decided right then and there she wasn't worth grieving over. If he hadn't had to come back on account of his nieces and nephews, he wouldn't be here now.

Reining his horse to a halt, Cade eyed the Bradshaw General Store, located down the street past the butcher shop. It looked almost the same with only one difference.

The mare shied, her tail swishing away a pesky fly as he stared at the wooden sign creaking in the breeze above the store. The *Winterborn News* office had moved into the upstairs floor, where sleeping rooms had been. Addy had written that Zoe had kept the store after her husband's death and was living in the back quarters. Most likely that's where he'd find the children. He squirmed, dreading the thought of facing the spitfire after all these years. He'd sooner fight a wildcat bare handed.

Red. She'd always be Red to him. He chuckled. Heck of a woman.

Children's laughter caught his attention. Four boys and three girls played in front of the store, rolling a large hoop with a stick. Were some of them Addy's kids? How old were they now? He couldn't remember. He'd never seen them, let alone kept up with their birthdays.

Nudging the mare's flanks, he rode on. Red wasn't going to like his coming back and disrupting her life. But then, he had a strong hunch there wasn't much she did like about him anymore.

Chapter Three

"Brody Wiseman, come away from the window."

"Uncle Cade is comin'. I can see him—"

"Brody!"

"Golly, Zoe." Jamming the rest of a biscuit into his mouth, the ten-year-old boy turned away. "Someone's comin', and I bet it's him."

Zoe wiped moisture from her forehead and then cleared the supper dishes. The heat was suffocating. Flies buzzed around the screen, attracted by the aroma of the evening's cabbage. The small window barely allowed ventilation. Jim had thought the two cramped rooms were sufficient living quarters. She had agreed—for two people. Not for five and three pets.

A tight knot coiled in the pit of her stomach. So Cade had gotten her message. He was finally back. The last time she'd seen him he'd kissed her goodbye and said he was going in search of a wanted man who had a twenty-five-dollar bounty on his head. He wouldn't be gone long, he said. She didn't know what his conception of "long" was. In fifteen years, she'd received a few sketchy letters, a smashed box of fancy chocolates from New Orleans, and a Christmas doll with two broken legs and a cracked face.

His gifts were meaningless, except for the locket he had slipped around her neck before he left. Her fingers touched the small oval resting in the hollow of her bosom. She had needed *him*. She had ached to hear his voice and feel again the heat of his kiss and warmth of his arms—not eat smashed chocolates and sleep cuddling a doll with broken legs.

Over the years she had grieved for him until she could grieve no more. He'd pledged everlasting love and said nothing would ever separate them.

Nothing except a man with a bounty on his head.

As the years rolled by, she'd stopped believing he'd ever come home—except in a pine box. Addy told her he was just sowing wild oats and that he'd be back someday. Well, she didn't have his sister's faith. She had finally stopped looking out the window.

But now he was back, and how would she handle the situation? She wasn't the young, foolish girl he'd left behind. His return changed nothing.

Cade Kolby was a stranger, a cold-blooded predator. It was only a matter of time before someone with a faster draw killed him, and at one time, she told herself, that would have suited her just fine.

Brody shuffled over to the table and sat down, staring at the sugar bowl. Since Addy's and John's deaths, he had been quiet and withdrawn. Where was the lively youngster Brody had been a few short weeks ago?

"I know it's him." The boy laid his head down on the table.

Of course it was him. Who else would be late for his sister's funeral? Why, after all these years, did she want to run and peek through the windows like one of the kids? Had he aged? Was he still good-looking and twice as ornery?

"He won't get here any sooner by you looking out the window," she told Brody. "Besides, it's not polite to stare."

Her nerves were raw. Over the past few weeks, her orderly life had turned chaotic. Brody's and Will's bedrolls filled one corner of the kitchen. The children's scattered belongings so cluttered the two rooms that she could barely move around. And the children's pet dog and cat came and went, inside and out, adding to the confusion.

Sleep was just a fond memory. Little Missy insisted on sharing her bed. The five-year-old had elbows like water witching sticks.

Zoe carried freshly laundered sheets to her bedroom off the kitchen, tripping over eight-year-old Holly's pallet at the foot of the bed. Stacks of clean children's clothes were piled about the disheveled room. The place looked like a hovel, but at least she felt as though she had a family now. She had toyed with the thought of keeping the children from the moment Addy drew her last breath.

Finding the money to clothe and feed them wouldn't be easy, but she could pinch a penny harder. In addition to the washing and ironing she took in, she would start a bookkeeping service. She prided herself on being good with figures.

It was highly unlikely that Cade would stay in Winterborn and raise them, and Zoe would die before she would allow him to take them with him. Nor would she allow him to give them to complete strangers. John's great-aunt Laticia was the only other relative the children had, and she was much too elderly to assume their care. Cade had little choice but to let Zoe have them.

She recalled how John disciplined the children by fear, threatening to send them to Aunt Laticia if they didn't behave. The photograph on Addy and John's dresser portrayed a grim, no-nonsense matron sitting straight as a poker, with a stiff white ruffled collar that looked as if it were the only thing holding up her head.

Zoe had visited with the matriarch on the rare occasions when she came to town to see her nephew and his family. Aunt Laticia wasn't as bad as her picture suggested, but no one could convince the children of that. They hid under their beds when she was there. Addy admonished John for making the children afraid of his aunt, but he only laughed and said he was half scared of her himself.

"When can I look?" Brody asked.

"When he gets here. It might not even be him." But Zoe knew it was. The quiver in the pit of her stomach told her so.

Stepping to the mirror, she tidied her unruly hair. Why was red hair always so frizzy and hard to control? Dark circles under her eyes reflected the difficult past few weeks. Addy's and John's illnesses and then deaths had been hard. Comforting the children had been harder. They wanted their ma and pa.

The back door banged open, and a breathless Holly came in carrying a basket filled with plump, shiny tomatoes from the garden. Tendrils of dark brown hair were plastered to her sweaty features. "Somebody's comin'."

Little Missy entered the room behind her sister and raced to the window to look out. "Oooohhh, he's all diwty. Is that my Uncle Cade?"

"Come away from the window, Missy, and wash your hands." Zoe adjusted the starched curtain. Frowning, she moistened the tip of a dish towel with her tongue and wiped an imaginary speck off the already glistening pane.

At the sound of running feet thundering through the store, she folded the dish towel neatly and hung it on a peg. "Will? Is that you?"

"Zoe, come quick! He's here! I heard Mr. Mallard say 'There's that little ruffian, Cade Kolby!'"

Gracious. It seemed that Herschel Mallard hadn't forgotten that silly incident years ago when Cade had put a bonnet on one of his prize bulls. She hid a grin. The animal had looked ridiculous pounding through town with Herschel on its heels.

Zoe heard Will running back to the front door and racing outside. Shoving his chair back from the table, Brody jumped up and followed. Holly's and Missy's eyes were as round as tea saucers. Clutching rag dolls to their chests, the two girls hung back rather than running after their brothers.

"It's all right, girls." Zoe reached for their hands, getting a firm grip. "Your Uncle Cade won't bite."

Lifting her chin, she took a deep breath as they walked together toward the front door. She likened the moment to pulling a tooth. Painful but unavoidable.

Chapter Four

Lifting her hand to shade her eyes against the blistering sun, Zoe searched the approaching rider. No wonder Missy had said "oooohhh." Cade Kolby's appearance was disgraceful. Long reddish-brown hair and a week's growth of beard made him look as sinister as his reputation. She could see why he struck fear in the hearts of wanted men. He was leaner, meaner, and more blatantly male than she remembered.

Yet, beneath the trail grime, he was still as handsome as the young man she'd loved all her life. The years had treated him kindly.

Warmth spread through her like sweet molasses. She felt hot, intensely hot, then cold. She knew why she had never forgotten him. The man was unforgettable.

Walking his horse to a stop, his gaze met her eyes. She reminded herself to breathe when his mouth turned up in a faint smile. "Hello, Red."

Here it was, the moment she'd been dreading since the day she'd sent the wire, and already she was reacting to him as if she were a smitten schoolgirl.

"You need a shave," she said, ignoring the mischief in his eyes as he leisurely perused her.

"I see you've still got your red curls."

Stiffening her spine, she looked away. She'd eat dirt before she'd let him know she had been waiting fifteen long years for him to come home. She'd been waiting all those years to tell him what she thought of a man who lied, how his father had lived in shame knowing that his son took lives for money. "Your watch stop, Cade?"

His slow, easy smile did little to temper her foul mood. "I kept in touch, didn't I?"

"Three letters in all these years? That's your idea of keeping in touch?"

He scratched his beard. "Can't remember the last time I shaved. Must have been somewhere between here and the last town."

Appalled by his lack of sensitivity, she shook her head. Fifteen years, three months, and four days since he'd ridden away with a pledge to be back soon. The promise never left her, but *he* couldn't remember the last time he shaved. "Well, at least you made it," she said, turning to go back into the store.

Brody grabbed her arm and stopped her. His eyes silently pleaded with her for civility. The boy wanted her to invite in the long-awaited uncle. *For his sake,* she thought, *only for Brody's sake.* Swallowing her pride, she turned back to find Cade's eyes still on her.

"Come on, Red. You thought I wouldn't come?"

"You didn't come for John and Addy's wedding. Or your mother's or father's funerals."

He looked away. She'd hit home. When he looked back his steady, midnight blue gaze impaled her, and the invisible hand around her throat tightened. "You missed your sister's burying too. We've already laid her and your brother-in-law to rest."

If she hadn't loved Addy so much, she would have felt a measure of satisfaction as pain flashed across his features.

"I came as soon as I got your message."

She lifted her chin. "I wasn't sure you'd get it. You're the only person I know who uses a saloon as an address."

How like him to miss the important things. Always chasing the almighty dollar and leaving responsibility to others. He might be hurting for Addy, but so was she.

When she glanced back, he was still focused on her. A smile played at the corners of his mouth. "What happened to your freckles?"

"I outgrew them." Just as he'd outgrown his boyish imperfections, she noted with dismay. She tried not to look at him, but it was impossible.

Hours in the sun had colored his skin to a rich, dark hue. A growth of heavy beard with a hint of crimson covered once-youthful skin. His shoulders were broader than she remembered. He filled every inch of his mustard-colored duster. Sinewy thighs flexed as he shifted his weight in the saddle, drawing her attention to the tools of his trade. A Colt Peacemaker was strapped to his thigh. The dying sun glinted off the butt of a Winchester rifle resting in the scabbard attached to the saddle.

Her gaze traveled to his blue denim shirt, open at the collar to reveal a curly thatch of dark chest hair. Beneath a sweat-stained black Stetson, wavy, chestnut-colored hair hung past his shoulders. She reminded herself to inhale when she realized she was holding her breath. She was going to drop at his feet in a dead faint if she didn't get control of herself.

The reins rested lightly in his gloved hands as he forced her eyes to meet his.

"You always were the prettiest girl in Kansas."

Now she refused to look at him. As God was her witness, she would never let him affect her again. But the children—she had to be civil for the children. "You need a bath."

The youngsters gathered in a silent huddle, tongue-tied and fidgety, somewhat in awe of this dark stranger and yet itching to meet him. Cade so favored their mother in looks.

Cade's eyes moved from one waif to the other, and she realized too late that she should have checked their appearances before coming outside. Brody had biscuit crumbs on his upper lip, and one of Holly's stockings was bunched around her ankle. The front of Missy's dress was water spattered, and her braids were escaping their ribbons. Will's nose, in constant need of wiping, ran a stream. Before Zoe could hand

him her handkerchief, he swiped the sleeve of his shirt across his face
and took care of the problem.

"They're all Addy's?"

She nodded. "If you had come home more often, you'd know."

The jingling of Cade's fancy silver spurs caught the children's attention as he swung out of the saddle. Pulling off his gloves, he smiled at
the youngest, who cowered behind Zoe's skirt. "What's your name?"

Urging the girls to the forefront, Zoe introduced them. "This is
Missy. She's five." She gestured toward her sister. "And Holly. She's
eight."

His gaze centered on Holly. "She looks like Addy."

"This is Brody. He's ten and the oldest. And Will is six."

Gathering the youngsters protectively to her, Zoe took a deep breath
and then said, "Children, this is your Uncle Cade."

The four pressed deeper into her skirt, clearly overwhelmed by the
rugged stranger.

She met Cade's eyes, pleading for help. "Addy thought Will favors
you."

"Is that good or bad?"

Ignoring his humorous attempt, she shrugged. "She never said."

"How come you're not keeping the kids at Addy's house?"

"The furniture and contents have been burned." When he frowned,
she explained. "Because of the fever, the doctor thought it best to
destroy all of John's and Addy's belongings."

"Was it the pox?"

"Doc Whitney's not certain, but he didn't want to chance spreading
whatever it was. The Wilson family all perished from a similar illness
a few months back. Other than John and Addy, there've been no new
cases, but Doc's still holding his breath."

Cade took off his hat and tapped it against his leg. Dust filtered to
the ground. "Losing both parents must be rough on the kids."

"They're doing well, considering."

Gawkers gathered in the street, eyes and ears glued to the homecoming. Zoe knew these busybodies were more curious about her and

Cade than they were about the children's welfare. Cade fell into step as she herded the children back into the store. There was no need for a public spectacle.

As they entered the building, Cade tossed his hat onto the counter. The pungent smell of a round of cheese on the ledge next to the till blended with the aromas of spices, coffee, and dye from the yard goods. Pickles, apples, and soda crackers filled barrels beneath the counter. "Show me where to stash my gear, and I'll wash up for supper. Is that cabbage I smell?"

Zoe never broke stride as she walked toward the living quarters, past tall shelves of canned goods and cooking utensils, and a table of linens and fancy ribbons. She sidestepped two bushels of fresh vegetables and a bucket of blackberries. "Supper's over. You'll need to find a place to sleep."

Her tone was snappish and she meant it to be. He had no right to march in and assume nothing had changed. Everything had changed, especially where he was concerned.

Brody suddenly grabbed Will around the neck and wrestled him to the floor. "Give me back my slingshot. I know you took it!"

"Did not!"

"Did too!"

Will set up a howl as Zoe waded in and broke up the scuffle. "Will did not take your slingshot, mister. I put it away. You've broken two windows and a slop jar this week."

Brody hung his head. Will punched him in the arm. "See. I told you I didn't take it."

"For heaven's sake, boys! Isn't there enough commotion going on without this? All four of you children go out back and play. Nicely."

Holly glanced at Cade, who was watching the fracas. "But what if he leaves again?"

"He's not going anyplace," Zoe said. "Go out and make sure the boys don't get their clothes dirty. They've changed twice today already."

"I don't wanna go outside," Missy said, twirling a long blond braid. "Bwody tied my haiw to the pump handle yestewday."

Zoe gave Brody a withering look that made his head dip even lower. "Go on, Missy. I want to talk to your Uncle Cade alone. I can assure you, Brody will not tie your hair to anything." She looked at Brody. "Isn't that right?"

He jammed his hands into his pockets. "Yes, ma'am."

The children left in a noisy flurry as Zoe returned to the front of the store. Cade followed close behind her and helped himself to a handful of crackers and a chunk of cheese.

Grinning, he lifted a brow at her playfully. "Make sure they don't get dirty? Isn't that asking a lot of boys?"

"You don't have to do the wash."

"Looks like John and Addy did a good job with the kids."

"They're bright and intelligent children." She watched his face sober.

"Why did Addy leave their welfare up to me?"

She shrugged. "You're the only family left."

"Did Laticia die?"

"No, but she's seventy-five years old. She and Abraham are hardly in a position to raise children."

"Abraham? Is that old black driver still around?"

She nodded. "Still answering Laticia's beck and call."

A glint of humor twinkled in his eyes as he bit into a cracker. "You're a little tense, Red. Boys can't get dirty? No supper, no room? What kind of hospitality is this?"

Grabbing a cloth, she furiously wiped the counter, her patience at an end. "What did you expect, Cade? That you could waltz back in here and things would be exactly as they were when you left?"

He slipped a piece of cheese into his mouth. "Still as prickly as a porcupine."

She snapped open a linen table napkin and refolded it. "Would it have hurt you to clean up a little before riding into town?"

He grinned, slipping another piece of cheese off the blade of the knife. "You want to draw me a bath?"

Her posture stiffened. "Frank Brighton has a hog trough you're welcome to use." She ignored his laugh and went on wiping the counter.

Swallowing the cheese, he reached for an apple, studying her. "Addy wrote that you married Jim Bradshaw. How come?"

The cleaning cloth hit the counter with a *whack*. "I waited nine years, Cade! Did you think I'd wait for you forever?"

He took a bite of apple. "You said you'd wait for me, Red. Forever. Those were your exact words. What happened?"

She turned to glare at him. "'I'll be back.' Those were *your* words. What happened?"

He shrugged. "Just because I haven't come back doesn't mean I wasn't going to. When you jumped the gun and married another man I figured why waste the ride."

He was blaming her? Anger inflamed her—directed not so much at him but at her for being so vulnerable. No matter how often she told herself that seeing him again would make no difference, it did, and she hated it.

"Speaking of forever, didn't we take a blood oath we'd never marry anyone else?" He winked as he reached into the pickle barrel. "Looks like I'm the only one who took the vow to heart."

"You have a heart, Cade?"

He sat down and propped his dusty boots on a barrel. "Sarcasm? Not like you, Red."

Years of frustration begged to be released, but she forced the urge aside. The children needed him. Their needs were foremost now. She walked past him and shoved his feet to the floor with a noisy jingle of spurs.

"It's late. You need to find someplace to light other than on my pickle barrel."

He got to his feet, shaving off another piece of cheese. "I thought I might bunk here for a few days."

"You thought wrong."

He helped himself to more crackers. "It's not like we're strangers—"

Whirling, she hurled the rag at him. "I'm not seventeen anymore, Cade Kolby! And stop eating my food!"

He ducked, and the cloth sailed to the floor.

"And don't act as though you left yesterday!" How dare he come in and assume that he owned the place!

When he looked at her as if she'd lost her mind, she grabbed the cleaning rag and began polishing the counter harder. "And don't think you'll be hanging around here, with me doing *your* wash and cooking *your* meals. Just because I loved Addy doesn't mean you can take advantage of me. Is that clear?" Turning around, she met his stare. A muscle twitched in his jaw. "Don't stand there eating my cheese and looking at me like that."

"You've changed."

"You're right. I have."

It surprised her when his eyes softened. "Let's try to keep this civil, Red." His tone turned cajoling, soft. Dangerous.

"Don't call me Red."

"That's your name, isn't it?"

"Not to you, it isn't."

"All right. Mrs. Bradshaw, is it?"

"Zoe."

He nodded. "Zoe." He sliced off another hunk of cheese. "So, what do you want me to do, Zoe? Jump off a cliff? If you're mad because I didn't come back right away, I always intended to come back for you."

"When? When exactly did you plan to come back for me?" She wasn't amused by the twinkle in his eye. If he found the situation funny, then he had a misplaced sense of humor.

"I'm back now, aren't I?"

Oh, he was exasperating. A woman would be a fool to fall for his ways, but she felt herself warming. *Stop—now!* common sense screamed.

She stored the rag under the counter. "You made a long, useless ride if you've come back for me. You'd best be thinking about the kids."

"That's why I'm here. Tell me what you want me to do." He reached into a jar for a stick of horehound candy.

When she frowned, he took the stick out of his mouth. "How much?"

"Ten cents."

Digging into his pocket, he fished out a coin and flipped it to her. "Highway robbery. I buy them in Wichita for a penny a stick."

She smiled. "I charge a penny to anyone but you. How long do you plan to stay?"

"As long as it takes."

He walked around the counter, and she backed away, realizing what he was about to do. "Cade, I forbid you to try anything foolish—"

He caught her around the waist and pulled her up close. The warmth of his breath on her cheek unnerved her.

"Calm down, wildcat." She squirmed, and he pulled her tighter against him. "You have a right to be angry. I'm sorry. I apologize."

No matter how many times she'd told herself he would have no effect on her, he could still make her weak in the knees. She clamped her jaw shut and turned her face away. He was so near that she felt the scratch of his beard against her cheek. "It's too late, Cade. You're fifteen years too late."

He smiled. "Come on. Let's not fight. You've always been the one woman in my heart. How about a kiss for Cade? For old time's sake."

Goose bumps rose on her arms as his hands slipped to the small of her back. He was more persuasive than she remembered, more appealing.

"I'd rather eat rocks."

She freed herself, picked up his hat, and jammed it on his head. Planting both hands in the middle of his chest, she backed him toward the doorway. "Get yourself cleaned up, and then come back to visit your nieces and nephews. And don't wait fifteen years to do it. And don't expect me to be here when you get back. I will have Gracie oversee your visits. Make your decision about the kids and leave, Cade. The sooner the better."

He stumbled backward, surprised when she slammed the door in his face.

She slid the bolt home. Then, on second thought, she jerked the door back open and snatched the cheese out of his hand.

She banged the door shut and jerked down the *Closed for Business* shade, hoping he'd get the message.

Chapter Five

Chalmer Winslow polished his sheriff's badge with the tip of his kerchief tied around his neck when Cade walked into the jail.

"Hey, Pop. Good to see you."

As a kid, Cade had often hung around the jail. There wasn't a lot of law-breaking in Winterborn, so parents allowed their children to play there while they tended business. Pop never had kids of his own, which was why he took to all the youngsters, handing out horehound candy sticks when they came to visit.

"Well, well. Cade Kolby." The old man got up to shake hands. "Heard you were coming back." Chuckling, he studied Cade from head to toe. "You've grown a bit."

Cade clasped Pop's hand affectionately. "I was born taller than you," he teased. Actually, the last time Cade had seen him, the sheriff had been thirty pounds lighter and had fewer wrinkles.

"Aw, I'm falling apart, but at sixty-eight, who's complaining?" He smoothed his mustache with his forefinger and then rubbed the bald spot on top of his head.

"I thought you might have turned in your badge by now."

"Nah, I'll be here until they throw dirt in my face." A wide grin split the older man's face. "Look at you." He squeezed Cade's bicep. "All muscled up. Hard to believe you were that tall, scrawny whipper-snapper who used to come in here, nosing into everything."

Cade glanced at the empty cell. "Looks like business is booming."

Pop laughed. "Chicken thieves are about it. Oh, and there was that bank robbery last year that got Zoe's husband killed. We had that criminal for two days. Poor Jim Bradshaw. Just standing there making a deposit and bam! Shot dead."

"Addy wrote me about that. Zoe must have taken it real hard."

"You know Zoe. She's tough as a boot."

Cade smiled. She certainly hadn't had any trouble expressing herself a few minutes ago. His gaze roamed the small room. The jail hadn't changed. It had the same battered wooden desk, potbellied stove, a couple of straight-backed chairs, and one cell that, if things were still as they had been before, wasn't used much.

Sitting down again at his desk, Pop propped up his feet and crossed his arms at the back of his neck. "So. Heard you got Luke Biglow."

Cade straddled a chair and sat down. "Luke and I bumped into each other around Houston a few months ago."

"Heard the reward was mighty hefty."

"Some people are worth more dead than alive."

"Tell me about it. Look at this." Pop held up a handful of wanted posters. "Half my time's spent nailing these up around town."

Cade took the notices from him and leafed through them, handing them back without comment.

Pop's features sobered. "Sure sorry about Addy and John. Sad for those young'uns. Zoe's had her hands full lately."

"Maybe that's why she's in such a foul mood. She just threw me out of her store."

"She did? And you lookin' so pretty." Pop winked. "How long you stayin'?"

"Not long."

"You plan on raising the kids? If not, there's an Amish couple over near Salina that might be interested. But, you know, the Brightons sure do want 'em."

"The Brightons? Frank and Helen? Aren't they a little old to take on four youngsters?"

"Not Frank and Helen. They're close to sixty now. Frank's youngest boy and his wife, Seth and Bonnie. They got three of their own, but they want more. They've sent word they'd sure like to be considered. Seth's building another room on and said he wants to have a whole houseful."

Cade got up and moved to the window. His gaze traced the town where he'd spent his youth. "I can't keep them, Pop. I know that's what Addy hoped I'd do, but I can't."

Pop dropped his feet to the floor and leaned forward. "I guess it's a jolt to have four kids dropped into your lap."

Cade watched a wagon pull up in front of Zoe's store. "They'll need a better home than I can give them." Pa and Ma had gone to their graves thinking their son had turned away from God. He hadn't turned away, but he sure wasn't the son Pa deserved. When he'd ridden away that day, he thought he was smarter than most. There were pennies on the dollar to be made around Winterborn. His family needed much more. The boys in this town could stick around and farm if they wanted, but he was looking for a better way to support the family. Pa pastored the local church until he took sick in Cade's teens. Cade had been left to provide for the family. Sure, the congregation did all they could, but most folks in town had a hard time seeing to their own needs. He'd been proud after he nailed his first criminal. Arrogant. He'd made more money in that one arrest than he'd seen in his whole life. So he'd gone after another. And another. When he had to kill the first man, he'd cried, knowing what Pa would say. But money had a way of getting in your soul, under your skin, soothing the conscience. When word reached his folks of his new occupation, they refused the money. Wouldn't touch a cent. It now sat in the local bank. Every red cent of it. Pa called it blood money.

After every kill he promised it would be his last. Then he'd read a poster, see the price on the man's head, and all of Pa's teachings seemed distant, unrelated to the circumstance. He figured he was doing society a favor.

"I think a lot of you, boy, but I have a tendency to agree. Those kids need some stability in their lives. You don't stay in one place long enough to fry an egg, let alone raise a family."

Cade removed his hat and ran his fingers through his hair. Pop was right. His home was a campfire and a bedroll. Children needed schooling, a roof over their heads, clean clothes, and three meals a day. What did he know about rearing kids? What did he know about family life, period?

"It'd be hard for a man with your reputation to settle down even if he set his mind to it," Pop said. "Some no-good would always be tryin' to get you before you get them."

Cade agreed. "Hart McGill. Heard of him?"

"McGill? Who hasn't? He and his gang have terrorized half of Kansas. There ain't a woman safe around any of 'em. What's he done to you?"

"Other than being a plague to society? He's out to get me."

"What's it to you? You've watched your back for years."

"I shot his baby brother."

"That'll do it every time."

"It was either me or him. I chose me." Cade returned to the chair and sat down. "Someday I'm going to settle down, have my own kids and my own little parcel of land, but that's not in the immediate future. You're right, Pop. There's always someone out there looking for a fight. I don't want to bring my trouble to Winterborn." He owed that much to his family's memory.

Pop nodded, looking past Cade to the posters on the wall. "There're some mean cusses out there, all right. But where could you go to escape them?"

"I won't. My past will follow me wherever I go, but someday I'm going to be too old for this and I'll have to quit. I've got a good nest egg put away. I wouldn't be hurting for money. Maybe get a place down by the border..." Cade's voice trailed off.

"Mexico? Ain't far enough, son. You'd still have to watch your back."

Cade knew that. He just didn't like to think about it. "I'm going to need a place to sleep tonight, Pop."

Pop brow's lifted. "That ain't all you need. You could use a haircut. Walt's raised his prices. Twenty-five cents. He's got a gun to our heads, but we have to pay it. The baths out back don't come cheap, either."

Cade laughed. "Zoe won't let me near the kids until I clean up. I suppose Glori-Lee is still renting rooms?"

"Not as many as she used to. It's all she can do to keep up with the café. Anyway, she's full up, I heard. You can either come home with me or take the bunk upstairs. It ain't much—just a cot and a wash-stand. You'd have to take your meals elsewhere, but seeing as how you're not going to be around long, it won't matter."

"Zoe wants me to wrap up my business and clear out. Yet she also expects me to spend time with the kids."

"It's not going to be easy. I don't know anywhere you can keep them with you. If Glori-Lee had a room available, it wouldn't be big enough to cuss a cat in, and my place can't accommodate the five of you."

"I won't be here long enough to set up housekeeping. My stay in Winterborn will be brief. McGill thinks I'm in St. Louis, and I want to keep it that way."

"Well, I'll help you all I can. You want to come home with me?"

"The bunk upstairs is fine." Zoe would have to keep the kids until he could make arrangements for their adoption. "I don't want to stay with you, anyway. You snore too loud."

Pop cackled. "Don't you be spreadin' a rumor like that, boy!"

"Rumor? When Addy and I used to play in here, you'd be reared back in your chair, raising the roof."

Pop heaved his bulk out of the seat, put his arm around Cade's shoulders, and walked him to the door. "You square-dance?"

"You asking?"

"Still full of it, aren't you? There's a dance over at the hall every Sat-urday night. I know it ain't proper for you to come tomorrow night, so soon after Addy's death, but keep it in mind. You could ask Zoe. You two used to be sweet on each other, weren't you?"

Cade smiled. He'd be the last person Zoe would dance with. He hadn't lied to her. He had been so busy collecting rewards he hadn't realized how many years had passed. Then Addy's letter had come, saying Zoe was about to marry Jim Bradshaw. Cade was stunned by the news. Zoe was his. She had always been his for as long as he could remember.

As it happened, he didn't get his man, but Zoe got hers. The next letter from Addy described the wedding. All the regret in Kansas hadn't been able to blot out the loss he'd felt. Why hadn't he gone back? He'd loved her. Was it the endless quest for money? He had all the money he wanted, and he wasn't wallowing in contentment.

He shoved the thoughts aside. Why dredge up ancient history? He couldn't turn back the hands of time. He couldn't change a thing.

He settled his hat on his head. "I don't know about the dance, Pop. I'm a little rusty."

"Oh? I thought dodging bullets kept a man nimble."

Cade poked Pop in his fat belly. "You should've been dodging biscuits and gravy."

Pop patted his stomach. "I've worked hard to get this. Got to have strength for sheriffin' in Winterborn."

"Guess you're right about a haircut. I'll stow my gear upstairs, and then I'll go see Walt."

Sniffing the air, Pop added, "Don't forget the bath. You smell worse than a polecat. No wonder Zoe threw you out."

The men parted at the front door. Pop reached into his shirt pocket for a horehound stick. "Here you go, boy. Something to sweeten you up."

As Cade caught the piece of candy in midair, he suddenly felt like a kid again. He thought of the times he and Addy had scrambled after the treats. Grief blinded him as the reason for his homecoming sliced razor sharp, deep through his gut. Addy was dead, and four kids with his blood running through their veins were homeless.

Chapter Six

A light breeze filtered from the open door Saturday morning, turning the overhead fan blades in Bradshaw General Store. Zoe was balanced on a ladder, dusting the top shelf of canned goods when the mayor's wife came in. Next to Addy, Gracie Willis was Zoe's closest friend, despite the twenty years' difference in age. Gracie, with her silver hair and cheerful nature, was as young in mind and spirit as a schoolgirl.

Giving a cobweb a final swipe, Zoe turned with a smile. "Morning, Gracie. You're out and about early today." Gracie usually did her shopping in the afternoon.

"Didn't sleep well last night," Gracie conceded. "Kept seeing Addy, lying there in a pine box next to John—I can't get her out of my mind." She took a handkerchief from her handbag and wiped her nose. "I'm sorry. I know you miss her too."

The emotion in Gracie's voice brought a lump to Zoe's throat. She took a deep breath, willing her tears away. She'd already cried herself dry. "Losing Addy is going to take some getting used to, all right. We were together nearly every day of our lives. The longest we were ever apart was when Jim took me to Wichita on a buying trip."

During Addy's and John's illnesses, she'd gone to their house three times a day, fed and bathed them, washed their sweat-drenched bedclothes, and watched them die. There was nothing anyone could do but try to make them comfortable. The fear in their voices as they agonized over the children's welfare still haunted her.

When she closed her eyes, she saw Addy's worried face and felt her fevered hand in hers. She heard her weak voice pleading with her to send for Cade. Addy's faith in her brother had never wavered.

Zoe watched Gracie inspect fresh ears of corn heaped in a bushel basket beside the counter. "Heard about your visitor yesterday."

Climbing off the ladder, Zoe tucked the dust cloth into the waistband of her apron. "I expect everyone in town's heard about him."

"How does it feel to see him after all these years?"

"Haven't thought much about it."

Gracie glanced up from perusing a china teapot. "You were real smitten with Cade Kolby when you were young."

"Was I? Well, you know what they say about schoolgirl crushes. Here today, gone tomorrow."

"I wish his mother had lived to see this day." Gracie sighed. "Senda was proud of her boy, though she didn't approve of his doings." She dropped three ears of corn into her basket. "Lawrence was talking about Cade just this morning, surprised he turned out as good as he did."

"If you call killing men for money good."

"Senda and Pastor Mac were fine people, just dirt-poor. Most of us have to watch our pennies, but after Mac took sick, that family lived hand-to-mouth. Cade wanted a better life for his folks. That was evident when he quit school to work for Clarence Redding, God rest his soul. Cade chopped wood and hauled hay fourteen hours a day for whatever Clarence saw fit to give him."

"I understand why he took to the job, I just don't approve of it." Zoe frowned as she rearranged bags of sugar. "He used to look at Pop's wanted posters all the time and talk about what he'd do if he had money. It really didn't surprise me when he didn't come back. What surprises me, though, is that he's still alive. I thought he'd have been gunned down by now."

Nodding, Gracie added a tin of sorghum to her basket. "He certainly tried to make life easier for Mac and Senda. Not a month went by without Cade sending money home. Just before his ma died, Cade sent her a brand-new Home Comfort cook stove. Law, I was so envious I thought I'd die. It had a warming oven twice the size of mine. Pastor Mac didn't want her to accept it, but Senda stood up to him. Said if her boy wanted her to have it, so be it."

Zoe smiled at the memory.

"I never tasted anything as good as that first pan of cornbread Senda baked," Gracie continued, shaking her head. "We ate the whole pan between us. Mac came in and asked what smelled so good, and Senda told him she'd ruined the cornbread and thrown it out to the hogs. He caught right on to the joke, asking how the 'hogs' enjoyed it."

Zoe nodded, grinning. "I miss Senda." Her merriment slowly faded. "She was like a mother to me."

"I always thought it was good the way the Kolbys took you under their wing after your ma died. I know it wasn't easy on you, being an only child and your pa being gone so much."

"Papa worked himself into an early grave for me. Selling Bibles was a hard way to make a living, though he never complained. But I did get lonely. I guess that's why my years with Jim were so good. He was always here, and home and family meant a lot to him."

"It's a shame you two never had children."

The thought pained Zoe. Jim would have liked to have had many, but he'd known it would never happen.

Gracie glanced around the store. "Where is Cade this morning? I thought he'd be here with the kids."

"He's been and gone. The children are playing out back. They didn't want to go with him today. I think they're a little frightened of him."

"Well, I'm disappointed."

"I told him you would supervise his visits with the children. I have other things to tend to—"

"Zoe Bradshaw! I'll do no such thing. It won't hurt you to spend some time with him—not that I don't want to see him. Walt said it took an hour and a half to get him shaved, barbered, and cleaned up.

Lilith saw him ride into town and said he was as good looking as ever, even with all the trail dust." Gracie turned. "Is he?"

Lifting a shoulder, Zoe fibbed. "Looks the same to me." When he'd shown up that morning, clean shaven, hair cut to a respectable length, wearing fresh clothes and smelling of Edna Mews's homemade soap, she'd had to remind herself to stay calm. But when he'd helped himself to the biscuits and jam without being invited, she'd snatched the biscuit away and given him a tongue-lashing, reminding him that Glori-Lee served breakfast at seven.

"Didn't notice he's changed a bit, huh?" Gracie dropped a tin of peaches into her shopping basket. "Lilith says he's a fine figure of a man. Strange you missed that."

"Sorry. Didn't notice."

"Goodness, I think you've been taking Reverend Munson's 'shalt nots' too much to heart."

Zoe busied herself rearranging a display of cast-iron skillets, refusing to rise to the bait. Cade was a perfect "shalt not." He was a fine-looking man, but who wanted someone who was here today and gone tomorrow? A killer. There was more to a man than the way he looked. Her husband had not only been handsome; they'd shared the same values. He'd been there when she needed him. Jim was a godly man.

Pausing before the rutabagas, Gracie tested them for firmness. "So you didn't notice? 'Thou shalt not lie.' That's what the Good Book says."

Finally Zoe couldn't stand it anymore. "All right!" she blurted out. "Yes, he's so good looking it makes my teeth ache. Is that what you want to hear?"

"If that's how you feel." Gracie dropped the vegetable into her basket and moved to the linens.

"So he's matured. He's still Cade."

Perusing the shelves, Gracie mused, "Refresh my memory on why that's so disturbing. What's wrong with him? Pop says he goes out of his way to bring a man in alive."

Zoe hardened herself to Gracie's words. Whether he brought them in dead or alive, he collected money on other people's miseries. "They're not always alive, are they? If you want to quote the 'shalt nots' don't forget 'Thou shalt not kill.'"

Gracie dropped the pillowcase she was holding. "He's just doing what the law requires, no more. You know as well as I do that outlaws must be stopped."

"There are marshals and sheriffs for that."

"And a bounty hunter is different how? He doesn't have a badge?" Gracie moved to a shelf on the far side of the store and changed the subject, calling over her shoulder, "Is he going to keep the children?"

"I doubt it. That would mean settling down, and I can't picture that."

Gracie examined a jar of fancy jelly. "How much?"

"Fifty cents. You ask that every week."

"I keep hoping you'll lower the price."

"Can't. It comes all the way from Kansas City."

Gracie set the jar back on the shelf. "Lawrence thinks Cade will probably find a good home for the children and move on."

A dark premonition flooded Zoe. Of course he'd move on. Didn't he always? "It's hard to believe he'd give away his own flesh and blood."

"Well, to be fair, he can't take them with him."

"He'd have to give up bounty-hunting."

"Give up bounty-hunting? Lawrence says a man can't just walk away from something like that, especially a man with Cade's reputation. There's no telling how many he's angered."

Zoe sighed but said nothing.

"Lawrence's cousin was a bounty hunter," Gracie went on. "He always sat with his back to the wall when he came to visit. Said he slept with one eye open and his gun under his pillow. I remember telling Lawrence it must be sad to be always looking over your shoulder. No sane man would involve innocent children in that way of life."

Zoe stared out the front window, trying to imagine Cade as a father, let alone a "sane" one. It was like trying to imagine Reverend Munson as a saloon dancer.

What would happen to the children? She was a second mother to them. If Cade took them away from Winterborn, it would break her heart, yet she knew it was his right.

"There are always the Brightons," Gracie offered. "They'd give the children a good home, and you know how much Bonnie wants them. It would be a shame to take them away from everything they've ever known."

Sighing again, Zoe walked behind the counter. "Nothing against the Brightons, but the children would be better off with me. Good heavens, Gracie, they're little people, not sacks of flour."

Gracie frowned. "You can't keep them, Zoe. Why, you're barely holding on now. How could you think of taking on the responsibility of raising four young children alone? Those kids need a father."

Zoe's chin came up. "And a mother."

"Then maybe you and Cade ought to give those children a home." Gracie quirked a brow. "Have you thought about that?"

"You're out of your mind." Zoe turned her back on her friend and straightened the coffee bin.

"My, my, aren't we huffy today?" Grinning, Gracie picked up a spool of ribbon. "I don't think it's such a strange idea. Cade is single, you're widowed—why do you suppose he never married?"

"I didn't ask." Weary of the subject, Zoe grabbed the jar of fancy jelly. "Here. You can have it for thirty-five cents."

"Bribery? I like that in a person." Gracie dropped the jar into her basket and put it on the counter. "Is he going to be taking his meals here?"

Writing up Gracie's purchases on a pad, Zoe kept her temper in check. Gracie was trying her best to ruffle her feathers, but it wasn't going to work. She was onto her tactics.

"Gracie, you didn't come here to shop. You're here to be nosy. Okay. No, Cade will not be taking his meals with us. His coming back has not sent me into a girlish titter, nor do I stay awake nights pining over lost love. His return to Winterborn will not change my life, other than to make it easier. When he rides out in a few days, which he no doubt will, I don't think I will even notice, other than to wave goodbye to the children, should he choose to keep them. There. Have I answered all your questions?"

A smile crept over the older woman's face. Sampling a cracker, she mused, "These are a little stale. Would you sell them for half price? Lawrence does so love soda crackers."

Moving around the counter to the barrel, Zoe scooped up a bagful and stuck it in her friend's basket. "Here. My gift to the mayor. Will that be all?"

Walking over to a stack of yarn, Gracie said, "I hate to miss the dance tonight, but I don't think it's proper for us to go so soon after Addy's death—even though I promised her I wouldn't mourn for her. Much. What about the checkers game Thursday night? Do you think Addy would mind? She never missed one until she got sick."

"She told me she didn't want us missing anything, and she said for you to keep a close eye on Lilith Wilks. She cheats."

"No!" Gracie exclaimed, turning toward Zoe.

"Addy saw her king her own checker. Twice."

"Why, imagine! A woman her age cheating at checkers." Shaking her head, Gracie dropped baking soda and brown sugar into her basket on the way back to the counter. "Now that we're on the subject, I've had my suspicions about Willa Baker."

Zoe totaled the purchases, shaking her head. "Willa doesn't cheat. She's just forgetful."

"She's also the champion and as sly as a fox. I say she bears watching."

Zoe handed the bill to her. "Two dollars and fifty cents."

Leaning close, Gracie whispered, "You've shorted yourself. You know I was just trying to get a rise out of you, asking for bargains. I'll pay full price for the jelly, and the crackers are perfectly fresh." Straightening, she sobered. "That's your problem, dear heart. You are too giving. No wonder you're going broke."

"A little off the jelly and free crackers aren't going to change my financial situation."

Unfortunately, the store ledger contained more debts than Zoe had assets, but she couldn't deny credit to needy families. Times were hard. When the gristmill closed down last year, many a man was caught unawares. She didn't intend to sit by and watch children go hungry. When desperate neighbors came to her looking for credit to feed their families, how could she refuse? Jim had never turned anyone away, and she didn't have the heart to start now.

"Jim was the most caring man in the world," Gracie sympathized, "but he was a poor money manager. His daddy was the same way."

Shaking off a feeling of impending doom, Zoe wrapped Gracie's purchases. "I'm falling farther behind every day."

"And you think you can feed four kids and keep them clothed?"

"I'll do what I have to."

"Have you thought any more about selling out? Frank Lovell wants your store. He's not my favorite person, but he has the money to buy it."

"Where would I go? I have no family."

"It's a shame Addy and John couldn't have helped with the kids' expenses, but after the mill closed, John could barely feed his family. If they'd asked, Cade would have helped them out."

"The last thing John or Addy would have done was ask Cade or anyone else for money."

"Well, you know Lawrence and I will help if we can. We've got a little set aside, if you need it."

"Thanks, Gracie. I appreciate it, but that isn't the answer. Money is tight, but when that shipment of yard goods comes in, I'll make a decent profit—enough to see me through another couple of months." After that, she didn't know what would happen, but the last thing she wanted was for Cade to know about her shaky financial situation. Zoe handed her friend her purchases. "I know I can count on you."

"And I know you. You're like Addy and John. Pride will keep you from ever asking for help."

"I have no desire to be a martyr. Don't worry. I'll ask if I need it. Just don't mention it to Cade."

"You don't think you can keep something like this quiet in Winterborn, do you?"

"I will only have to keep my money troubles from Cade a week or less. I'll be shocked if he's around that long."

As the door closed behind Gracie a moment later, Zoe climbed back up the ladder to finish cleaning.

She hoped she would never have to ask friends for money, but with suppliers breathing down her neck, and being two months behind on the bank payments, she couldn't hold out much longer. She was already taking in washing and ironing. When would she find the time to do anything more? She dusted harder, blinking back tears. Taking charity wasn't something she liked to consider anymore than losing the children. She couldn't trust Cade to be sensible. Heaven knows she had reason to believe he wouldn't be. Would he do the right thing and let her have the children? Ha! He'd never done the right thing in his life.

Still, maybe he understood how limited his options were.

She knew one thing for certain. Those children were hers. If he refused to recognize it, he would be in for the fight of his life.

Chapter Seven

Cade opened his eyes Sunday morning to the sound of rain dripping off the eaves. A damp-smelling breeze ruffled the rumpled curtain at the open window. He stared at the dingy, water-stained ceiling. Thunder and lightning had kept him awake most of the night, and the heavy downpour had left a puddle in the middle of the warped pine floor. Late summer rains. They helped the crops but did little for thoughts of the upcoming winter.

Cade stretched full length, recoiling as his feet encountered soggy bed linens. The old jail roof was leaky as a sieve. Poking a foot out from under the sheet, he closed his eyes. If he'd wanted this kind of misery, he would have slept outside. He put off getting up and lay listening to the sounds of the awakening town.

The church bell rang in the distance, calling morning worshippers. The smell of frying bacon and fresh coffee drifted to him. He inhaled, smiling when he heard the unmistakably shrill voice of Hattie Thompson shouting to Woodall that he was going to be late for church. No doubt, Woodall was dallying as he finished his morning ritual.

Funny how everything had changed, but nothing was different.

For no reason at all, a childhood incident popped into Cade's mind—the time he and Addy had sneaked some of Pa's communion wine. Pa would have skinned them alive if he'd known how his children had gotten tipsy in the barn loft that day. He grinned. Zoe had refused to be a party to the nonsense. She'd stayed sober and covered for them, telling his folks they were sick from eating too much sweet potato pie at dinner and had gone to bed early.

He sobered. They had paid dearly for that trick. His temples still throbbed thinking about the miserable thumping headache he'd had the next day.

Zoe blackmailed him, making him answer to her for a full week. He'd rolled out of bed before dawn in the biting January cold and waded through snow up to his hips to gather eggs and muck out her daddy's barn.

Cade shifted his hip on the thin mattress. It hadn't been so bad, though. Zoe had brought him cinnamon rolls fresh from the oven and steaming cups of black coffee. They'd sat in the warmth of the barn stalls, surrounded by dry hay and milking pails, and talked for hours. There wasn't anything he couldn't tell her in those days. They knew everything there was to know about each other.

"Addy," he whispered, "why would you pick me, of all people, to decide your kids' future?"

Rolling out of bed, he sat on the edge of the bunk and scratched his head. He still smelled like a lily from all the soap and shampoo Walt had used on him Friday night. He shook his head, trying to dilute the scent of Edna's fancy bar soap. He didn't know what she made it with, but the flowery scent stuck to him like a burr.

He got up and dressed, strapping his gun belt around his waist. Sidestepping the rain puddle, he moved to the battered washstand and poured water from a chipped pitcher into a bowl.

He lathered his face with soap, and then he reached for his straight razor. Cade couldn't believe he was shaving again. Twice in one week. He never thought about it when he was on the trail, but because of Red and the kids, he now had to worry about his appearance. His hand froze when an almost imperceptible sound caught his attention.

He slowly moved the razor to his left hand, letting his right slide to his gun. He stared back at his reflection in the mirror and shifted slightly so he could see each kid.

Four small children stood there, staring at him as if he were the bogeyman.

Cade's tension subsided, and his hand casually dropped from the holster. Setting down the razor and picking up the soap mug, he whipped up a rich lather, pretending to be oblivious to his early morning visitors.

Brody stood straight as an oak, twisting his hat in his hands. Red jelly rimmed Will's upper lip, and he held a biscuit in his hand. Holly's and Missy's wide eyes sized him up.

He found the intense scrutiny amusing. Should he break the ice and let them know he saw them, or just allow them to satisfy their curiosity?

Carefully drawing the razor over his lathered cheek, he talked to his image in the mirror. "Well, Cade, your sister sure has left you a passel of fine-looking children."

Will quickly covered his mouth to stifle a giggle. Brody elbowed him sharply. Holly's face turned as red as a hot poker. Missy buried her face in her sister's side.

Tapping the razor on the rim of the bowl, Cade continued talking to himself. "A man would be right proud to have kids like that."

He bent closer to the mirror to shave under his nose and then down his left cheek. "I'd like nothing better than to stay here in Winterborn and be their pa, but I can't. I travel from town to town and never know where I'll lay my head at night. Good kids like that need roots. They need a ma and a pa who can fry chicken, bake biscuits, and tuck them into bed at night."

Sloshing the razor through the water, he paused. "Pop says the Brightons would love to have them. Don't know much about Seth Brighton, but I heard he's a fine pa to his own kids. Seems to me he'd make a fine pa for Addy's kids."

He frowned when he saw Holly's bottom lip jut out like a sore thumb. Brody didn't look any too happy about the prospect, either. The looks on Will's and Missy's faces pulled at his heartstrings.

Drawing the razor back through the water, Cade said, "I hear Seth's got a fine bunch of ponies at his place. I could talk to him and see if the boys could have a horse of their own."

Brody's and Will's faces momentarily brightened.

"And Bonnie raises those cats. Hear she's got a new litter that's cute as buttons."

Holly and Missy expressions turned vaguely interested.

"Yes." Cade finished shaving and laid the razor aside. He studied the children's reactions in the mirror. "All and all, I'd say the Brightons would make a fine ma and pa for Addy's kids."

Four chins lifted with open hostility. Reaching for Missy's hand, Holly nodded to Brody, who in turn grabbed Will by the collar, and they marched out as soundlessly as they had arrived.

Cade dried his face on a rough towel, glancing toward the empty doorway. Something close to loneliness came over him. He hadn't experienced the feeling often. He wasn't accustomed to needing anyone. His horse and the open road were his family, yet it was as if Addy spoke through Holly's eyes, a silent reminder that he wasn't getting any younger.

A man his age should have namesakes of his own. He needed a reason to come home at night. He should certainly have more than one horse. He should have several, plus more cats than old Bossy could provide milk for.

But the kids needed more than ponies and cats. They needed love. He could give them love; what he couldn't give them was permanence.

He'd ride out and talk to the Brightons, see if they had enough love and permanence to go around.

His choice seemed easy enough. So why wasn't it?

Chapter Eight

Zoe glanced up from her bookkeeping Monday morning to see Cade standing on the back porch. She ignored her quickening pulse. She blamed the strong coffee in front of her for her sudden heart palpitations.

Peering through the screen, she frowned. Early morning was the only time she could work on the store's ledgers without interruption. What was he doing here before seven? His smile caught her breath, and she hurriedly turned back to the ledger. Numbers danced before her eyes, and she couldn't remember what five times seven was.

"The children aren't up yet," she said.

"Good. I came to talk to you."

Wonderful. A shoot-out at daybreak—just what she needed. Laying her pencil aside, she got up and unlatched the screen door. Sunrise glistened off early morning dew, scattering diamond patterns across the grass. Honeysuckle trailing up the building's back wall perfumed the tiny kitchen.

When Cade entered the room, the limited space got even smaller. His presence seemed to fill every corner as he pulled off his hat and looked around.

Glancing toward Will's and Brody's pallets, he whispered, "Looks like a houseful."

Zoe knew he'd expect a cup of coffee, but she'd had to scrape the can this morning to make her own. There'd be no more coffee for her this month. She sat back down at the table. "You wanted to talk to me?"

Hooking his hat over the chair back, he took the seat opposite her. "Yes. About the Brightons."

She totaled a column. "Bonnie and Seth?"

"What kind of people are they?"

"Good people. You remember Seth's folks, Frank and Helen?"

"I remember the old man being strict. He was quick to take his kids behind the woodshed and use a hickory switch on them."

Her pencil paused in midair as she thought about it. "I don't know that Frank's like that now. He seems to be a reasonable man, and his children are all responsible, hardworking adults."

"Do you think Bonnie and Seth would make a good home for Addy's kids?"

Zoe sipped her coffee, facing him over the rim of the cup. "Yes, but I don't think that's the best place for them."

He glanced toward the stove. "Any more of that coffee?"

"No. This is the last of it."

"The last of it?" He shifted slightly in his chair. "Don't you own a general store?"

"I do, but I have to pay for my coffee like everybody else."

He reached across the table and took her cup. Their hands touched, and she jerked back as if she'd encountered a hot stove. He flashed a disarming grin as he took a long sip. When he handed the cup back to her, she deliberately wiped the rim where his lips had been.

He chuckled. "Afraid of me, Red?"

She got up and took her cup to the sink. Wild horses couldn't make her put her mouth where his had been. She wasn't playing games with him. He was trying to evoke memories that were better left alone. "When have I ever been afraid of you?"

"If you're not, the kids are." He turned the ledger she was working on and scanned the long rows of figures. "So far they haven't said a word to me. They can talk, can't they?" He moved back when she returned to the table and snapped the book shut in his face.

She stuck the ledger into a drawer. "The children are intimidated at the moment. They'll eventually warm to you."

"*I* don't have time. How do I get them to open up to me now?"

"Give them a few days." An edge of impatience crept into her voice. "You surely have a few days, don't you?"

"Very few. They did come over and watch me shave yesterday morning."

Zoe opened her mouth and then quickly shut it. It had been the wee hours of the morning when she'd finished Mrs. Penscott's ironing and then fell into bed. She mentally groaned when she recalled having slept later than usual and let the children fend for themselves. They had gone out early and come back wide eyed, chattering about their uncle's strange behavior and how they had missed Sunday school and weren't happy about it.

"They didn't know I saw them," Cade added. "I got the feeling that if I'd turned around and said 'boo' they'd still be running."

She picked up the whistling tea kettle and poured hot water into the dishpan. "They thought you were a bit strange, talking to yourself about the Brightons and their supposed ponies and litters of kittens. That's deceitful. We don't mislead the children."

"I didn't lie to them. Pop told me Seth and Bonnie have a good-sized farm and chances are they have cats and horses. Seth's made his wishes known."

"He has, but that doesn't mean Addy would want Seth to have them."

His features sober. "Exactly where does Addy want them?"

She scrubbed a pot, bracing herself. "They'd be better off with me."

"With you?"

The skepticism on his face assured her he'd never even considered the option. Before her confidence wavered, she went on. "Apparently you've decided not to keep them."

"I can't keep them, and I can't believe you'd want them."

She turned to confront him. "And why not?"

"You don't have a husband. If Seth and Bonnie take them, they'll have both a mother and a father."

Tears welled in her eyes, and she resented her fragile emotions. Fighting the tight knot in her throat, Zoe struggled to keep her feelings in check. He knew how to get under her skin, but she wouldn't let him. There was too much at stake to let him intimidate her.

"No one could love those children more than I do. I was there the day each one was born. I helped deliver Missy and Will. They're like my own. I'm the one who nursed Addy until her last breath, and believe me, Cade, I would never have sent for you if it wasn't your sister's dying wish. Next to you, I'm the closest thing to family the children have, other than John's Aunt Laticia. I won't let you give them away!" She heard her voice choke with emotion. He'd gotten to her again. How dare he sit there and calmly discuss Addy's children as if they were nothing more than strangers in need of a roof over their heads.

"*Won't* let me? Aren't you forgetting that I'm their uncle and I can do what I think is best?"

The tone of his voice forced her to meet his defiant gaze. "You don't know them, not one thing about them. How could you? You never once bothered to come home and meet them. Do you think the presents you sent at Christmas made up for your absence? I don't know what Addy was thinking when she put her children's welfare in your hands—a man who doesn't care whose feelings he steps on. A ruthless killer."

He didn't waver. "I'm all they've got right now. And I'll decide who raises them."

She swiped her nose with a hanky. "You had better make the right choice."

"Look, Red, I'm not trying to hurt you..."

"Of course not. I don't have a price on my head. Why would you waste time on me?" Her eyes held his, refusing to break contact.

Brody and Will stirred on their pallets. The last thing she wanted was to involve the children in their quarrel. Lowering her voice, she whispered, "Addy's dead, and her children need a home—a home I can give them, a home I *want* to give them. Please don't take them away from me, Cade. There's no reason to uproot them from everything they've known. Let them stay here with me. I can raise them as well as Seth and Bonnie can."

Arms crossed, she stepped to the window, watching a sparrow flit in and out, building a nest under the kitchen eaves. At the moment, she envied the bird. The only problem it faced was today. She had years of loneliness ahead of her if Cade took the children or, worse yet, gave them to the Brightons. If that were to happen, she would be relegated to being a doting "aunt," bringing gifts at appropriate occasions but never really sharing in their lives.

When she turned to face him, she saw his anger, as well as…disgust and pity? *Please, God, not pity. Not from him.*

"I'm not saying you wouldn't love them," he said, "but look around you. How can you raise four children? You're practically walking on kids."

Zoe cringed as he sized up the room, his gaze lingering on the old, worn-out furnishings. She bit her lower lip, aware of her faded dress and obvious lack of means. If he were to guess just how badly off she was financially, he would never let her have the children.

"I know what you're thinking," she said, "that I wouldn't be able to afford them—but things are picking up. As soon as I get the new shipment of yard goods, I'll make a tidy profit."

"Money isn't the only consideration. I can provide you with all the money you'll ever need."

Rinsing a dish, she said softly, "I don't want your money."

"Too dirty for your taste, Red? I wasn't offering you my money. I was talking about the kids. Whoever has them, I'll see that they're taken care of financially. But I want them to have a mother and a father. That's what Addy would want."

"So if I had a husband, you'd let me keep them?"

"Do you have someone in mind?"

"No. Merely asking."

"You surely wouldn't marry someone in order to keep the kids. You wouldn't take a vow to God and not keep it?"

"You don't know me at all, Cade Kolby. Any vow I would take I would keep. There are plenty of men who would welcome a ready-made family."

"Name two."

"Perry Drake and Ronald Fell."

"Drake? The banker?"

"Yes. He's a wonderful man."

"Who's Fell?"

"A man—a very nice man who bought a farm east of town a few years back."

Cade leaned back in his chair. "Funny. Addy never mentioned Ronald Fell. Maybe I'll bump into him while I'm here."

"You won't. He's…back East on business." Actually, she'd never met Mr. Fell. Perry mentioned that the bank held the mortgage on the Fell farm. For all she knew, Ronald was married or too old to care, and as far as Perry was concerned, he'd taken her to the Saturday night dance a couple of times, but that was all.

Straightening the sugar bowl, Cade cleared his throat. "I know you mean well, Red, but if Addy wanted you to have the children, she wouldn't have involved me."

She jammed a skillet into the dishpan. "Oh, yes, I forgot who I'm dealing with. Cade Kolby, Prince of Uncles—Prince of Lovers—Prince of—"

He slammed both hands on the table and got up. The warning in his eyes said she'd made her point.

Brody stirred on his pallet, opening one eye. When he spotted Cade, he quickly shut it.

Cade reached for his hat. "I'm taking the kids swimming today. Is that all right with you?"

She shrugged. "Why ask? Addy made you king, not me."

He put his hat on and adjusted it low on his forehead. "See that they're ready in an hour."

Zoe turned and flung a wooden spoon at him as the screen door slammed. The spoon ricocheted off the wire mesh and took a hard bounce onto Brody's pallet.

Brody picked it up and looked at her. Will lifted a tousled head and rose on an elbow, sleepy eyed and yawning.

Staring at the screen door, Zoe slowly counted to ten. Clenching her hands into fists, she silently ranted and railed, calling Cade every name under the sun. Throwing a spoon at him had probably lessened her chance of keeping the children, but she didn't care. It was hard to control the anger that simmered inside her, anger that *he* provoked.

Brody and Will were still focused on her. For their sake, she would pretend their uncle wasn't the most impossible man on earth. Turning from the door, she met the boys' curious stares brightly.

"Guess what? Uncle Cade is taking you swimming!"

Chapter Nine

Cade left the Bradshaw store and walked down the street to the jail. When he opened the door, he found Pop sprawled on the cell bunk, white faced and moaning.

"Pop! What's wrong? Are you sick?"

The sheriff drew his knees up to his chest with a groan. "Gooseberry pie," he rasped.

Cade entered the cell and knelt beside him. The old man's face was nearly as white as his mustache. "How much did you eat?"

"Three, maybe four pieces. I lost count."

Cade shook his head. "Green apple quickstep. That's rough."

"Dadburn that Lilith! She knows better than to let me make a hog out of myself on her pies!" Pop doubled over again.

Cade glanced around the empty office. "What can I do to help?"

"Just get out of my way, I'm coming through." Pop hauled himself off the bunk and made a bee line for the back door.

Sidestepping the sheriff's hasty departure, Cade called, "Maybe next time you'll stop at one piece!"

Moving to the desk, Cade sat down and leafed through the wanted posters. He laid two aside, knowing he had already collected the rewards on them. Hot bile rose to his throat when Hart McGill's picture came up. He stared at it long and hard. They had upped the reward another five hundred dollars. The worthless being was overvalued. When he thought of Owen Cantrell, shot in the back walking through his own front door, it turned his stomach. Owen had been gunned down for no reason other than because he was Cade's friend. The image of Bess Cantrell, grief stricken as she was carried away from the graveside by her two sons, would stay with Cade for as long as he lived.

Pushing bitterness aside, Cade moved to the window and thought of more pressing matters. If Hart got wind that Cade had loved ones in Winterborn, their lives would be worthless. He'd talk to Seth and Bonnie about getting the kids settled as quickly as possible.

The back door opened and Pop returned, carefully easing onto the nearest chair and releasing a sigh. "That was close."

Cade grinned and sat down. "You going to live?" Pop's face was white as a sheet, his strength obviously drained.

"For a few minutes…never know when the next bout will strike. You here for any particular reason? Thought you'd be busy with the kids."

"Actually, I did have a reason for stopping by. The roof's leaking like a sieve, and I'm not looking forward to sleeping in a wet bed again. I could move the bunk, but the roof's dripping in so many places that it wouldn't do any good. I can see daylight through the cracks."

"Yeah, I know about the leaks. Just haven't had time, money, or manpower to fix 'em."

"You're in no shape to fix anything right now."

Pop moaned. "That's a fact. How are you and the redhead gettin' along?"

"We're not. I need to finish my business quickly and move on."

"Too bad. Zoe needs a man like you—someone who won't let her run roughshod over him. Jim was too patient. Zoe got the best of him at times—" Pop's expression corkscrewed. "Hooboy. Nature calls." He bolted toward the door calling over his shoulder, "Don't leave! I got a favor to ask."

While Pop was tending business, Cade browsed through the gun cabinet. He took out a Henry lever action rifle and examined it. The guns hadn't been used for some time. They needed a good cleaning.

"Whew, doggies!" Pop said, entering the room again. "If I ever look at another piece of gooseberry pie, shoot me."

Cade slipped the Henry back into the cabinet. "You need a favor?"

"I've got a problem over in the next county, but I'm not in any shape to go. Thought you might take care of it for me."

"Sure. What do you need?"

"Hague Pearson got all liquored up a couple of nights ago and got shot. Someone needs to go over and bring his body back."

Cade frowned. "Hague Pearson? The old hermit who lives near the county line?"

Pop nodded. "That's him. Me and Mooney Adams got a bet going. You remember old Mooney, sheriff of Suffox County?"

"I remember Mooney. Mean, but honest."

"Whoever has the least crime on his record at the end of each year wins a prize. It ain't much, more like a prestige thing. We ain't got any crime here in Winterborn, so it's a pretty sure bet I'll win, but Hague could put a kink in the plan. I want you to take the buckboard over there, pick up the body, and decide exactly where Hague got shot. Mooney says Hague was shot on our side of the line and dropped dead on his side. I say Hague was shot in Suffox County, period. I don't want that death on my record, and Mooney don't want it on his."

"I'm guessing Hague didn't want it on anybody's record."

Pop chuckled. "Don't mean no disrespect. Hague was an ornery sort, but he always let me hunt on his property. I'll see he gets buried proper-like. I'd be much obliged if you'd drive over there and get it sorted out for me."

"Sounds like a good way to get shot."

"Nah, Mooney knows he's in the wrong. He's just trying to win that prize."

"I'm taking the kids swimming today. Can it wait until tomorrow?"

Pop shrugged. "Don't see why not. Old Hague ain't goin' anywhere."

"I need to talk to Seth and Bonnie, anyway. Someone said they live on the old Brighton place north of town?"

Pop nodded. "Yep. Just down the road a piece from Frank and Helen's place."

"I'll pick up Hague then. Kill two birds with one stone. I'll stop by and talk to the Brightons on the way back."

"Want to satisfy your conscience that they'll make a good home for Addy's kids? They will, you know. Seth's a hard worker."

"So I hear." Cade got up and stretched. "Cheer up. By tomorrow you might feel like taking care of the Suffox County trouble yourself." Cade laughed when Pop's stomach rumbled so loud they both heard it.

"Son, there ain't enough outhouses between here and Suffox County for me to chance it. The rate I'm going, you'd be bringing back my carcass alongside Hague's."

Chapter Ten

Leaning against a tree, Cade listened to giggly splashes. One by one, the three oldest kids dropped into the cool water from a rope knotted to the jutting branch of a walnut tree. Missy waded along the rocky bank.

Glancing across the stream, Cade silently conceded he'd missed home more than he thought. It was peaceful here. He, Zoe, and Addy had spent hours at the swimming hole as kids.

A hawk cried overhead, drawing his attention. Was it the money or the thrill of the chase that kept him away? He'd made a lot of money, but money was worthless when you're six feet under. The incident near Laredo last month was as close as he'd ever come to dying. The outlaw had been a hair quicker than he had. His hand absently went to the nagging pain in his right shoulder, a reminder that his luck would play out someday.

Missy squealed and he straightened. Twigs snapped beneath his boots as he raced to the water's edge. He found Addy's youngest sobbing and holding a bleeding foot.

"What happened, sweetheart?" He picked her up and examined her toe. A tiny nick oozed a thin trickle of blood.

"Something bit me!"

"Nothing bit you. You stepped on a sharp rock."

"Thwow it away!"

"All right." Still holding her in his arms, he waded into the water and pretended to single out the culprit. "Wait a minute—yes, there it is. Come here, you rascal!" He picked up a rock and hurled it to the opposite bank, laughing when his heroic theatrics induced a giggle from Missy.

"You're going to get in trouble, Uncle Cade." Holly pointed at his wet trousers.

"Yeah," Brody added. "One time Will and I waded through a puddle of water and just about ruined our shoes. Zoe made us polish 'em for an hour."

"A hunnert hours," Will corrected.

"Maybe she won't notice." Cade waded out of the stream, carrying Missy, and settled her in a grassy spot on the embankment.

"It huwts, Uncle Cade."

He wrapped his kerchief around the tender spot. She hadn't spoken directly to him until today. Her voice was tiny and sweet as spring hyacinths. "I know, honey. It'll stop in a minute."

Holly ran up the grassy knoll, breathless. "Should I go get Zoe?"

"Missy will be fine." He smiled at the eight-year-old as he held out his hand. "Come here. Don't be afraid of me."

Holly hesitated, and then she walked slowly toward him. After a moment, she sat down beside him, staring. "You look kind of like Ma."

"Think so?"

"Uh-huh. Did you pull Ma's hair like Brody and Will do mine and Missy's?"

He chuckled. "I'm sure I did. Isn't that what brothers are for?"

Will shot out of the water with Brody chasing after him. The boys ran up the hill, intentionally shaking water on the girls.

Missy yelled, "Quit it! You'll get my sowe toe wet! Uncle Cade bandaged it fow me." Cornflower blue eyes turned in his direction, and Cade heard the voice of an angel say, "Thank you, Uncle Cade. You'we a good boy."

Will shook water on her again. "He ain't a boy. He's a growed man."

"Yeah," Brody said, eyeing Cade. "He shoots a pistol. I'm gonna shoot a pistol when I learn how." He looked at Cade straight on. "Will you teach me?"

Cade knew Addy wouldn't mind if he taught her boy to shoot, but he thought Zoe would have his hide. "Have you ever shot a gun, son?"

"My pa let me shoot his shotgun one time when he took me squirrel hunting." He rubbed his shoulder. "It hurt."

Cade turned him in the direction of the water. "You can learn to shoot when you're older. Right now, you're wasting swim time."

"Can I get in the watew again?" Missy held her foot high in the air, waving it.

"Don't know why not." He carefully unwrapped the handkerchief and saw that the bleeding had stopped. "Just don't step on any more sharp rocks."

Holly took hold of her little sister's hand. "I'll watch her, Uncle Cade."

"Thank you, Holly. I'd appreciate it."

As they walked away, Missy turned around and grinned. For the first time, he noticed she was missing a front tooth.

"Awe you glad I'm talkin' to you, Uncle Cade?"

He winked. "Real glad."

Noisy chatter erupted as he leaned back against the tree again. Addy and John must have been proud of their children. Settling his hat lower on his forehead, he thought of Zoe, stirred by her love for his sister's kids. If he hadn't ridden off all those years ago, he and Red would be married, and those would be his kids playing on the swing. The thought didn't sour his stomach. If he let himself, he could think on that a while.

An hour passed. Pushing his brim up, he realized it was getting late. The sun was setting, and the children had missed dinner. Zoe would wonder what happened to them. Before he could call them in, the sound of snapping twigs brought his hand to his holster. Quick as a flash, the Colt centered on the intruder.

Zoe froze at the edge of the clearing, her gaze riveted on the weapon. He heard her suck in a deep breath as her face turned tense with cold disapproval.

"Don't ever sneak up on me like that," he said, slipping the gun back into his holster.

"It's getting late. I was worried." Her voice was chilly with condemnation.

"Sorry. The time got away from me."

"Why doesn't that surprise me?"

"Hey. We've had a peaceful afternoon and I'm feeling generous." He pointed to the ground beside him. "Might as well sit down."

After a bit, she seated herself a safe distance away. "Are you getting along with them?"

"No. We've been bickering like thieves."

"Very amusing."

"We're doing fine. Stop worrying."

"Better call them in. Supper's ready."

Cupping his hands to his mouth, he shouted, "The redheaded boss lady says you've had enough for one day!"

A bevy of groans and complaints went up as the children sloshed out of the water and trudged up the embankment.

"Hi, Zoe!" Holly said.

"We swimmded all day!" Will grinned from ear to ear.

"Hello, children."

Brody's lips quivered as Zoe wrapped a large towel around him. "Ow! That hurts!" he cried.

Zoe lifted the towel and examined Brody's reddened shoulders. When Will, Holly, and Missy crowded around to see, Cade realized they all looked like cooked lobsters.

"Cade, how long have they been in the sun?"

"I don't know. All afternoon, I guess." He frowned. "A little sun's good for them."

"A little sun? They're blistered!"

He pressed a finger to Brody's sunburned skin, leaving a white indentation. "What do you do for this?"

She picked up the kids' strewn clothing and helped Will put on his shirt. "Never mind, I'll take care of it. Come along, children. I'll give you a vinegar bath to take out the heat."

"A vinegar bath! Pee-eew!" the children chorused.

Cade stepped back as she gathered the quivering children and herded them up the embankment. "Hey," he called. "I'm taking them to Glori-Lee's for supper."

"That won't be necessary. I have chicken in the warming oven."

He caught up with her in two long strides. "Look, Red, this is my day to have them."

She slowed and let him pass. "Nothing was mentioned about meals."

"Having them for the day includes feeding them."

"Oh? What did you feed them for dinner?"

He stopped in the middle of the path. "They weren't hungry."

Brody turned to look over his shoulder. "I'm hungry. I'm starvin'!"

"Me too!" the other kids chimed in. "Starvin'."

"Oh, my. Uncle Cade forgot to feed you." She picked up speed and passed him.

He easily caught up with her. "I intend to feed them. I was about to call them in when you showed up. How long are you going to hold this grudge?"

Her steps quickened. "How long are you going to be here?"

Latching onto her arm, he stopped her and turned her to face him. "It's my day, and I'm feeding them."

"You can just hold a gun to their heads and order them to like you."

"A gun? Is that what the cold shoulder's about?"

"I don't hold with killing. You know that. You knew that when you rode out of here." She jerked away from him, rubbing her arm. "How could you do that to your poor father?"

She was spoiling for a fight, but he wasn't going to oblige her. His profession didn't concern her. "You sent for me."

"Addy sent for you. Not me."

He grabbed her arm again, grasping it tightly. "Only because of Addy?" Their gazes locked in a heated duel, and he shook his head. "You were never good at lying, Red."

She didn't back down. "When the children are recovered from being burnt alive, you can take them to wherever you're staying and spend time with them."

"That's big of you. I'm sleeping over the jail. I have a leaky roof, a bed, and a washstand. All five of us can't get in the room, let alone socialize."

"That isn't my problem."

"Look. I need your help and you're shutting me out. You have a right to be mad at me, but that's between us. Right now, let's worry about Addy's kids." He glanced at the children, who had wandered ahead, chasing a frog down the path.

Zoe stopped and brushed a lock of hair from her cheek. "I wish it would rain and cool things off."

"I'd appreciate it if you'd stop wishing for more rain. I'm not sleeping in a wet bed another night."

"Stay with Pop."

"Pop doesn't feel like company."

She turned accusing eyes in his direction. "What's wrong with him?"

"Gooseberry pie."

Her cheeks bloated as if the thought sickened her. A smile started at the corner of her mouth and then quickly faded. They stood for a moment in awkward silence.

Children's laughter filled the clearing, and Cade considered the situation. He used to have fun with her; it should be a happy time now. Instead, it was war.

Sighing, she said, "I wish you had been here for the funerals. The children needed a man to lean on."

"I tried. Sorry I didn't make it." He'd ridden for twenty-four hours straight hoping to arrive in time. If he'd ridden any harder, it would have killed his horse.

"When are you going to talk to the Brightons?"

"Tomorrow. I'm doing Pop a favor in Suffox County. I'll stop at the Brightons' on my way back."

"I wish you wouldn't."

"We've already had this argument. If it would make you feel better, you're welcome to come with me. We can talk to Bonnie and Seth together."

She stared into the distance, her face void of emotion. "I'll fight you on this, Cade."

"Why doesn't that surprise me?" Cade watched Will grab the frog, admiring the boy's quickness. "Fight me all you want. You're young— you need to think about remarrying and starting a family of your own. A woman with four kids isn't going to attract a whole lot of men...with the exception of Fell and Perry Drake. If those two turn you down, you're out of luck."

He watched her swell with indignation. She needed an explanation as to why he wouldn't give the kids to her. This was as good as any—a lot better than the truth.

Will ran back to them and thrust the frog in Cade's face. "Uncle Cade, Uncle Cade, look! I caught him!"

Taking a stumbling step back, Cade dodged the slimy offering. "Don't stick that thing in my face."

"Put the frog back in the water," Zoe ordered.

The boy's disappointed expression made Cade want to let him take the frog home with him, but instead he watched them take it to the water's edge and give it its freedom.

"How do you say no to them?" he asked.

"You have a lot to learn about children."

Taking her by the shoulders, he forced her to look at him. "That's why I intend to spend time with them. The kids and I are eating together tonight, either at Glori-Lee's or your house. You decide."

Zoe pulled away and kicked the dirt. "They're burnt to a crisp, half starved, and exhausted. What they need is a vinegar bath, supper, and bed."

Missy ran back and tugged at Zoe's dress. "Please, we nevew eat at Glowi-Lee's!"

"I want to eat at the café," Will joined in. "I'm not crisp or the other thing you said!"

"We're not 'accosted,'" Holly blurted. Cade wanted to laugh at Holly's mispronunciation, but he knew that if he so much as smiled, Zoe would slap him silly. "I want to eat with Uncle Cade at Glori-Lee's too!"

Cade's gaze locked with Zoe's. *Get out of this one gracefully.* "You're outnumbered, Red, so you might as well join us."

She tossed her head. "That would be a waste of money. I have a perfectly good chicken waiting for me at home."

He glanced at the kids and grinned. "Come on. You prefer a chicken's company to ours?" The kids burst into giggles. Zoe didn't.

"Before the meal's over, a chicken's company will look good, Cade Kolby. Have you ever eaten in public with four children?"

"No, but eating's eating, isn't it?" He winked at the kids. "They're big enough to feed themselves. What's the problem?"

"Fine," she said. "Pick them up in an hour, and may I remind you *again* that my name is Zoe, not Red."

Her sudden acquiescence made him wary. His smile faded. "Why won't you come with us?"

"I have chores, thank you. Come along, children."

Zoe stalked off as the youngsters hung back, trailing behind her and waving shyly to him. Cade lifted a hand and waved back. How hard could feeding four children be?

Chapter Eleven

Reeking of vinegar and smeared with baking soda paste, Cade marched his brood into Glori-Lee's café a little past seven. The tiny, birdlike widow glanced up and sniffed the air.

"Who tipped over the pickle barrel?"

Cade took off his hat and held it in front of him. "You're a sight for sore eyes, Glori-Lee. You're even better looking than when I left."

"You better believe it!"

"You got a man yet?"

"Been savin' myself for you."

Cade laughed. "You surely can do better than me."

She kissed him on the cheek. "You're too old for me anyway. I got my eye on one of the Pointer boys. He's young enough to raise the way I want him."

"You're a fickle woman, Glori-Lee."

Grinning, she motioned him to a large table near the front window. A vase of roses sat on a freshly ironed red-and-white checked table-cloth. The savory aroma of pot roast and baking bread drifted from the kitchen. A couple of the male diners smiled as the kids fought over chairs. The women gave Cade the cold shoulder, holding their napkins to their mouths as if they were protecting themselves from unsavory riffraff.

The children took their seats, and Cade sat down at the head of the table, admiring his newly acquired family. Despite their blistered skin and pungent odor, they were a handsome lot.

He studied the handwritten daily specials on the menu. Everything looked good. "What do you like to eat?" he asked the children.

"Peach pie," they chorused.

"Pie and what else?"

"Cream!"

He thought for a moment. "Don't you usually eat something before having pie?"

"Chocolate cake!" Brody answered.

Cade leaned back in his chair. "Okay, cake and pie it is." He was thinking more along the lines of the roast beef and potatoes, but they ought to know what they wanted to eat. After all, it was a special occasion.

"Peach pie, chocolate cake, and a pitcher of cream," he told Glori-Lee.

The woman frowned. "Have they had their supper?"

"Not yet. We're ordering it now." He'd sometimes eaten sweets for dinner, and it never killed him.

"Pie and cake!" the kids chorused.

Glori-Lee took the order and then stuck her pencil behind her ear as she ambled off toward the kitchen, grumbling, "Zoe ain't goin' to like this."

The smiles on the kids' faces were worth a tongue-lashing. Cade laid his hat on the table. "Well, now. Tell me about yourselves. Got any pets?"

Missy's eyes lit up. "We got a tomcat, Womeo, and Butch. He's ouw dog. And Bud."

"Bud? Who's Bud?"

"Bud lives in a jar," Will explained.

Missy solemnly nodded. "He's a bug. He's nice."

Cade lifted his brows. "A nice bug that lives in a jar. Anything else?"

"Nope," Brody answered. "Just Romeo, Butch, and Bud. I wanted a pony, but Zoe says she can't afford to feed one more thing."

The statement "can't afford" disturbed him. The general store had been in the Bradshaw family for three generations and should have left Zoe well off, but from the looks of the place, she wasn't. Her dresses were old and faded, and the furnishings were the same ones Jim's parents had had. She was still using the old cookstove.

He temporarily set the thought aside. "What about school? What grades are you in?"

Holly volunteered, "Third. Brody's in fifth."

"Guess school will be starting before long."

"I might not go back to school," Brody announced.

Holly slapped him on the arm. "Yes, you will. Zoe'll make you."

Cade intervened. "You have to go to school, son. You need an education."

Brody scooted forward in his chair. "Ma said you never finished school, and you know stuff."

"You need to know more stuff than I do. Besides, I had to quit. My pa got sick, and I had to go to work for a farmer to put food on our table."

Will sat up straighter. "You know plenty of stuff. Pa said you're the best there is at shootin' bad guys."

"Yeah," Brody said. "A boy at school said you shoot 'em dead. You hardly ever bring 'em in alive."

Cade frowned, disturbed by the boy's misconceptions. While he did what was necessary to collect a bounty, he'd always given his prey fair warning, and he'd never shot a man in the back.

Holly stared at him with eyes so like Addy's, it was chilling. "Ma said killin's nothin' for a man to be proud of."

"Your ma's right, but there're times when it's necessary."

"Ma said she prayed for you every night, prayed you'd come home and we'd all be a family again."

"We are a family," Brody insisted.

"Yeah," Will said. "Can I hold your gun?"

Cade shook his head. "No one holds my gun but me."

Glori-Lee returned with a whole pie, a large cake, and a big pitcher of thick cream. "Help yourselves, young'uns. Heaven help you. You'll all get bellyaches."

The children proved well mannered and polite, and Cade felt an uncle's pride as the meal progressed smoothly. He had to admit that a meal of pie, cake, and cream was a change from his usual beans and hardtack.

"I need to ask you kids something. We have to decide where you're going to live."

Missy's face clouded. "We don't want a kitten. We want to live at Zoe's."

Will looked up. "I want a pony, but I want to live at Zoe's too."

"That's what we need to talk about," Cade said. "If you couldn't live at Zoe's or the Brightons', where would you want to live?" He studied the children's sober looks.

"Not with Aunt Laticia," said all four at the same time.

"What's wrong with your Aunt Laticia?" Granted, he didn't relish the disgruntled crone.

Brody put his fork down and stared. "She's scary lookin'."

Will wrinkled his nose. "And she smells funny."

"We want to live with Zoe and you," Holly said. "You're our ma's brother. Ma always said Zoe was like her sister, so that makes her your sister too. Ma said brothers and sisters stick together."

Cade cleared his throat. "I'm afraid that's not possible."

"Why not?" Will asked. "Do you have to go shoot bad guys again?"

"I might, but not until we get you settled." He glanced at Brody when the child reached for a third piece of cake.

Licking his fork, Brody said, "Pass the cream, please."

"If you have to go shoot bad guys," Missy said, blinking heavy eyelids, "why can't we stay with Zoe?"

The sun, the swimming, and the long day were taking their toll on the little ones. Red was right. The kids needed a bed as much as they needed supper.

Will yawned. "Did you shoot that bad guy that shooted Zoe's husband?"

Cade avoided the boy's question and changed the subject. "Finish your supper, Will. You're getting sleepy. Look at your little sister. She's already asleep—oh! She's fallen into her pie." Springing to his feet, he grabbed Missy and lifted her head from her plate, pulling peaches out of her hair.

"Uh-oh." Brody pushed back from the table and doubled over. "My belly hurts."

"Mine, too." Will groaned. "And my skin's on fire!"

Glori-Lee rushed over to help as the children's moans increased. Cade was aware of unhappy expressions on the other diners' faces as the complaints escalated. "These young'uns are in pitiful shape. They need a hefty dose of castor oil and then their beds." Still grumbling, Glori-Lee wiped Missy's peach-covered face with a dishcloth. "Law, feeding these babies cake, pie, and cream. Kolby, where's your brain? You're gonna kill 'em."

Cade frowned, stepping around the table to check on Holly. "Are you all right?"

She got up slowly, her face pasty white, her balance unsteady. She shook her head. "I feel kinda sick."

He hoped there were enough bushes along the way home to accommodate his poor judgment. Pie, cake, and cream. He should have known better.

"I'll take them home," he told Glori-Lee.

Shaking her head, she said, "I'm glad I'm not the one to take them back to Zoe in this condition."

He lifted Missy into his arms and took hold of Holly's hand, trying to herd Brody and Will ahead of him as he left the café. Outside a clap of thunder rattled the sidewalk seconds before the heavens opened.

Glancing up, he frowned. *Man alive.* A stiff wind whipped the treetops and sent tumbleweeds bouncing haphazardly across Main Street.

Walt Mews shouted hello to him as he locked the barbershop door and then made a dash for the livery stable, holding a *Police Gazette* over his head.

Cade glanced toward the land office as Woodall Thompson consulted his watch and closed the upstairs window.

Jagged lightning lit up Ben Pointer's metal weather vane as Brody broke for the bushes, Will close on his heels.

Whimpering, Missy buried her face in Cade's neck. Using his hat as a shield, he covered her head, and then he pulled Holly close and wrapped one side of his vest around her head and shoulders.

"I don't feel good, Uncle Cade," Holly moaned.

"I know, honey. I'll take you home as soon as the boys," he glanced at the bushes, "finish up."

Missy snuggled closer, her breath sweet against his face. "I don't want the lightning to get me."

"I'll protect you, sweetheart. Nothing's going to happen to you while Uncle Cade is here."

He winced as the rain fell harder. Looking up, he released a noisy breath. *Is this your way of setting me back on the path of righteousness?*

Within seconds he was drenched to the bone, and so were the children. They turned piteous eyes on him, their lips quivering. Their noses were sunburned, they were worn out, and their bellies ached. It didn't take a crystal ball to tell him he wasn't cut out for fatherhood.

And the worst was yet to come. He still had to face the redhead.

Chapter Twelve

"You ordered rain? You got rain." Cade's voice broke through the downpour.

Zoe held the lamp higher and stared at the sopping assemblage standing at her back door. Cade held Missy in one arm, and Holly's head was tucked under his vest on the other side. Brody and Will were green around the gills, and there wasn't a dry thread to be seen on any of them. Water streamed off Cade's hat brim onto Will's head. Blinking, the boy swiped at the running stream.

Cade shifted Missy on his hip. "Are you going to make us stand out here all night? We're not getting any drier."

Hurriedly sliding a rag rug to the door with her foot, Zoe unlatched the screen. "Wipe your feet." Cade brushed by her and carried Missy into the kitchen. The other kids followed, quickly wiping their shoes on the rug.

"If you'll excuse me?" Cade turned and walked back out the door and threw up on Zoe's rosebush. Supper hadn't set real well with him, either.

"It's stowming, Zoe. I was scawed, but Uncle Cade didn't let anything happen to me," Missy informed her.

Zoe set down the lamp and led the little girl to the sink. She started to peel off her wet clothes.

"Holly, help Will. Brody, get out of your wet things and put them in the sink."

Instead of doing as she was asked, Holly sank to the nearest chair and laid her head on the table. "I don't feel so good."

"Me, either," Brody seconded.

Will didn't have to say a word. Zoe could see he was sick as a dog. Cade walked back into the kitchen. "What did you feed these children?"

"Supper."

Exasperated, Zoe plucked a slice of peach from Missy's wet hair. "What's this?"

"Supper."

Will groaned. "We ate peach pie and chocolate cake."

"And cream," Brody added. "A great big pitcher of it."

"Oh, Cade!" A vein throbbed in Zoe's temple as she watched him lift Missy to the counter and strip off her wet shoes and stockings. What would happen if he took a notion to assume full responsibility for them?

Missy reached up to Cade, holding out her arms. He bent toward her, and she kissed him on the cheek. Cade's expression softened and he kissed her back.

"We had a good time, didn't we, Uncle Cade?"

"A very good time."

"You can call me Sunflowew. That's what Pa called me."

He hesitated and then obliged. "All right. Sunflower it is."

Zoe brushed by him on her way to wring out the wet clothing. He knew it irked her that even though he wasn't pa material, the children took to him like flies to molasses.

He trailed her to the sink. "I'm sorry. I made a mistake feeding them all those sweets. I wasn't thinking—but it was a special occasion."

Rinsing peach juice out of Missy's dress, Zoe grumbled, "Anyone with a lick of sense knows you don't feed kids peach pie, chocolate cake, and cream."

"It's not going to kill them to eat what they want once in a while."

"Oh, no? Look at them. They look half dead to me."

He glanced at the children. "Have you forgotten the time Addy and I got into Pa's communion wine?"

"No. Have you forgotten that you thought you were going die?"

"That's my point. We didn't. And I learned my lesson." And his stomach hurt too.

She turned to face him. "What? Not to drink half a bottle of wine?"

"No. Not to let you catch me."

She wrung out Missy's dress and hung it near the cookstove to dry. "Haven't you got somewhere to go?"

"As a matter of fact, I don't. I haven't been to the jail since this morning, but I can tell you that bunk is floating in water."

"Too bad."

"Yes, it is. I'm not sleeping there."

"Then go over to Pop's. It'd serve him right for not fixing that leaky roof months ago."

She shooed the children to the bedroom for their nightclothes, and then she bent over to pick up wet towels, bumping into a broad wall of warm chest.

Cade smiled as she slid up his length, her senses simmering.

"Will you kindly get out of my way?"

"Can't. Room's too small. No place to go." He tweaked her nose and she shrugged away.

"Cade—"

"I don't want to stay with Pop. He might be contagious."

"Gluttony is not contagious."

Brody came out of the bedroom buttoning his nightshirt. "He can sleep with me and Will."

Will jumped up and down. "Yeah! That would be fun!"

"I'll fix you breakfast, Uncle Cade," Holly offered. "I can cook eggs almost as good as Ma."

Missy ran into the kitchen and latched onto her uncle's leg. "I want you to sleep with me and Zoe so we won't be scawed of the stowm."

Patting the child on her head, Cade grinned at Zoe. "On second thought, I'll sleep with the boys. Your bed is a little short for me." He eyed Zoe. "And a little cold."

"Uh-uh," Missy said. "It's wawm…weal wawm."

Zoe lifted a brow. Sleep with the boys? That quick, and he'd moved in. Taking her for granted, never thinking she might have enough on her hands as it was. She didn't like it, but there was no point protesting. She was outnumbered.

"No one would get any sleep if you slept with the boys."

Cade grinned. "What a dilemma."

Zoe threw a dirty towel on the table. "Jim kept a cot in the mercantile. He favored naps. For tonight *only*, you can sleep there. Be careful. I keep my mother's figurines close by."

Brody smiled. "We ain't allowed to play near them cause they cain't be bought again. Ever."

"On account we might break something," Will clarified.

"A tiny cot?" Cade asked.

"There's the floor. Take your pick. You're only going to be here one night." She strode past him, speaking in a low tone. "Don't get too comfortable."

After dosing the children with castor oil to ease their bellyaches, Zoe rounded up an extra pillow.

Leading Cade to the cot, she warned again, "Be careful of my figurines."

He glanced at the assortment of delicate angels, swans, and butterflies sitting on a table to one side.

"I heard you."

"Just so you understand." She closed the door. A second later she heard something hit the floor. Clamping her eyes shut, she held her breath before yanking the door open.

Cade was down on his knees in front of the counter with the broken lid to the pickle jar in his hand. "I'm hungry."

Slamming the door shut, she went to bed.

Chapter Thirteen

Fierce wind battered the old store with the force of a gale. Cracks of lightning lit the room. Zoe got up several times to put vinegar on the fretful children's sunburned shoulders. She tried to stay calm, but the store's worsening financial situation upset her.

Sporadic thunderclaps shook the tiny rooms. She heard can goods falling off the store's shelves. It had been years since a storm like this had raged through Winterborn. She nearly jumped out of her skin when a limb split off the huge oak in the backyard and slammed against the porch. Butch howled and scratched incessantly at the back door, wanting to come in. Romeo's meows escalated to frantic yowls. She couldn't remember spending a more miserable night.

Around four o'clock, nerves frazzled, she finally fell exhausted into bed.

She'd closed her eyes only a moment when a clap of thunder roused her. She was barely aware of Missy sliding out of bed and whispering something to Holly. The two girls left the room, and Zoe dropped into a deep sleep.

Toward dawn she rolled over and found Missy's side of the bed empty. She shot up and noticed that Holly was missing.

Donning her robe, she glanced out the window toward the outhouse. Maybe they were still sick. She groaned when she saw that the outhouse door had blown off and half of the back fence was down.

Alarmed, she stepped into the kitchen, and her heart leaped to her throat when she saw that the boys weren't on their pallets, either. "Brody! Will! Holly! Missy!"

She ran through the kitchen and opened the door to the mercantile, coming to an abrupt halt when she saw Cade, the kids, Butch, and Romeo clustered in a heap around the cot, all sound asleep.

Her hand went to her throat when she saw Bud, the children's pet tarantula, out of his jar and perched in the middle of Cade's chest. Missy must have taken off the lid again.

Zoe stood for a moment, uncertain what to do. She could let Cade wake naturally and…no, that was plain mean. She'd wake him quietly without disturbing Bud.

Tiptoeing to the cot, she whispered, "Cade."

He opened one eye and smiled at her. He opened the other eye and came face-to-face with Bud. Jerking upright, he flailed his hands at the tarantula, knocking it into the center of the room.

Stunned, Zoe couldn't believe how quickly a man could vacate a cot. Before she could explain, he was chasing the creature around the room, trying to smash it with stocking feet.

Butch sprang to life, barking and leaping over the end table. His tail caught two of the figurines and sent them to the floor with a crash. Romeo yowled and shot like a streak across the room.

The girls scrambled toward Cade, hanging onto the seat of his long johns. Missy squealed, "Quit dancing, Uncle Cade! You'we scawing Bud!"

Cade shouted, "Bud *who*?"

"Bud, the bug," Zoe yelled.

"The bug?" Cade ceased prancing and dropped into a chair. Running a shaky hand through his hair, he let out a breath. "That thing is a *pet*?"

Sickened, Zoe slumped to her knees, staring in despair at her broken figurines. She should have known to put them away.

Brody and Will raised sleepy heads. "Is it still storming?" Will asked.

Missy ran to Bud and scooped him into the jar. Screwing the lid on, she looked at Zoe. "Did the stowm scawe you too, Wed?"

Zoe struggled to keep a straight face. The very idea of Missy calling her "Wed"! She finally burst out laughing, slapping her hands on her knees. "No, Sunflower. The storm's over. I just wondered where you all were."

Once the excitement had died down, Zoe carefully picked up the broken pieces of a swan and a butterfly.

"I'm sorry about your figurines," Cade said, stooping to help.

"It's my fault. I should have put them away."

"I'll buy you new ones."

"Don't be silly. They're irreplaceable."

Zoe kept her eyes averted. The sight of him in his long johns distracted her more than she cared to admit. Who would think a man in his underwear could evoke such provocative feelings, even if he did look silly in stocking feet? "The storm was pretty bad. The backyard has a lot of damage. I haven't looked out front yet."

The children scampered out of the room and ran to the back door. Will hollered, "The outhouse is tore up."

"There's a big tree limb in the yard!" Holly said. Zoe and Cade joined the children, surveyed the damage, and then they walked back to the front of the store, where Cade opened the door.

"What's it look like?" Zoe asked, trying to see around him.

"Looks like I'll be sleeping on the cot a couple more days."

"Why?"

Her first glimpse of Main Street answered her question for him. The jail's roof had been blown off and was now perched on top of Woodall Thompson's sycamore tree. Surrounding businesses had missing shutters, and the street was strewn with signs and boards. *Ben Pointer and Sons* was stuck in Glori-Lee's window box. Mayor Willis, in his nightshirt, surveyed the carnage.

Cade called to him. "Anybody hurt, Lawrence?"

Zoe was mortified when she saw Lawrence glance up and do a

double take at Cade standing at the door in his long johns and her in her robe.

Lawrence glanced away. "Not that I know of. Is that you, Cade?"

Cade stepped back. "I'll be out shortly."

Lawrence shook his head. "No hurry. Take your time." Frowning, his eyes slid back to the long johns.

Appalled, Zoe yanked Cade back inside and slammed the door. "Why didn't you explain?"

"Explain what? That I slept on the cot in a mercantile with four kids, a dog, a cat, and a tarantula?"

Wheeling, she marched to the kitchen, knowing the incident would be reported all over town before breakfast.

By eight o'clock, the sounds of hammers and saws rang up and down the street. According to Lilith, it would take days for the town to return to normal.

Missy shot in the back door, dancing on her tiptoes. "Uncle Cade, I gotta go."

Cade glanced up from his breakfast plate. "Go where?"

Zoe dished two eggs out of the skillet and put them on Brody's plate. "She needs to use the outhouse."

"It don't have no doow on it. Evewybody will see me!"

Cade scraped his chair back from the table and got up.

Zoe frowned. "Your breakfast will get cold. Can you wait a moment, Missy?"

She hopped on one foot and then the other. "Noooooooo! Now!"

"Give me just a few minutes, Sunflower, and I'll have you back in business."

Missy skipped out behind him, and the screen door banged shut. Zoe carried Cade's plate to the warming oven. Raising the window for some air, she paused with her hand in mid-motion when she noticed Cade stripping off his shirt. Powerless to look away, she stood frozen to the spot, drinking in the sight of his muscular back glinting in the morning sun. Sinewy cords rippled as he lifted the heavy outhouse door into place. Seeing him this way brought back memories of the night that had changed her life forever.

She smiled as Missy held her hands between her legs and jumped on one foot. Cade hoisted Will up on his shoulders to get the fallen limbs off the roof of the outhouse, while Brody and Holly hammered nails into a cross board on the door. There was no denying it. Cade loved the kids. Zoe nearly laughed out loud when he set Will down and chased him around the outhouse. Cade was a kid at heart.

Family. This was her family now. Her smile faded when she realized their child could have been helping repair the outhouse. How old would the child be? Almost sixteen? Approaching adulthood, almost the same age Cade had been when he left. She quickly looked away, swallowing the lump crowding her throat.

Missy's impatience grew. "Huwwy, Uncle Cade! Huwwy!"

Cade grabbed a hammer and started pounding. "I'm hurrying, Sunflower—can't you use the bushes?"

Zoe grinned when she heard Missy's indignant, "No!"

In a few minutes, the outhouse door had been repaired enough for Missy to seek relief, and within an hour nearly all the broken limbs had been cleared from the yard. Brody, Will, and Holly worked like beavers alongside Cade, while Missy issued orders with the gusto of a cavalry officer.

Around noon, Cade stuck his head in the kitchen doorway and called to Zoe, "I'll be at the jail."

She glanced up from the ironing board, her gaze meeting his and catching until she smelled a scorched odor coming from the chemise. She quickly folded the garment and put it back in the dirty clothes basket. "Are the children going with you?"

"They're going to help Lawrence Willis clear Main Street."

"Tell them not to get in the way."

"You tell them. Missy would court-martial me."

Chapter Fourteen

Crossing the street, Cade spotted Pop standing in front of the jail assessing the damage.

"Boy, wind took her off slick as a whistle." Pop stared, hands on hips, at bare rafters where once the spare room had been. "Ain't got the money to build it back proper-like."

"The town doesn't have the money for a new roof?"

"Nope. Never thought about having it blown clean off," Pop confessed. "Suppose we'll just do enough to keep the jail dry and not worry about that room overhead. Hardly ever used it anyway."

"I was sleeping there," Cade reminded him.

Pop's eyes widened. "You weren't in there during the storm, were you?"

"No. By then, the bunk was so wet that I stayed the night with the kids in the mercantile."

Pop chuckled. "The kids?"

"Zoe wasn't crazy about the idea, but she let me sleep on a cot."

"Women. They can be merciless, can't they?"

Cade stuck Pop's hammer and nails in his back pockets, and then he grabbed a rung of the ladder leaning against the building. "Round up a couple of extra hands to help me put on a makeshift roof before it rains again."

"You got time to do this?"

"I'll have to pick up Pearson tomorrow."

"Hope they got him in an ice house. You be sure and remind Mooney that Hague's death's on his record, not mine. Don't let him pull one over on you."

"Not many men pull one over on me, Pop."

"I'd go myself, but I got more troubles. I broke out in hives. Can't quit itchin'."

Cade nodded, noting the angry red patches on Pop's face. "What did you eat now?"

"Hard tellin'," Pop said, scratching his hip.

"Maybe the Pointer boys will help with the roof. If you've got a minute, can you get them for me?"

Pop hurried off, and Cade climbed the ladder. His "brief" stop in Winterborn was getting longer every day.

Toward dark, his head was throbbing from the ring of hammers driving nails through wood. Signs had been reattached to storefronts and broken windowpanes replaced. It was gratifying to see small children lugging wooden carts through town, picking up scattered branches and other debris. Brody and Will piled their cart high, and then they hauled it to the end of town and dumped it.

The jail had a roof again, though it was nothing to brag about. The salvaged shingles were old and would probably leak like a sieve. The overhead sleeping space had been torn down and used to patch a hole in the town hall.

Cade returned to the general store that night sunburned and with blistered hands. The aroma of frying chicken scented the air. When he opened the screen door, a fly buzzed past him.

Zoe jammed her fists to her hips. "Where'd that fly come from? I told you kids to watch that back door!"

"Don't blame the kids. I let it in."

"Well, shut the door before we have a houseful. I suppose you're hungry."

"I'm worn out, and I don't feel like going over to Glori-Lee's." Cade watched her eyes soften, and he knew it was a dinner invitation.

"Wash up. Supper'll be ready in a few minutes."

Missy raced around the table and pulled out his chair. "Aftew you wash youw hands, Uncle Cade, you sit by me."

He stepped toward the sink as Zoe moved away from the stove. They bumped hips. She spun to face him.

"Sorry," he muttered.

He sat down at the table and removed his hat. Holly had buttered his corn and poured him a glass of milk. "Thank you, sweetheart." His gaze focused on Zoe's as she slid a pan of biscuits out of the oven and carried it to the table. She still had that little wiggle when she walked.

Taking her seat, Zoe reached for Brody's hand and bowed her head. "Holly, I believe it's your turn."

"Dear Lord, thank you for this good food. And for Zoe letting Uncle Cade sit at the table. Amen."

After grace, Zoe passed the biscuits while Brody doled himself a hefty portion of potatoes. "When are you going to teach me to shoot a pistol, Uncle Cade?"

Will grinned. "Me too."

Spooning string beans onto his plate, Cade could feel Zoe's eyes on him. He knew how she felt about guns, so the subject was a delicate one. "You both need to be older before you shoot a pistol, but I'll show you how to handle a shotgun."

Zoe ladled gravy over her potatoes. "At their age, why do they have to know how to shoot any gun?"

"They need to know, Red. Boys turn into men. Men feed their families." He winked at the males.

Zoe passed the butter. "I saw that."

Grinning, he reached for another biscuit. "Remind me to have a discussion with you about men being men."

Without looking up, she said, "I know about men being men."

He bit into his chicken. "What is it with you and guns?"

Brody craned his neck in Cade's direction. "Ma said she's been like that ever since Jim got shot in that bank holdup."

Cade switched subjects. "You gonna eat all those potatoes? Pass a few to me."

Seth Brighton was mending harness when Cade drove into his barnyard early Wednesday afternoon.

He swung down from the buckboard, and the two men shook hands.

"Well, I declare. Cade Kolby." Seth grinned from ear to ear. "We heard you were back." The man's eyes moved to the pine box lashed to the wagon bed. "What you got there? A man with a price on his head?"

Cade fell into step with the younger man as they walked toward the house. A couple of towheaded kids played in a dirt pile near the back.

"It's Hague Pearson. He was shot and killed in Suffox County. I'm picking up the body for Pop."

Seth shook his head. "That's too bad. Hague never caused no trouble around here. Kept to himself."

"That's what I hear. By the way, one of your hogs was out. A couple of your boys helped me chase it back into the pen."

"That'd be Eddie Lee and Bruce. They're a big help. Storm blew the fence down, and the hogs got loose," Seth said as they climbed the steps to the porch. "Sure was sorry to hear about John and your sister. They were good people."

"Yes, they were."

"Say, I'll bet you're parched. How 'bout a glass of lemonade? Got some cooling in the spring." He raised his hands and called to one of the kids, "Jimmy! You go on down and fetch the lemonade!" He turned back to Cade. "For a boy jist gettin' over the measles, he can run like the wind."

"I can't stay, Seth. The business in Suffox County took longer than I thought, and I still have one more stop. I'd like to get back before dark, but I wanted to talk to you."

"Then maybe we'll just sit in the shade a spell." Seth ushered him to a chair on the side porch. "Sue Ann," he called, "you run in and check on your mama."

Seth settled in the seat next to Cade's. "Guess I know what you're here about."

"Pop said you and your wife were interested in taking in Addy and John's children."

"We sure are. That's a fine bunch of kids. John and I were friends a good many years."

Jimmy returned with a jug. He sat it down and ran up on the porch to stand in front of Cade. "Are you Will and Brody's uncle who shoots bad guys?"

Seth took the lemonade and set a hand on the boy's shoulder. "You go on back and play, son. Your pa's talking business."

When the boy was out of earshot, Cade said, "I want to get the children settled as soon as possible." The man's children appeared happy and well cared for. Pop was right. The Brightons would provide a good home for the kids. In time they would love it here. Seth and Bonnie could give them what he couldn't. A ma and a pa.

Seth shifted in his chair. "Could be a few weeks before we're able to take them. Bonnie needs to get back on her feet."

Cade frowned. "Is your wife ill?"

"Come down with a fever during the night."

When the young man's face sobered, Cade wondered how high of a fever.

"We're expectin' it'll pass real quick."

"You want me to send Doc out to look at her?"

"Sent for him first thing. Sawyer said he had to be over the county line for two, three days." Swallowing hard, he blinked. "I'm taking the kids to my folks this evening. They're going to keep them, just in case…"

"Probably wise of you."

Seth rubbed his eyes with thumb and forefinger. "Bonnie will feel bad about this, knowing she could have them right away. She has her heart set on taking Addy's kids—and we still mean to take them. We're just gonna have to put it off for a few days…until we see how Bonnie comes along."

"Of course." Cade got up to leave. "Anything I can do to help?"

"No. I'd appreciate your prayers, though." Seth reached out to shake his hand. "We'll send word the minute Bonnie's up and about again. It shouldn't be too long…" Seth pointed to the south end of the house. "I'm building on. We'll have plenty of room for the young'uns."

Chapter Fifteen

It was late in the afternoon before Cade approached the outskirts of Winterborn. Pausing, he stared at the cemetery entrance. He'd put off visiting his family's graves for as long as he could. He'd avoided cemeteries most of his life due to putting many a man there himself.

He climbed from the wagon and leaned down to pick some blossoms from a clump of wild daisies. In the midst of prairie grass and scattered wildflowers, a lone cottonwood shaded the family plots. Addy would have been at peace knowing she and John would be buried here.

His gaze traveled to nearby headstones, reading the familiar names of those he had known from childhood, swallowing against the tightness in his throat. When he came to the inscription "Mac and Senda Kolby—Together in life, Eternal in death," his vision blurred. Ma's and Pa's graves.

Kneeling, he observed a moment of silence. He hadn't talked to the Lord much in the past few years. It seemed that if he didn't talk to the Lord, he might not have kept up on Cade's whereabouts. He moved to Addy's and John's fresh graves, where he laid the handful of daisies among the wilted bouquets left by other mourners. Rising, he removed his hat and tried to remember a prayer. Any prayer. It was hard. He hadn't prayed in a long time.

God, you're a whole lot better than I am, and I suppose you know what you're doing, but there's four little kids left with broken hearts.

Shame washed over him. When he was a boy, there hadn't been a Sunday when he wasn't seated next to his ma at the Good Shepherd Church, listening to Pa preach the Word. Senda Kolby had raised her children with an iron hand and a forgiving heart. She lived and died by the Ten Commandments, and expected others to do the same. Had she been disappointed in him? Was it her prayers that had kept him alive all these years?

The peacefulness was broken by the call of a meadowlark overhead. He glanced up as the bird flew away, and he envied its freedom. Addy's image swam before his eyes. The vivid picture of his little sister falling out of a toy wagon, tears running down her dirt-streaked face. He'd led her to the front porch and set her in the swing, wiping away her tears with his shirttail.

An emotional half chuckle escaped him. He had given her his prized slingshot, hoping it would make her feel better.

"Sorry, I'm all out of slingshots, sis." In his estimation, no one had been good enough for his sister. To Addy's dismay, he had run off more promising suitors than you could shake a stick at.

His gaze shifted to the grave beside Addy's. He wished he'd known John Wiseman. In Addy's letters, she'd praised the man she'd married. Through her words, he had felt her happiness, a happiness that was short lived.

The crunch of dry buffalo grass caught his attention, and his hand slid to his gun. Then he heard Zoe's voice call out, "It's me, Cade."

Turning, he watched her approach the graves, carrying a small basket of flowers. She was flushed from the walk. A few straggling tendrils of hair stuck to her face, glistening with tiny beads of sweat. She had a natural beauty that didn't require kohl or rouge to turn a man's head.

"This is the last place I thought I'd find you today." Setting her basket on the ground, she wiped her forehead with a handkerchief. "The children are looking for you."

"What do they want?"

"Nothing in particular. They're with Pop now. Why are your cheeks wet?"

He turned away. "It's hot here."

She picked up a handful of flowers. "I don't know why men are so embarrassed to cry. It's a natural thing to do under the circumstances."

"I'm sweating."

"You're crying."

His gaze met and held hers. "Do you always have to have the last word?"

"Only when I'm right."

Stepping around him, she laid flowers on Addy's and John's graves, and then proceeded to Jim's. Cade felt a pang of envy when he saw her somber expression. Had she loved her husband deeply? He hoped Jim had made her happy. It seemed that all he, Cade, had brought her was misery.

Standing before Jim's marker, she bowed her head. He wanted to comfort her, but it wasn't his place. She had enough pain to handle.

She laid flowers on Jim's grave and her parents' graves and then moved to his parents' resting place. She pulled long strands of grass away from their headstone, and then placed marigolds against the simple crosses.

"You come here often?" he asked, ignoring the guilt that swept him. Until today, he'd never put a flower on Ma's or Pa's graves.

"As often as I can."

"Do you always put flowers on my folks' graves?"

"I guess it's habit. Addy and I used to come here together."

"I appreciate it."

"It's no bother." Straightening, she dusted her hands, glancing at the sun. "It's a scorcher today."

"Real hot."

She smiled. "I know. You've been sweating. "

He turned to walk away, and she latched onto his arm. "We need to talk."

"Here?"

She shook her head, and he wondered if she guessed his reluctance to linger in a cemetery.

"There's some shade over there," she pointed to a tree outside the gate.

Their shoes kicked up puffs of dust. Grasshoppers jumped beside them as they trod the rutted path. The scent of dry hay hung thick in the stifling summer air.

Zoe's gaze went to Cade's horse and the sheriff's wagon behind. "I see you picked up Hague."

"Yes. I need to get him to the undertaker." Already the foul scent seeping from the pine box turned one's stomach.

Moving toward the tree, she motioned for him to follow. "Let's rest a moment."

Sitting on the grass, she leaned back against the tree trunk, fanning herself with her handkerchief.

He took a seat beside her, removed his hat, and hooked it over his knee. "What's on your mind?"

"You have to leave."

"Leave. What'll it be, Red? Leave or stay? You seem to reach a different conclusion every day."

"Leave. The kids are getting attached to you too quickly."

"Isn't that the point of me staying?"

"Regardless, I know you're not going to stay, so you have to leave."

He stared at her. "You confuse me."

"What's confusing about your leaving? You *are* going, aren't you?"

"Eventually."

"Then leave now before you do anymore damage."

He took a deep breath and released it slowly, choosing his words carefully. "I don't want to hurt the kids." When he looked into her eyes, he saw her misgivings. She didn't trust him. The thought stung, but he conceded that he had neglected his family. Her disapproval of him was his own fault. "I'll stay as long as it takes to find the kids a home."

"Not good enough."

Could he tell her about Hart McGill and not upset her? He couldn't.

Women didn't understand his profession. "It's the way it's going to be."

"Why do you have to go? If you're so adamant about me not having the kids, why not stay and raise them? Is Winterborn such a burden to you?"

"Do you know what's going to happen to this town when word spreads that I'm here?"

She sighed. "Trouble."

"'Trouble' is putting it mildly." There were men waiting to jump at the chance to gun him down in public. He wasn't going to subject Winterborn to hardened criminals, let alone Zoe and the kids. Coming home made him realize how much he missed the town. Pop, the old-timers at the barbershop, the smell of cookies baking at Edna Mews's house, young boys playing marbles in the street. He had been one of those kids once. Now his life was an endless succession of dirty cow towns, empty bedrolls, cold beans, and warmed-over coffee. Not much to brag about for thirty-three years.

He focused on the meadow opposite the road and watched sunflowers bob their heads in the breeze. He couldn't travel far enough to escape the enemies he'd made, but he wasn't going to endanger Addy's kids because of them.

The grizzly image of Hart McGill crossed his mind. He wouldn't rest until he, Cade, was six feet under.

"I'm just saying that if you don't plan to keep the kids, then the kindest thing to do is to leave. Right now." Zoe wiped her palms on her skirt. "The longer you stay, the harder it will be for them to give you up."

"They won't be giving me up. I'll be back on occasion."

She stood and brushed off the back of her skirt, jaw clenched, frustration written on her face. "Where have I heard that before?"

Trying to lighten the mood, he playfully tugged at the hem of her skirt. "Don't get yourself in a snit." He winced when he saw the stubborn tilt of her chin that always meant trouble.

"I made a promise to an old friend's wife. All right?"

"And she believed you?"

"You know what? I'm getting a little tired of your sass." He grinned when impatience flared in her eyes.

"Is that right? Well, let me tell you what I'm tired of—"

He reached up, took her hand, and pulled her down beside him, mocking her wide-eyed countenance.

"Cade Kolby, stop manhandling me."

Leaning close, he whispered against her ear, "You big enough to stop me?"

She stiffened and pulled away, but his arm slid around her waist and held her immobile.

"Don't think you're going to kiss me," she declared.

"How else am I going to shut you up?" He grinned at the surprise in her eyes and then lowered his head. He had forgotten how intoxicating she smelled. Too many years had passed since he had kissed her.

Just before their lips met, her fingers clamped around his ear like a bear trap. Words escaped through her clenched teeth. "I *said*, don't think you're going to *kiss* me!" She pushed him aside. "Answer my question."

She appeared unfazed, but her shaking hand and the blush on her cheek told him he still had an effect on her. "I forgot the question."

"When exactly are you leaving?"

Getting to his feet, he rubbed feeling back into his ear. "When I'm good and ready."

She stood and faced him. "Those children should be mine, Cade."

"Do you remember how lonely you were as a girl with no mother? Your pa was gone most the time. Is that the kind of life you want for Addy's kids?"

"Of course not, but I wouldn't be gone. I would be here."

"I remember how good life was for Addy and me, growing up with both a mother and father. I want that for her kids. I know that's what she would want."

Zoe's eyes misted as she fumbled for her handkerchief. He reached for her hand and gently rubbed the back of it with his thumb. "I'm not trying to hurt you. I'm trying to do what I think is best for all concerned."

Seth and Bonnie were fine people and would do right by the children. As soon as Bonnie was well, the kids would go there to live. No use telling Zoe about Bonnie right now. He'd only further upset her and that wasn't his purpose. She was a fine woman, but the kids needed a pa.

She took her hand out of his and reached for her basket. "You're impossible."

Cade watched her walk briskly down the road, her backside flouncing with every determined step. He shook his head. A lot of sass. His grin widened. That's what he liked about her.

"I don't think so," he called, slipping his hat back on. "I've met worse."

He'd been worse. She just didn't know it.

Whirling, she flung her basket at him. Without missing a step, she marched on.

He thumbed his hat to the back of his head and took a deep breath. This felt good. Sparring with her made him feel like a kid again.

He sobered. It wasn't the kid in him that reacted to her. There had been other women over the years, but none caused the excitement in him like that female did.

Chapter Sixteen

Cade delivered Hague's body to Pop and then headed to the Brad-shaw place. Shadows lengthened. The moon had a ring around it. Rain by morning.

He'd missed supper at Glori-Lee's by an hour, and he assumed he'd go to bed hungry.

He had days, at most, to wrap up his business here. Hart McGill wasn't a fool. It wouldn't take long for news to spread that Cade Kolby wasn't anywhere near St. Louis.

Butch barked as Cade rounded the back of the store. He spoke the dog's name, and the mutt bounded over.

The door opened and Missy peeked out, breaking into a grin. "I'm glad you'we home, Uncle Cade. We kept suppew wawm for you."

Supper warm for him? It had been years since anyone had kept supper warm for him.

He smiled at the angel with the cornflower blue eyes. "You did?"

Missy nodded and then jumped up and down. "He's home, Zoe! He's home!"

Brody, Will, and Holly joined Missy in the kitchen. Zoe came in, pushing a lock of hair out of her eyes. The children dragged Cade to the table as she reached into the warming oven and took out a plate. Holly ran to pour a glass of milk while Missy buttered a thick wedge of corn bread and laid it on his plate. Brody hung over his shoulder, talking about the frogs he'd caught.

Overwhelmed by the attention, Cade sat down. When Zoe set the food in front of him, he said, "I expected to go to bed hungry tonight."

"It's not much," she warned. "Plain old beans and cornbread."

Beans and cornbread. At eight o'clock at night, with him not having eaten since early morning. The fare looked like turkey and dressing. He dug in, aware of the eyes suddenly focused on him.

His spoon slowed as he glanced up and met Missy's disapproving gaze. Crossing her arms, she shook her head.

He lifted his brows.

Leaning over, the child whispered, "You haven't *pwayed*."

"Prayed?" He glanced at Zoe.

"Blessed the food," she offered.

Stunned, he asked, "Me?"

"You're the one eating, aren't you?"

He bowed his head and clasped his hands together. He hadn't thanked God for anything in years. He looked at Missy out of the corner of his eye. "What do I say?"

"Just say, thank you fow the food, God, and thank you fow my family."

He glanced up and met Zoe's amused eyes. Bowing his head again, he prayed, "Thank you for the food, God, and thank you for...my family." The words felt strange on his tongue.

Kitchen warmth surrounded him as he ate. Brody wanted to know all about his day, so Cade explained about the trip to Suffox County. Will, Missy, and Holly huddled close to the table, listening.

Will straightened. "Did you shoot a bad guy today?"

Cade patted the boy's head. "I didn't shoot anyone."

Zoe brought her sewing to the table and darned socks, smiling at the children's occasional bursts of laughter. Cade regaled his rapt audience by telling them how he and Eddie Lee Brighton had chased a pig down the road, trying to capture it.

"Maddy had to stand guard over Hague's body while I chased that porker on foot for better than twenty minutes," Cade said, laughing. "Must have run off four pork chops and a side of bacon before she gave in."

Zoe glanced up at the mention of Maddy.

"Did some lady go with you?" Brody asked.

"No." He winked at the children. "Maddy's my horse. Short for Madeleine. Named her after a woman I knew in Wichita. Feisty little filly…" His gaze caught Zoe's and she looked away, sharply biting off a piece of thread

When the clock struck nine, she laid her mending aside. "It's bed-time."

In a flurry of commotion, the boys ran to make up their pallets. The girls disappeared into the bedroom, returning to Cade a few moments later for good night kisses.

Sending the children on their way, Zoe bustled around the kitchen, putting away dishes. Leaning back in his chair, Cade watched the way the lamplight shone on her hair. Her lithe figure hadn't changed much. Her waist was still so tiny he could span it with two hands.

"What did Seth and Bonnie have to say when you stopped by?" Her voice was soft, hesitant.

He'd deliberately avoided the subject, but it was open now and she had to know.

"How well do you know Bonnie?"

Zoe trimmed the lamp. "Not well. I see her occasionally at social functions and church. She stays to herself most of the time."

"She wasn't raised around here?"

"No. In Oklahoma. Why?"

"Bonnie's come down with a fever."

Zoe almost dropped a cup. "Why didn't you tell me earlier?"

"As soon as she's better…"

"The fever!" Zoe's hand flew to her throat.

"She's sick. It may not be *the* fever, just a fever."

"How can you know? That's what Addy first thought, it was just a fever. What does this mean for the children?"

"Frank and Helen have taken them—"

"Not Seth and Bonnie's children. Addy's children."

Getting up from the table, Cade carried his plate to the sink. "For the moment, it means I'll be in Winterborn a few days longer than I intended."

"Cade, if Bonnie has taken ill with the same fever that killed John and Addy—"

"We don't know that. Stop borrowing trouble. It could be a short illness. In a few days, Bonnie will either be better or worse. We'll look at the situation then."

"Cade—"

"No, Zoe." He answered her question before she asked. "Bonnie's illness doesn't change anything. It merely delays things."

When her face clouded with resentment, he reached out and tweaked her nose. "Thank you for holding supper for me. It's been a long time since you've done anything that nice for me."

The exasperated look she gave him before she walked out of the room made him suspect it would be even longer before he sat at her table again.

He spotted Holly in the doorway. "Hi, Sweet Pea. I thought you'd be asleep by now."

The child walked over to him and put her arms around his neck. "Don't be mad at Zoe. She's just tired."

Cade squeezed her against him. "I'm not mad at Zoe. We just talk mean to each other. I really kinda like her. Hey, I could use some help feeding Maddy tomorrow. Why don't you go into the store in the morning and get a carrot? I'll bet she'd love that."

The girl's eyes brightened. "Can I give it to her?"

"Sure can."

Dawn was streaking the sky as Cade and Holly put down fresh hay. He lifted the little girl up and sat her on the side of the stall so she could pet Maddy's mane.

"She sure loves carrots, huh, Uncle Cade?"

"She appears to be pretty partial to you too."

"Someday I'm going to have a horse like Maddy."

Cade winked. "You got a pretty smile, just like your mama."

Holly's eyes misted. "I miss Ma and Pa. Ma was always laughin' and singin'."

Cade lifted her down and picked up a pitchfork. "I miss my ma too. Reckon we always will, but it gets easier. Your ma wouldn't want us to be sad." He paused and tipped her face up with his finger. "Let's see that happy face."

Her lips trembled and then turned up in a sweet smile. "I love you, Uncle Cade."

He swallowed hard. "I love you too, Holly."

Chapter Seventeen

Lilith's shrill laugher could wake the dead. Once she got going, folks as far as Suffox County could hear her high-pitched squeals and intermittent snorts.

"King me!" Edna said, stacking Gracie's checkers in her growing pile and laughing along with Lilith until tears rolled down her cheeks. Though Gracie had just lost the game, she wound up laughing as hard as the other two women.

Zoe found herself joining in, giggling at the nonsense. If she were offered a king's ransom, she wouldn't be able to say what was so funny.

"Oh, my." Gracie wiped tears from her eyes as she got up. "I think it's time for cake and coffee."

Arranging her black pieces for a new game, Zoe smiled and asked, "Can I help with the refreshments?"

"You can cut the cake."

Lilith never looked up as she put another "won" mark in her column. "Just a small piece for me. Hubby says I've been eating too much lately."

"That man." Gracie laughed, waving her hand. "Anything my brother says should be taken with a grain of salt." Zoe followed Gracie into the kitchen, leaving the two women to squabble over their scores.

Gracie's kitchen smelled of perking coffee. Grandmother Willis's hand-crocheted white tablecloth covered the round oak pedestal table sitting near the bay window. A fresh bouquet of snapdragons from the flower garden sat in the midst of Gracie's best china. Her Stanley cookstove and white oak cabinets were the talk of the town.

Zoe breathed a sigh of envy. Someday she hoped to have a house like this one. She lifted the cake cover and sniffed. "Do you think Lilith won the last game fair and square?"

"Well, she may be my sister-in-law, but that doesn't keep me from keeping a close eye on her."

Zoe laughed. "I've never beat her, but I haven't seen her cheat."

While Gracie filled the creamer, Zoe cut thin slices of cake and arranged them on china plates.

"I've been dying to talk to you all day." Gracie glanced up and grinned. "What's this about Cade moving in with you? Lawrence said he saw him there the morning after the storm."

Zoe's cheeks burned. She wiped a bit of gooey burnt-sugar frosting off the knife and tasted it. "He didn't 'move in' with me. The jail roof had a leak in it."

"Lawrence says there are no sleeping quarters over the jail anymore."

"No, the storm took care of that. The children want Cade to stay with us, but that's impossible."

"There's always Pop. His place is small, but he could put up one more."

"Pop's under the weather."

"Edna said he ate eight pieces of gooseberry pie at the social. That's enough to fell an elephant." Gracie replenished the sugar bowl.

Zoe grinned. "No telling how many he actually ate, but then he broke out in hives. I guess he's had a miserable few days."

Gracie poured coffee into the server, wiping up stray drips with a clean cloth. "I don't suppose Glori-Lee can help. She's closed off half her rooms since she hurt her back last spring."

Arranging cups on a tray, Zoe sighed. She didn't know what she was going to do now that Cade had no place to go. He was ill-equipped for fatherhood, and one would think, after the café incident, he'd know enough to leave the child-rearing to her.

"Where's he sleeping? Land's sake, you can hardly move around the way it is."

"In the mercantile, on Jim's cot. It's all very proper. I could hardly turn away the children's uncle without explaining why, and I didn't want to get into that."

Not only crowded, it was much too close for comfort. She couldn't avoid Cade if she wanted to. This morning she'd been caught off guard when she walked out of the bedroom and found him bare chested, shaving at the sink. She'd caught herself staring. And he'd noticed. She'd pretended not to let it bother her, but he wasn't fooled. He took his sweet time putting on his shirt, his mischievous eyes never leaving hers. She wasn't about to back down, so she just stared right back.

Zoe shivered against goose bumps, recalling the effect he still had on her as she licked the knife and put it in the dishpan. "It's nice to see the children smiling again. When I left this evening, Cade was on the floor wrestling with Brody and Will. You should have heard Holly and Missy giggling, Gracie. They haven't done that in weeks."

"So they've really taken to him."

"Yes, I'm afraid they have. He'll break their hearts when he leaves, and they've had enough sorrow in their young lives. By the way, he stopped at the Brightons' to talk about the children. Bonnie's come down with a fever."

"You don't say!" Gracie frowned. "Like Addy and John?"

"They don't think so. Seth's worried, but Doc Whitney will be back in a couple of days. He's off in another county. I thought I'd take dinner to them tomorrow and ask if there's anything I can do to help."

"What about their young'uns?"

"Seth took them to Frank and Helen's, in case the fever's contagious."

Gracie paused. "How will that affect Cade's plans to let the Brightons adopt the kids?"

Zoe shrugged. "Not that I wish ill health on anyone, but it buys me some time. I'm going to do my best to convince him to let me raise the children. They're so much a part of me already."

"You're bent on keeping them, aren't you?"

"I've always wanted them, but I did what Addy asked. I sent for Cade. Now I wish I hadn't. I thought surely he wouldn't object to me raising them if he didn't intend to."

"Why does he object to your having them? Is it the money?"

"He doesn't know my financial situation. He says he wants the children to have a mother and a father, but I think he's just being spiteful."

Gracie raised her brows.

"Don't speculate," Zoe chided. "I just mean things are strained between us right now. He wouldn't let me have them if I were married to King Solomon."

"He said that?"

"Not in so many words. He said I needed to marry and get on with my life. Have my own family."

"You should."

"Those kids *are* my family." Tears stung her eyes. She threw a spoon into the sink. "I don't understand why Addy didn't give them to me in the first place."

"Hmm," Gracie mused. "A body would swear she was matchmaking, trying to bring you and Cade back together. After all, other than John and the children, you were the two people she loved the most."

"That's crazy. Even Addy wouldn't do something that far fetched." But privately, Zoe wouldn't put it beyond Addy to have thought that if Cade came back, it could be the same as before. Unfortunately, Zoe had gained enough sense to realize that loving him was like loving the wind.

Edna's voice resounded from the parlor. "Lilith! Where did that third king come from?"

Hyena-like laughing filled the parlor.

Zoe and Gracie broke into smiles. "Sounds like there's going to be a tiff," Gracie said. "We'd better get the cake and coffee in there."

Backing out the kitchen door, Zoe balanced the tray with both hands, four white linen napkins tucked under her chin. "Gracie, promise me you won't mention my financial situation to anyone."

Gracie chuckled. "Have you ever known me to gossip?"

"Only since I was born."

Chapter Eighteen

The next two days passed in relative peace. After the supper dishes had been cleared, Brody wandered into the kitchen. "It's Saturday night, Zoe. Are we going to the dance?"

Cade sat on the back porch, cleaning his saddle. He glanced up when the boy's question filtered through the screen door.

Zoe folded the dishcloth and hung it up to dry. "Not tonight, Brody. You need to go to bed early. We missed Sunday school last week, and I don't want that to happen again."

It was the first Sunday she'd missed in nine months. Ironing until the wee hours of the morning took its toll. If only the new yard goods would arrive, she wouldn't have to take in extra work. She had enough orders to make her bank payments through the coming winter months. The shipment was due any day.

Holly peered out the window. "The lights are on at the dance hall."

"I know, dear. Perhaps we'll go next week."

"I'll bet Mr. Drake will be there," Holly added.

"Mr. Drake will understand."

Brody snagged Will around the neck, noisily kissing him on the cheek. "Ohhh, Zoe, you're so preeetty with your long red hair!"

Will grabbed Brody back. "Oh, Perry, you're so strong and handsome."

"Boys!" Zoe admonished.

"Are you talking about Perry Drake?" Cade called.

Zoe felt heat rise to her cheeks. Cade was watching them through the screen, and she wished he hadn't heard the boys' teasing. He would make more of their playful remarks than he should. Perry had taken her to the Saturday night dance before John and Addy had taken ill, but it was nothing.

"Did Perry ever marry Jenny Parson?"

"Yes, Jim and I considered them two of our best friends." Zoe put a skillet away. "Jenny died of snakebite a month before Jim was killed." She ventured a glance toward Cade.

"So," he said, holding her gaze through the screen, "are you and Perry sweet on each other?"

She slammed the cabinet door shut. "The boys are teases." Banking occupied Perry's time and interest, and the good Lord knew that she had no time to socialize. Gracie thought Perry would make a suitable companion for her, but there was no love interest on her part. Only good company.

Holly moved to the table. "It's gettin' dark. Want me to light the lamp?"

"Why don't we use candles tonight?" Zoe suggested. There was barely enough oil left to last the month. She needed to be sparing with what remained. No coffee, no lamp oil—how soon would it be before Cade noticed?

"We can't see good with candles," Brody complained.

"A candle will do, Brody. Thank you."

"It's been weeks since we've gone to the Saturday night dance," Holly complained.

Zoe realized fun was a thing of the past for all of them. "I'll tell you what I'll do. After baths, I'll play the phonograph. You can hold your own dance." Addy had loved records, a new device that emitted music. She collected all she could get her hands on.

"Ouw own dance!" Missy said joyfully. "Can I tuwn the handle?"

"You may help." The machine was costly and required adult super-vision.

Brody hauled in the wooden tub, and Zoe put water on the stove to heat. While she hung a curtain to allow the bather privacy, she noted that Cade remained on the porch, keeping a safe distance from all the commotion.

By eight o'clock the kids were spanking clean, their hair washed and smelling of New England rum, a solution Addy believed kept the hair shiny and free from disease.

Cade grumbled, consenting to a bath but refusing to put rum on his hair. "I'll drink it, but I'm not wearing it," he said.

Afterward, he refilled the tub with clean water, and then disap-peared into the store with the kids.

Zoe bathed in peace, listening to the sound of music coming from the mercantile. Cade's booming laughter nearly drowned out the strains of "Little Brown Jug" as the kids and he thumped noisily across the floor.

Smiling, she closed her eyes and slid deeper into the hot water. What were the children going to do when Cade left? To his credit, he'd been truthful with them, telling them outright that he couldn't stay. However frank he'd been, his departure wouldn't be any less painful. At times she wondered if they fully understood the implications of his leaving and that they could be living with another family soon. She dreaded the emptiness she would feel once they were gone.

Picking up the sponge, she lathered her arms, shoving her gloomi-ness aside. Judging by the racket coming from the store, the children were having too much fun for her to be having maudlin thoughts. She smiled when she thought how just a few short weeks ago she'd lived a life of solitude, evenings when you could hear a pin drop, it was so quiet.

Wincing when she heard Butch bark and Romeo yowl, she hoped her mother's priceless figurines were surviving the rowdy goings-on in the next room. Unfortunately, when Cade moved in, so had the animals.

She stood up, reached for a towel, and dried off. Tying the sash of her robe, she poked her head into the store and smiled when she saw Missy standing on Cade's feet, dancing to the strains of "I'll Take You Home Again, Kathleen."

The boys were dancing together, arm in arm, mocking Cade and Missy. They pranced around the room, making faces at each other.

Holly sat on the settee, hands folded, seemingly awaiting a turn around the dance floor with her uncle. Butch and Romeo lay on the floor next to her feet, their eyes following the dancers.

Cade had never looked more masterful or graceful as he glided around the floor clasping Missy's tiny hand in his large one. Zoe felt an uncharacteristic pang of envy. When, where, and with whom had he learned such niceties? In whose parlor had he last danced so elegantly? Whose hand had he been holding at the time? She doubted it was a five-year-old's.

Cade glanced up, smiling at her. "Care to join the fun, Red?"

She pulled the collar of her robe higher around her neck. "I don't think so."

"Come on," he coaxed. "The boys need a little refining." His eyes indicated Brody and Will, who were stumbling over each other's feet.

"Come on, Wed, it's fun," Missy encouraged.

"Well." Zoe stood for a moment, debating the advisability, and then she quickly decided it couldn't hurt. The children needed a little diversion. She went back to her room, put on a clean dress, and joined the fun.

After scooting the table of figurines to a safe corner, she held out her hand to Will. "May I have this dance, kind sir?"

Will's face turned beet red, his gaze shifting to the ceiling, but he walked into her arms.

The phonograph played, and the dancing couples swirled to the music. Holly took her turn with Cade, and Missy made Brody dance with her.

When the music ended, the dancers collapsed in nearby chairs, laughing and breathless. Brody hurried over to rewind the phonograph.

Zoe held up her hand, protesting. "Brody, it's getting late."

"Just once more," Holly pleaded.

Missy grabbed hold of Cade's hand and pulled him to his feet. "I want to dance with you again."

He turned to Zoe and winked. "Women. They just can't get enough of me."

Zoe had no trouble seeing why. "Really?" She winked back. "There's no accounting for taste."

His eyes said, "Touché." They broke into friendly grins.

The music played on as Cade took turns dancing with Holly and Missy. The young girls' flushed faces and sparkling eyes were well worth the party

When the clock chimed nine thirty, Zoe put a halt to the festivities.

"No more. It's way past bedtime."

Holly and Missy showered Cade's cheeks with kisses. "It's the best dance we ever went to," Holly proclaimed. "The very best!"

The girls scampered off to bed, humming the strains of "I'll Take You Home Again, Kathleen" under their breaths.

Will shuffled off toward the kitchen, grumbling, "I hate dancing with Brody."

Brody shoved him on his way out. "I hate dancing with you too."

"Boys, stop bickering. I'll be in shortly to hear your prayers."

Reaching for the candle, Zoe turned to Cade. "I left clean sheets beside the cot."

"Thank you."

Her face burned as his gaze skimmed her. "Good night."

She let Butch and Romeo out and then listened to the boys' prayers, touched when they asked God to make their Uncle Cade stay. The girls' prayers were the same. It was too late to worry about them getting attached to him.

They already were.

Chapter Nineteen

Pulling the sheet closer, Zoe closed her eyes. Tonight was the first time since Jim's death that she felt alive. The laughter, the winded fun had been missing ingredients in her life. Like cake batter without baking powder, her life had fallen when her husband died. Jim's familiar face swam behind her closed lids. Boyish, not strikingly handsome, but solid. His compassion for others shone through his doe-brown eyes. She loved this good, faithful man. Guilt crept into her consciousness. *But did you love him the way you love…loved Cade?* She'd been a different person then, an idealist, so certain that Cade was the man God had destined for her that she never questioned the one night she had set her values aside. But sin had a price. It always did. God had forgiven her because she'd asked him to, but sin had a way of seeking payback long after the act was over.

The faint sound of music drifted from the mercantile. *Holly.* The child was fascinated with the phonograph.

Zoe checked the pallet Holly slept on. The little girl sighed in her sleep and rolled to her side.

Sliding out of bed, Zoe slipped into her robe. She peered around the bedroom door and saw a flickering light in the mercantile. Had she forgotten to snuff a candle?

"Cade," she called softly. When he didn't answer, she quietly left the bedroom and padded into the store. There wasn't one candle burning; there were several.

He's lit every candle I own!

Inside the doorway, a strong arm caught her around the waist and pulled her into the room.

"I believe this is our dance."

She struggled to free herself from his grasp, his low voice affecting her good sense. "Aren't you worn out from dancing with all your 'women'?"

Drawing her closer, he whispered, "Ah, fair lady, I have yet to dance with the prettiest one of all."

She wrenched free and wet her fingers, extinguishing a candle. He stopped her.

"You still look beautiful in candlelight, Red."

Dear Lord, this is so unfair. Help me! Candlelight only made him more handsome.

"And still as feisty."

She squirmed against his embrace but her struggles were in vain. Giving in, she settled into his arms like an old friend. His warm breath brushed her temple as their feet slowly matched the strains of a waltz. What was she doing? She was a widow and mourning the death of her best friend.

But this was Cade. The one man who had ever given real meaning to her life.

Forgive me, Jim, Addy. One dance. One impossible moment to shred this awful mantle of grief and responsibility.

He smelled clean and soapy. Her fingers itched to touch his hair, but she didn't. Once she touched him, she would never stop. Everything about him was familiar, and so hopelessly wrong.

Resting her head on his chest, she listened to his steady heartbeat. "Why didn't you come back?"

"When I rode out that day, I had every intention of doing just that."

"But you didn't. What do you want from me? You've already won the children's hearts. Can't you let me be?"

His hold tightened. Not improperly, but certainly with a sense of possession. "It's one dance together. Why do you interpret my every move as significant? If it weren't for Addy, I wouldn't be here."

"Do you think that I don't know that?"

"You know what I mean. Once I heard you were married, I made up my mind to forget you."

"Well, a woman can't hear that enough."

"Did I say I forgot you? I made up my mind to, but it didn't happen. I thought about you every day."

Her eyes closed, and she struggled with emotions. Love. Hate. Resignation.

Fear.

Did he remember every breath, every word, and every vow they'd exchanged? She did.

His breath brushed her ear. "We were so young, Red. Our lives are different now. If I could turn back time, I would."

"It's never too late. Give up bounty-hunting and become the children's guardian. Raise Addy's kids."

"You make it sound so simple."

"You have all the money you could ever need. Can't you find it in your heart to make a home for your nieces and nephews? That's what Addy desperately wanted."

"No." He paused, shifting her to meet his eyes. "That wasn't her sole purpose for getting me back here."

She looked away. "I know what she was doing, but she loved you, and she wanted the best for you and her children."

"You think a bounty hunter is an ideal choice for fatherhood?"

Their feet fell back in step with the music. Their gazes locked in the flickering candlelight. "Listen to me, Red. I could give it up right now, this moment, and nothing would change. I'll always have to guard my back. Do you think I want that for Addy's kids? Do you want them to have to watch their backs too? The enemies I deal with don't give a rat's nest. They'd just as soon gun the kids down as they would me."

Sickened, she jerked away. "Killing. You're whole adult life you've been immersed in killing."

"That's what bounty-hunting's about. Occasionally it requires killing for the better good. Read your Bible, Red. God doesn't coddle evil. Would it make sense to you if I wore a badge?" He shook his head. "I'd be looked up to then, wouldn't I, and be considered a hero by many. Why does a piece of tin make what a marshal does right and the lack of it make what I do wrong? I've killed many a man, but I've never murdered anyone."

Zoe's fists balled in anger. The life he chose was one that would eventually destroy him. Couldn't he see that? He was being given a chance to change his ways. And he refused.

She turned to go, suddenly unable to breathe. The situation was hopeless. When would she accept that he was a man who couldn't, or wouldn't, be tied down?

Pausing in the doorway, she said quietly, "I hope you leave soon."

He set his jaw. "As soon as my work is done."

Pugnacious. The man was hopeless.

Chapter Twenty

Monday morning Zoe was in the kitchen ironing Mrs. Penscott's petticoats when she heard the tinkling bell over the front door. Gracie ran through the store and into the back rooms, breathlessly blurting out, "Have you heard? Pop broke his leg."

Mouth agape, Zoe set the iron on the stove. "When?"

"Saturday night at the dance. I thought maybe someone told you at church yesterday. Lawrence and I missed the service. His gout was acting up."

"No one said a thing, but I left right after the sermon. The kids were eager to get back. Cade took them fishing. What happened?"

Gracie snickered. "Pop allemanded left when he should have allemanded right. He took poor Clara Simms down with him."

Zoe's hand flew to her mouth to cover her amusement. The mental image of Pop and the puritanical Sunday school teacher sprawled in the middle of the dance floor leaped into her mind.

"Was she hurt?"

"Just embarrassed. Her crinoline flew up over her head and got hooked on that silly comb she always wears. It took two of us to get it untangled." Gracie dumped her packages on the table and helped herself to lemonade. "Pop didn't know he'd broken anything until he tried to get up. With Doc out of town, nobody knew what to do except Sawyer. He'd set many an animal's leg, so he put the bone back in place, steadied Pop's leg with a couple of splints, and bound up everything securely."

Zoe walked to the front window of the store and looked up the street to the jail. "The kids and Cade went over early this morning to see Pop. I'm surprised they haven't come back and told me."

"They're probably too busy waiting on him. You know Pop. He likes attention."

"Don't all men?" Zoe stripped off her apron as she hurried behind the counter. "I'll take him some nut bread. That should make him feel better."

Gracie sat down and propped her feet on a nearby stool. "I'm going to sit here and finish my lemonade." She shuddered and puckered her lips. "Great day, it's tart. You out of sugar?"

"Just running a bit low. While you're at it, finish the ironing." Zoe slipped two loaves of sweet bread into a wicker basket and covered them with a towel.

"The kids are attached to Cade's hip," Gracie mused as Zoe scurried past her. "You see one, you see the other."

"I know. That's what worries me." Walking out the door, she called over her shoulder, "Watch the store for me. I'll be back in a minute."

Crossing the street, she spotted Will running from post to post, ripping down wanted posters.

"Will," she hollered, "what are you doing?"

The boy hung his head and shielded the evidence behind his back as she approached. "Nuthin'."

"You're doing something." Zoe tried to see around him. "What's that behind your back?"

"Nuthin'."

"Will?"

He twisted the toe of his shoe in the dirt.

"William Wiseman?"

He slowly brought out the posters from behind him and handed them to her. Her brows lifted in question. "What's this all about? You know better than to destroy public property."

Teary-eyed, he jutted out his bottom lip. "If there wasn't any bad guys wanted, Uncle Cade would stay here with us."

Her shoulders dropped. She knelt to console him. His wrenching sobs broke her heart.

"He told…us…he…had…to go get…a bad guy. That's…why…he can't…keep us."

Anger surfaced. Cade could have been a little more tactful. She'd like to wring his neck like a Sunday chicken!

"Even if he does go, he'll come back."

"No, he won't," Will sobbed. "Mama said he's hard to pin down."

Zoe took the towel off the sweet bread and used it to dab at the little boy's tears. "Well, let's not worry about it now. Uncle Cade is here, and I don't think he's going after bad guys any time soon. Now, I want you to take these posters to Pop and tell him you're sorry for pulling them down."

Nodding, Will sobered.

"That's my sweet boy." She kissed his cheek and watched proudly as he marched into the jail, carrying the posters.

After folding the cloth, she laid it in the basket and slowly followed him, giving Will time to complete his apology before she arrived.

A few minutes later, she let herself into the jail. It was so crowded, there was barely standing room. Two tittering young ladies had cornered Cade. She did a double take. Judy Farnsworth? When had she started dressing like a strumpet? Zoe wondered if Judy's mother knew she was out in public in that garb.

She recognized the striking brunette with Judy as Lilith Wilks's niece, Susan Tetherton. Just a short time ago, Susan had been in pigtails and overalls, playing marbles with the boys.

Well, her mind wasn't on marbles today.

Forcing a smile, Zoe got a grip on her emotions as Susan said, "Cade Kolby, I've heard about you all my life, but Aunt Lilith never told me you were so downright handsome." Susan leaned in close, smiling.

A silly giggle escaped Judy's painted lips. "Told you, Susan. Told you he was tall and positively breathtaking."

Zoe glanced at Pop and the children, who were sitting behind his desk, gorging themselves on cookies.

"Hi, Zoe," Brody called. "Want a cookie? Judy and Susan baked them for Uncle Cade. They're good."

Closing the door, Zoe set the basket on the corner of the desk next to Pop's propped-up leg. "Brody, don't talk with your mouth full." She glanced at Pop sympathetically. "How are you doing?"

"Ain't worth a plug nickel."

"Did Will apologize for taking down the posters?"

"Yep." Pop laughed, ruffling the boy's hair. "He sure likes his uncle. Can't see the attraction myself. How 'bout you?"

Missy hopped off of Pop's lap. "Zoe, my belly huwts again."

Cade excused himself from the young women and, grinning, scooped Missy up onto his shoulder. "Before Zoe gets mad at us, tell her I said only one cookie."

"He did. He did, Zoe," Holly confirmed. "I only got one too."

"Brody had four," Will said.

The accused hung his head, withholding comment.

Pop lifted his splinted leg and eased it to the floor. "They'll live. Here, Zoe, try a piece of Lilith's rhubarb pie. Woman talks a lot, but she sure can bake."

Zoe smiled. "I thought you'd have sworn off pie by now."

Judy and Susan flashed dimpled smiles toward Cade. Their fresh beauty and bouncing curls were a sharp contrast to Zoe's faded calico dress and wayward hair, frizzed from leaning over a washboard doing never-ending laundry. Her gaze shifted to Cade, wondering if he was making the same comparison.

She turned back to Pop. "I won't stay. I just wanted to check on you. I thought you might enjoy some of my nut bread."

"That's real hospitable of you." He leaned forward and sniffed the basket. "You gotta try some of this, Cade. She makes the best nut bread in town."

"I use applesauce in all my baking instead of sugar." At least these days she did.

"Sugar or applesauce, whatever you use, it's the best bread I've ever eaten." Pop helped himself to a second slice.

Cade reached over and accepted a piece. "You don't have to convince me. I eat her cooking."

Loud voices erupted outside the jail.

Pop tried to get up but fell back in his chair. "What in the tarnation's going on out there?"

The door flew open, and Zoe saw Cade's right hand automatically go for his gun even as his left hand moved her to safety behind him.

A short man, white-faced and grimy with dust, burst through the doorway, barely able to talk. "The stage has been robbed!" Catching his breath, he collapsed onto the nearest chair. "Four men. Looked like the Nelson gang, but cain't be sure." The man dropped his head and covered his face with hands that trembled like leaves in a storm. Zoe's stunned gaze moved to his skinned and bleeding knuckles and torn shirt.

"Good grief, Troy!" Pop exclaimed.

"Anyone killed?" Cade stepped to the door, where his eyes swept Main Street.

"No, but we shore thought we were goners." Troy Becker accepted a cup of water from Zoe, nodding his thanks.

She glanced outside to see a group of curious onlookers converging on the jail. "You're about to have more company, Pop."

"Has something happened to the stage?" Walt Mews asked. "I saw it coming into town like a scalded cat. My shipment of hair tonic from Boston is on it."

"It ain't no more." The stage driver got up, set his cup on the desk, and looked wild eyed at Walt. "It's gone, along with Mrs. Bradshaw's yard goods."

Zoe groaned. "Oh, no. The whole shipment?"

"It ain't my fault. They come outta nowhere!" Troy exclaimed. "Never saw nothin' like it!"

Cade stepped forward. "Exactly what happened, Troy?"

"I was approachin' Rider's Pass when all of a sudden, here they come. First I thought it was Injuns, the way they were whoopin' and hollerin', but then I seen they was white men. They grabbed the money sack and, before they left, took every bottle of your tonic, Walt, poured it all over Mrs. Bradshaw's cloth, and smashed the bottles. Didn't see the sense of that—but that's what they did. You never saw such a mess in all your born days."

Zoe took hope. "You mean my shipment is still out there in the road?" Maybe she could salvage part of it. She had to salvage part of it. It meant financial ruin if she didn't.

The driver met her expectant expression. "You could say that."

Cade frowned. "What do you mean? Is it there or not?"

"It's there, all right, but I don't think she'd want it. The horses didn't take kindly to the stink of that tonic. They got all excited and..." His face turned crimson. "I hate to tell you, but that ain't all they did on it."

"Oh, dear." Heartsick, Zoe sank onto a chair. This was the end. Without the money the yard goods would bring, she was bankrupt.

Cade frowned. "Is the fabric that important to you, Red?"

"Most important," she admitted, hoping her desperate tone didn't reveal her financial woes.

Struggling to get out of his chair, Pop fumed, "Just when something excitin' happens, I got a broken leg and can't do a thing about it."

"Stay where you are, Pop." Cade reached for his hat. "I'll take care of it."

"Cade!" Zoe protested, following him to the gun cabinet. The men in the Nelson gang were hardened criminals. She reminded herself that he was used to chasing outlaws across the country, but she wasn't used to witnessing it firsthand.

"Better send someone out there to clean up the mess," Pop warned. "Don't let the trail get cold before you form a posse."

Cade glanced at Zoe. "I'll be gone a while. You'd better take the kids home and stay there in case there's trouble."

Zoe frowned. "Trouble?" She didn't want him back in her life, but she didn't want him dead, either. Her eyes searched his for a sign of assurance. This sort of trouble might be commonplace to him, but it was foreign to Winterborn.

He grasped her shoulders and turned her toward the door. "Take the kids and go home. I'll be back as soon as I can."

Before she could protest, he solicited help from several of the men and then doled out rifles.

"Go home, Zoe," he ordered.

She started to argue. Then she clamped her mouth shut. Hurrying the children out the door, she glanced back as the small office quickly emptied, the young tittering girls now silent. Cade should not get involved. That's all the children needed, for their uncle to get shot.

Zoe waited for Cade at the hitching post. The posse formed and decided on a plan of action. As he was about to mount up, she reached out to him.

"This is insane. What happens if those thugs are just waiting for a posse and they shoot you?"

"I suppose I'll fall off my horse and—"

"This is nothing to be light about!"

He met her steady gaze. "Go home."

"You can't tell me what to do."

"Then don't go home. If that material's so all fired important, I'll go get it for you."

"With horse urine and manure on it!"

"I didn't say it was important. You did." Cinching the saddle tighter, he said, "Zoe, please take the kids home and stay there."

She grabbed his arm. "If you insist on doing this, promise me you'll be careful." Her breath caught in her throat when his deep blue eyes met hers. She thought she saw a hint of amusement.

"Worried about me, Red? I thought you didn't care."

Frowning, she backed away, crossing her arms. "Don't be silly. I'm thinking of the children."

He swung onto the mare. "You worry too much."

She gave him an irritated glance and noticed his face sober at her concerned look.

"You got my word. I'll be careful. I'm thinking of the kids too." Reining his horse to the right, he tipped his hat and rode off.

His word indeed.

Chapter Twenty-One

Cade patted Maddy's neck, frowning as he took in the stinking site. Flies buzzed the piles of fresh horse manure scattered over bolts of once-colorful cotton. Broken glass sparkled on the dry ground. He glanced at Walt Mews and the barber wrinkled his nose. There was nothing left of his hair tonic to salvage.

Zoe Bradshaw's yard goods picked a heck of a time to show up at the junction between Suffox and Miller Counties. Rider's Pass was little more than a narrow bend in the road, obscured by a heavy thicket of elm, hackberry, and tangled underbrush, the ideal site for an ambush.

Red would throw a fit if she were here to see her fancy bolts of cloth in this condition. Covering his nose with a gloved hand, he reined Maddy aside. It would take a better man than him to sort through the mess.

"Walt, take your men and ride south. Roy, take a couple of men and go west. Ben, take your boys and head east. I'll ride north. Let's meet at the jail around sundown, and be careful. We don't know who we're up against."

The posse wheeled their horses and galloped off in a boil of dust.

Cade prodded Maddy up the road, wondering how much the lost the shipment would set Zoe back. He didn't know her financial situation, but from what he'd seen, he was sure it wasn't good.

The sound of swiftly rolling wagon wheels caught his attention, and he moved a safe distance into the brush, watching the bend in the road as the pounding of hoofs grew louder. A buckboard whipped wildly toward him. As the wagon flew by, he noted the driver was slumped over on the seat. Wheeling Maddy, he sent the mare galloping after it.

Maddy gained on the wagon, her longer stride and lean body a definite advantage over the stocky quarter horse team.

"Easy, girl," Cade said as they paced the two out-of-control horses. Leaning to his right, he grabbed one of the flapping reins and pulled back. "Whoa! Whoa there!"

The rig ground to a halt, and Code drew his gun, dismounting to check on the driver. If this was a McGill setup, he was ready for him. He cautiously stepped up to the seat of the wagon and hopped on. Pointing the barrel of the gun, he called, "You there!" A man lay unconscious. Easing closer, he bent and searched for a pulse.

A young woman was laying on a blanket in the back. He stepped over the seat and knelt beside her. Putting a hand on either side of her head, he stilled her tossing and turning. She was burning with fever.

"Who are you?"

"Sick..." she rasped. "Where's Bruce?"

He noticed the wedding band on her finger and assumed the driver was her husband. "He's here. I'm going to get you to the doctor."

"Bruce...sick...need help."

Cade stepped back over the seat to rouse the unconscious young man. "Wake up." He shook the man's shoulders, and he moaned as Cade pulled him upright. "Can you tell me what the problem is?" The young man's head lolled to one side.

Scanning the area, Cade half expected lightning to strike him dead. If one more thing went wrong...Pop and his broken leg, Bonnie sick, Zoe on his back to give her the kids and get out of town. One delay after the other, and now he was chasing nobodies without prices on their heads when he should have left Winterborn days ago.

A cold bedroll, a lonesome trail, and hardtack were beginning to sound good. And he would be able to shave and cut his hair when he wanted to.

He stepped into the wagon bed, lifted the unconscious man into his arms, laid him next to the woman, and then whistled for Maddy. After tying her reins to the back of the buckboard, he climbed onto the driver's seat and clucked to the team.

Zoe glanced up from sweeping the front porch when she heard the rumble of a wagon coming into town. People scattered for cover as the buckboard wheeled toward the mercantile. Her jaw dropped when Cade jumped down from the rig and took the steps two at a time. "Is Doc back yet?"

"I haven't seen him—his business away must be taking longer than he expected." Her gaze swept the wagon.

"I've got two sick people here." Cade motioned to the back of the wagon. "Do you know them?"

Zoe's eyes focused on the prostrate couple. "It's Bruce and Ida Evans. What's wrong with them?"

"Don't know, but they've got a high fever. I found their team running wild about an hour ago. They need Doc's help."

Zoe turned as the stench of chewing tobacco caught her attention. Sawyer Gayford walked up. "Sawyer, do you know when Doc will be back?"

"Nope."

Cade muttered under his breath. He slapped his hat against his thigh with one hand and smacked the door frame with the other. Frustration flashed in his eyes.

"What's wrong?" Glori-Lee called from the café.

Sawyer shouted back, "More sick folk!"

Cade turned. "More? There are others?"

"Yep." Sawyer spit again. "Clyde Abbott and his oldest boy come down with fever and spots this morning."

Cade turned to Zoe. "What should I do with Bruce and Ida?"

"Do with them?" she asked. "I don't know what to do with them. That would be up to Doc, if he were here." She glanced up and down the street. "Take them to the jail for now."

She started back to the store at a run, calling over her shoulder, "I'll get water and sponges." Cade jumped into the wagon, turned it around, and headed for the jail.

Zoe burst into the store, breathless. "Holly, you're going to have to watch Missy for a while. Brody, can you take care of any customers who might come in?" The boy's eyes lit up. Pausing, she pointed at him. "I know what you're thinking, and you may have one piece of penny candy. No more."

"How do you always know what I'm thinking?"

"I just do."

Holly put her dolls aside, walked up to Zoe, and tugged on her skirt. "What's going on?"

"Bruce and Ida have a fever." Concerned about the fear she saw in the young girl's eyes, she added, "We don't know if it's the same fever that took your parents." She threw towels and sponges into several buckets and basins. "I'll be at the jail if you need me."

Missy appeared in the doorway, tears welling in her eyes. "Don't die like my ma, Zoe."

"Come here, honey." The child walked over, and Zoe hugged her. "I'm not going to die. This fever may be nothing at all."

Brody handed his sister a peppermint stick. "You can help me run the store, Missy." He turned to Zoe. "Go on. She'll be all right."

"Thank you, Brody." She touched his cheek, proud of the young man he was becoming.

Her mind spun as she ran up the street, thankful she didn't have to endure another crisis alone. She wished Cade had been here for Addy and John, but he was here now, and she was thankful for whatever help he could give.

When she walked into the jail, Cade's tight expression relaxed. Obviously, he didn't want to handle the situation alone any more than she did. "Where's Pop?" she asked.

"I don't know. I sent Sawyer to find him. If the jail's going to be turned into an infirmary, Pop needs to know."

"What about my yard goods? Can they be salvaged?"

He shook his head. "Sorry."

Zoe rolled up her sleeves. She'd worry about it later. Dealing with bad news was old hat to her by now. She handed Cade a sponge. "You bathe Bruce, and I'll see what I can do for Ida." Her heart went out to the stricken couple who tossed about on the floor of the single cell, calling out to each other. When Ida tried to get up, Zoe restrained her and eased her back to the pillow. "Bruce is right here, Ida. Lie still. The cool water will help. We need to get your fever down."

"Sick...so sick."

"Shhh," Zoe soothed. She turned at the sound of boots scraping across the floor. Sawyer shuffled in with Pop hobbling along on his crutches behind him, breathing hard.

"Someone said the Evanses are sick."

Cade sponged Bruce's forehead with cool water. "We'll have to use the jail for a few days. There's no other place to put these folks."

"No reason they can't stay here," Pop said. "Cell hasn't been used for years—unless the posse comes up with someone."

"Ain't much chance they'll catch the gang. If it's the Nelson bunch, they're probably long gone." He leaned closer to examine the ailing couple. "They look mighty sick."

"I found them on the road earlier. They must have been trying to get to Doc." Cade poured more water into the basin. "Better keep people away, Pop. They're burning up with fever."

"Yeah, that's a good idea." Pop backed up, maneuvering out of the cell on his crutches. "I'd offer to help, but I'd just be in the way. I'll be at the house if you need me."

"Sawyer, you stand guard at the front door, and don't let anyone come in," Cade ordered.

The old man nodded and stepped outside, hollering, "Stand back. Kolby said no one's to come in. This stuff might be catchin'."

Zoe knew what this new outbreak meant to the town of Winterborn. Everyone still felt John's and Addy's loss. She prayed there wouldn't be a panic.

Missy's words echoed in her mind, "Don't die like my ma." When

Zoe had nursed John and Addy, she hadn't given a thought to catching the fever herself. She glanced at Cade. What would happen if they both came down sick? "Do you think it's the same sickness that took John and Addy?"

"I don't know."

"Dear Lord, grant us mercy," she murmured.

Chapter Twenty-Two

Within the hour Zoe heard Sawyer warning Perry Drake to keep his distance. Standing in the street in front of the jail, Perry called out, "Zoe! Do you need an extra hand?"

Leaving Ida, Zoe stepped outside. She should have known Perry would be one of the first to offer his help. "Thanks for coming. It's Bruce and Ida. Cade brought them in earlier."

He smiled. "I've missed you at the dance the past Saturday nights."

"Thank you. I've missed going." Which wasn't exactly true, but Perry was a nice man and she didn't want to hurt his feelings.

The concern in the banker's eyes was so typical of him. She glanced toward Cade, who leaned now in the doorway, watching the conversation. The curiosity in his eyes pleased her. She sidestepped along the side of the building, moving the banker farther away from the open doorway.

"I left the bank as soon as I heard," Perry said.

Before she could respond, Cade stepped outside, motioning to her. "Zoe, Ida needs you."

She was certain he was only trying to break up the conversation. What had gotten into him? Years ago he and Perry had been schoolmates. She graciously stepped back, saying, "Excuse me, Perry. Ida requires my attention."

He detained her. "Tell me what I can do."

"Find Doc. We'll need him as soon as he can get here."

"Of course. I'll go right away."

Perry gave her hand an affectionate squeeze, and Zoe watched disapproval cross Cade's face.

"I'm concerned about you," Perry said. "Should you be around the illness?"

"I nursed John and Addy and didn't catch the fever."

Other than a lack of sleep and worries about a pile of ironing big enough to choke a horse, she was fine. Perry left, and she returned to the sick. Ida was sleeping soundly, just as Zoe had left her. Frowning, she turned to Cade. "I thought you said Ida needed me."

It irked her that he refused to look at her.

"Looked to me like she needed you."

Snatching up a water bucket, she walked out of the jail as a buggy rumbled to a stop at the hitching post.

"Uh-oh," Sawyer sang out. "Looks like we got another one. Make room!"

Zoe turned around and marched back in, pulling the remaining blanket from the shelf outside the cell.

Seth Brighton came through the doorway carrying Bonnie, his face ashen. "Somebody's got to help her. She's talkin' out of her head."

Zoe motioned to Cade. "Shove the desk aside to make room for another pallet." It was going to be a long night.

Around sundown, Zoe heard the beleaguered posse ride in. Sawyer's voice filtered into the jail as he yelled for the men to ride on.

"What's wrong?" Roy Baker called.

"The whole town's come down with fever!" Sawyer shouted.

The whole town? Zoe shook her head. If they weren't careful, Sawyer would incite mass hysteria. She turned. "Cade?"

Cade rose to his feet. "I'll have a word with him."

Bruce moaned, twisting on his pallet.

Cade opened the door and left the room. Gracie entered a moment later carrying a large tray of food.

"Gracie, you're a godsend," Zoe said gratefully.

"It's nothing. Just chicken broth for the sick and beef stew for the healthy."

"You shouldn't be here. We don't know for certain what we're fighting."

"Nonsense. I want to help." Gracie set down the tray, glancing at the patients. "Maybe if we get a little broth into their stomachs, they would feel better." When Gracie picked up a spoon, Zoe stopped her. "Go outside. Cade and I will do it."

"Law, I'm as capable as anybody—"

"Outside!" Zoe ordered.

Gracie rattled on and unloaded the tray. "I've checked on the children, and they're fine. Stopped by the store just before I came, and Brody had everything under control. They can spend the night with me. That'll be one worry off your mind."

"That won't be necessary. I'll be going back to the store in a little while." She was relieved when Cade came back from talking to Sawyer.

"Are you sure? I'd enjoy their company."

"It would be helpful if you'd feed them supper, but I want them with me."

Gracie left, and Zoe rubbed her temples. "We're going to have a mess on our hands if this thing spreads." She poured a cup of hot tea, glanced at Seth kneeling by his wife's pallet, and lowered her voice. "By the way, you were rude to Perry."

"I thought you said there was nothing between you two," Cade whispered back.

"There isn't. We're just friends."

"That's not what he thinks."

"How do you know what he thinks?"

"I'm a man."

Her lips thinned. Yes, he certainly was a man. She couldn't argue with that. But watching him minister to Bruce allowed her to see a side of him she'd forgotten existed. A strong compulsion came over her to reach out and touch him... She gave herself a mental shake.

He was also a man who acted like a jealous suitor but wanted no kindred responsibility.

She spooned warm tea into Ida's mouth, and then knelt on Bonnie's other side. She felt the woman's forehead. "Your temperature is still quite high."

"My children...I have to take care of my children..."

"You can't take care of the kids, Bonnie. You can barely lift your head," Seth argued.

Rising, Zoe said gently, "Seth, you need to go home and get some rest. We'll send someone for you if there's any change."

"Maybe I'd better. I've got chores to do." Seth leaned down and kissed his wife. "I'll be back first thing in the morning."

Later, Zoe sat against the outside of the building, tipping her chin up and closing her eyes as she ate cold stew. Her back hurt, and she had a blinding headache. "I need to check on the children."

Cade poured a cup of coffee and handed it to her. "You should have let Gracie take them for the night."

Sighing, she lifted the back of her hair to let her neck catch the faint breeze. "I want them with me for as long as possible."

"There's no reason you can't go home and stay there. I'll take care of things here."

"You'll need help now that there are three sick people. I'll go see about the children and then come back." She pretended not to see his indignant frown. "What?"

"I'm their uncle. I'll go."

"For now, I'm their caregiver. You stay here, and I'll check on them—"

"Fine. If you get sick, I can't run your store."

Nor can you iron, she thought resentfully, remembering the bushel basket of ironing waiting for her in the kitchen. It wouldn't keep until the Evanses and Bonnie Brighton got better. The bank payment was due next week. Besides, it wouldn't do any good to protest. The look in his eyes promised an argument.

He pitched the remains of his coffee to the ground. "It's settled. I'll stay, and you'll go home. If we can keep the outbreak contained, the crisis should be over in a few days."

"You two argue over the silliest things," Sawyer butted in, stepping out of the shadows and spitting a stream of tobacco juice. "You go, I go. What difference does it make who goes?"

"Why don't you go, Sawyer?" Cade said. "Come back in the morning if you want to help."

Zoe guessed the man took the hint, because he abruptly left in a huff.

Bone tired, she watched Cade study the rim of his cup. Sympathy washed over her when she noticed lines of weariness around his eyes. If he'd thought his visit to Winterborn would be brief and uncomplicated, he was mistaken. Of course, he could leave. Would he? Or would he have the gumption to stick it out until the sickness subsided?

Chapter Twenty-Three

Zoe was outside hanging laundry early Tuesday morning when Cade rounded the corner. She quickly looked away as he stripped off his shirt and began to wash up at the rain barrel. She tried to focus on her work, but her gaze kept straying in his direction.

"Who's watching the patients?" she asked.

"They're all asleep. I thought I'd bring over the dirty sheets and clean up."

She pinned a pair of overalls to the line, feigning indifference to his state of undress, yet she was anything but oblivious to him. Water ran off his chest, trickling through the mat of curly dark hair. Muscles flexed in his bare arms. She saw the power of the man rather than the boy she had loved so fiercely long ago. He'd changed in so many ways that at times she wasn't sure she'd ever really known him.

When he caught her gawking, her cheeks turned hot. Ducking behind a row of billowing sheets, she reminded herself she was thirty-two years old, not one of Winterborn's dewy-eyed schoolgirls hoping to win a man's attention. Susan and Judy were a disgrace. They were downright shameful in their pursuit of him. Were he to change his ways and decide to take a wife, he could marry either girl and have a mother for Addy's children in the time it took to say "Which one?"

She stuck a clothespin between her teeth and leaned over to pick up a wet towel. A twig snapped behind her. The moment she turned, two large hands grasped her around the waist, and she felt her feet leave the ground.

Squealing, she shoved against Cade. He laughed, letting her feet dangle in midair. Spitting out the clothespin, she whacked him on his chest. "Put me down!"

He held her closer. "Widow Bradshaw, I'm ashamed of you. Don't you know it isn't polite to stare at men with their shirts off?"

She was as helpless as Missy's rag doll in his arms. His power far overshadowed hers.

"Put me down," she repeated. "Brody and Will might see us."

He glanced toward the back of the house, where the boys were playing with the dog. "What if they do? Hasn't anyone told them that once their 'aunt' would have welcomed a hug from Uncle Cade?"

"No, and you are not to mention a word to them, do you understand?" She could imagine the version he'd give.

"My promises are conditional." His eyes gleamed with a playful light that she knew meant trouble, judging by his feisty mood.

She gripped his hard, bare shoulders, trying to push away, but his arms were like corded steel.

Struggling to keep her response impersonal, she spoke between gritted teeth. "I don't do anything on a conditional basis."

The smell of sunshine and drying laundry filled her senses as he lowered her until their faces were inches apart. She turned her head, averting her eyes. "Let me go. I'm hot and sweaty."

Playfully, he pretended to drop her. Instinctively her arms tightened around his neck.

"Stop it!"

He firmed his grip mischievously. "A gentleman would never drop a lady...especially a lady who looks good enough to kiss."

He set her gently on her feet and slid a hand behind her neck, keeping the other one around her waist. "I'm probably going to get my face slapped, but I'm going to kiss you."

Swallowing, she licked her dry lips. His brashness unnerved her.

Jim would have never taken such liberties, been so reckless. "Don't do this, Cade," she warned. "Let me go before the neighbors see you."

She squirmed in his arms but was unable to free herself. Specks of water beaded on his shoulders. She'd forgotten how the feel of his bare skin ignited emotion in her, emotion she didn't want to feel. His eyes softened, and she anticipated his kiss.

But she knew she couldn't let it happen, no matter how much she wanted it. One kiss, and the madness would start all over again. Had it ever really ended? Once it could have been so very good between them if he'd only come back. Would she have lost the baby? Would it have made any difference if he'd known that she carried his child?

Their gazes locked, and he must have seen something of her inner pain, because instead of touching her lips with his, he released her. She saw—what? Regret? Trifling indifference? But now that she was free, she was reluctant to leave the warmth of his embrace.

Finally she looked away, smoothing her skirt. "Will you be home for supper?"

"Is that an invitation?"

"I made an apple cobbler."

"How did you know apple's my favorite?"

"I still have my faculties." She refused to meet his flirtatious gaze.

He crooked his forefinger under her chin and tipped up her face so that she looked at him. "I'll be here."

Stepping away, she leaned and picked up a shirt and pinned it to the line. "No new cases during the night?"

"None that I know of."

She sighed and hung another shirt on the line.

Bringing his hands to his hips, he scanned the long rows of wash. "Did all this come from the jail?"

"Not all of it. Some are the children's things." She saw him mentally counting the skirts, petticoats, and feminine undergarments. The tally was large, even for sickness. She had to think quick—she couldn't risk him suspecting she was taking in wash for extra money. "I'm...doing

Mrs. Penscott a favor. She's down in her back with lumbago." She rolled her eyes heavenward, praying forgiveness for her fib.

"Daisy Penscott? Judge Penscott's widow? You'd think she had enough money to hire her wash done."

"You'd think. " Wedging a clothespin between his lips, she murmured, "Here, make yourself useful. Hang Will's long johns for me."

Chapter Twenty-Four

M r. Drake will see you now." Mary Beth Peters smiled as she ushered Zoe into the bank president's office late that afternoon.

Perry Drake might be president of the bank, but stout, middle-aged spinster Mary Beth Peters was his right hand, without whom Zoe doubted Perry would have risen past bank teller. Mary Beth's jolly demeanor was always good for the soul.

"I was just sick to hear about the yard goods," Mary Beth said. "I had my heart set on a new dress. Are you going to reorder?"

Zoe didn't have the money to order a handkerchief, let alone bolts of fabric. "I haven't decided, Mary Beth."

As the women approached Perry's desk, he rose to shake hands. "Zoe, you've been on my mind. I trust that you're not overdoing?"

"I'm fine. Cade stayed at the jail last night."

"That's good."

Perry had kept fit and lean. He wasn't as muscular as Cade, but was distinguished looking. His slighter build reminded her of Jim.

Mary Beth excused herself and returned to her desk.

Sitting down, Perry smiled. "I'm glad you stopped by. Are the children with you?"

"Gracie took them home with her this morning. I don't know what I'd do without her."

"She's a fine woman."

"That she is."

"I figured Cade would be gone by now."

Was that resentment in his features? "He will be soon. This fever outbreak delayed him."

Perry lifted his gaze. "I asked because there's been talk...him staying at your place..."

"Talk, Perry? I'm surprised you listen to gossip. The only reason he's staying in the mercantile is because the roof blew off the jail."

Perry leaned back in his chair, stroking his chin. "Has he found a home for the kids?"

"I'm hoping to keep them myself, even though Cade is dead set against it." The banker's brows lifted. "He thinks I should marry and have my own children."

"He's right. Not many men would want to marry a woman saddled with four children."

Saddled? She stiffened. Since when did Perry view children as a burden?

The bank's clock chimed the hour, sounding like the Liberty Bell in the awkward silence. Zoe pressed a handkerchief against her cheek, blotting perspiration brought on by the insufferable heat.

"I'd like to talk to you about increasing my loan," she said.

"Again?" Perry ran his finger along the inside of his collar.

She leaned closer, aware that he was embarrassed by the request. "A small amount, just enough to pay my bills this month. I've lost the yard goods. I'll need to reorder."

The banker steepled his fingers, gazing at her. "Would you consider a personal loan? I'm afraid the stockholders won't...that is, without more security..."

She sympathized with his position. It wasn't easy to turn a friend away. The remorse in his eyes was sincere but little consolation to her. "I wouldn't ask if it weren't absolutely necessary. I've gone over the books, and there's no other way. I counted on a profit from those yard goods, and now I'm not only out the price of the order, but I'll have to purchase more."

Perry lowered his voice. "If it were up to me, I'd loan you any amount you wanted. I know you're having a difficult time making ends meet, but my hands are tied without additional collateral."

Collateral. Zoe hated the word. She had mortgaged everything she and Jim owned, and still it wasn't enough. She fell farther behind every day. Sinking back in her chair, she worried the corner of her handkerchief.

"If you won't accept my offer," Perry went on, "then perhaps another private party. Frank Lovell is always willing to make loans."

"I'd never ask Frank for money." She pictured the town skinflint, who was known for the exorbitant interest he charged. She was tired of him coming around, trying to attract her with his wealth. All the money in the world wouldn't make him appealing. He already owned most everything in Winterborn. Let him be happy with that.

"I'd rather lose the store than go to Frank."

"Sell the store, Zoe. To someone." She stood to leave, but the seriousness in Perry's tone made her sit again.

"Your loyalty to Jim is admirable," Perry went on, "but you're in trouble because of his inability to handle business matters. Jim was too generous. I don't know anyone in town who went hungry while he was alive."

Zoe sighed. "That's part of my problem. I'm having a hard time saying no now when families counted on Jim for so long to see them through."

"Your problem is those four kids. Give them up, Zoe. You can't afford them."

Perry was a friend and confidant. She usually respected his advice, but not today. "I can't afford to give them up, Perry. They're a part of me. I can't imagine handing them over to strangers."

He got out of his chair, came around his desk, and laid a hand on her shoulder. "You get that silly notion out of your head. Cade will find the kids a good home, and you can get on with your life. Maybe even remarry. There's still plenty of time to have children."

No, there wasn't. Sadness washed over her. She would never have her own children. The miscarriage fifteen years ago had left her barren. Her sadness had evolved into biting resentment. Cade owed her Addy's children! Addy had known Zoe couldn't have other children, so why hadn't she given them to her?

Perry's voice drew her back. "The last thing you need are several mouths to feed. You're working yourself to death taking in washing and ironing, running the store, and looking after Addy's kids. If you sold out to Frank, your worries would be over."

"All the money would go to pay off the bank note."

Perching on the corner of the desk, Perry focused on her. "I'm sorry. I wish there was something I could do. You know how fond I am of you. If you would consider me a serious suitor—"

Vacating her chair, she moved to the window beside his desk. "Perry, please. You've been a good friend. Let's not spoil the relationship." She watched people go about their daily routine and thought about his offer. No. She could never marry him.

"Is it Cade? Is that whom you're waiting for? If so, you'll be an old woman by the time he settles down."

She shook her head. "Cade? Don't be absurd. I'm not that foolish."

"I'm glad to hear it."

He rose to join her. "Speak of the devil, there he is now." Cade passed by carrying a tray of food from Glori-Lee's.

"For a bounty hunter, he makes an admirable nurse," Perry mused. "Still, I hope he moves on soon. This town doesn't need the riffraff his type could bring in."

His words rankled. "I don't approve of his occupation either, but the children's welfare isn't something you can hurry. He has his faults, but Addy loved him and was confident he would do right by her children."

Her defense of Cade surprised Perry as much as it did her, judging from his sour expression. Cade wasn't an angel, but Perry had no right to judge him.

Perry snapped the shade closed. "Addy was blind to his faults."

How could she justify Addy's intentions when she didn't understand them herself?

Sobering, Perry took her by the shoulders. "You know Jim wouldn't want you to be alone or unhappy. He loved you more than life itself."

Her brave front began to slip as he drew her to him and held her close. Momentarily leaning into the comfort of his shoulder, she closed her eyes. Then she stepped back, trying to regain her composure. "I'm needed at the jail."

"Wait a minute." Perry returned to his desk and pulled a ledger from the top drawer. "I insist on writing you a personal draft sufficient to see you through the next few months."

Her hand flew to cover his. "I won't hear of it."

"Be reasonable. Your options have run out. What other choice do you have if you're intent on keeping the store?"

"I will not impose on my friends for financial help."

She turned around and walked out of the office. She might be broke, but she still had her pride. Not even financial ruin could take that away from her. And Perry, though he would deny otherwise, would expect matrimony prospects, something she wasn't prepared to offer.

Chapter Twenty-Five

"Stand back, Herschel, you cain't come in here!"

Herschel Mallard tried to push past Sawyer, but the old man blocked his way. Zoe, kneeling next to Bonnie, watched Cade walk over and break up the scuffle. "What do you need, Herschel?"

"One of my bulls is missing."

Cade grinned. "Maybe he's out socializing with the women."

"Ain't no time to be funny, Kolby. That bull cost me a pretty penny. Where's Pop?"

Sawyer butted in. "Pop's laid up with a broken leg."

"Who's takin' care of sheriffin'?" Herschel peered between the two men standing in the doorway. "What's going on here?"

Bruce raised his head, moaning. "Go away, Herschel. We all got the sickness."

Herschel abruptly stepped back. "The what!"

"The fever! And shut the door! That blasted light's blinding me."

Cade glanced at Zoe. "Can you handle things here while I help Herschel find his bull?"

She nodded as she patted Bonnie's brow with a cool cloth.

Cade rode with Herschel to the Mallard farm west of town, the home there a one-room shanty perched on a rocky hillside.

Riding the fencerow, Cade located the trouble toward the back end of the pasture.

Herschel swore a blue streak as he viewed the cut wire. "Rustlers."

"Most likely. Anyone else had trouble lately?"

"Clyde Abbott's brother, Saul, lost some steers a few weeks back. Pop never found 'em."

Cade stood up, dusting off his knees. "I'll take a look around, but I imagine they're long gone."

"Don't be bringing me back no bulls wearing bonnets."

Grinning, Cade took the reference to his childhood prank in stride. "You got my word on that, Herschel."

Nodding, the farmer said, "Good enough."

Toward dark, Cade rode to Saul Abbott's farm and knocked on the front door. The smell of meat frying drifted from the open window. It had been hours since breakfast. A young girl a few years older than Holly opened the door. The child was barefoot, her dress faded and threadbare.

"Are your folks home?"

The girl nodded. "They're layin' down, feelin' poorly."

A man appeared in the background, hitching his suspenders over his shoulders. A heavy growth of reddish beard covered his face. Squinting, he held up a hand to shade his eyes. "Is that you, Kolby? Heard you was back."

"Hello, Saul. Didn't recognize you for a second. Are you sick?"

"Me and the missus got somethin' bad. I cain't even look at the light without my head feeling like it's gonna explode."

"There's been an outbreak of the fever."

He took a step back. "The fever? Like John and Addy?"

"Don't know. Herschel said you had some cattle missing."

"Did you find them?"

"No. In fact, one of Herschel's bulls is gone."

"Those no-goods. Sure would like to get my hands on who's doing it."

The little girl pulled on her daddy's sleeve. "I'm cookin' side meat, Pa. Can we invite Mr. Kolby to stay?"

"'Fraid he can have it all, sis. Your momma and I don't feel much like eatin'."

"How many are in your family, Saul?" Saul was around Cade's age, so he could have a whole houseful of kids by now.

"Got three young'uns—two boys and Sis, here. Then me and the missus, 'course."

"Are the kids sick?"

"Not so far." Saul sank into the nearest chair and held his head.

"I think you and Mrs. Abbott should come with me. We have several cases at the jail."

"I'd argue if I had the strength, but I think maybe you're right. The missus is real bad. No need of the younger ones gettin' this." Turning to his daughter, he said, "Sis, you go to the barn and get your brothers. You'll have to see after things until me and your ma get back."

Around bedtime, Cade pulled the Abbotts' wagon to a halt in front of the jail. Saul and his wife lay in the back. Cade helped Mrs. Abbott out as Zoe stepped outside.

"Oh, dear. More?"

Cade nodded. "Two more."

Zoe managed to get Belle Abbott up the steps and into the jail. "I was getting worried. The children had to take supper with Gracie again since you weren't back."

"Sorry. I was detained."

"I told them you'd eat with us tonight."

He brushed past her.

Sawyer spat. "Here we go again. Same old tune. 'I want the kids.' 'You can't have 'em.'"

"Be reasonable, Red. I've got two more sick people. Stop harping and help me get Belle and Saul settled."

"Harping!"

"Harping," Sawyer confirmed.

With a sigh, Zoe returned to the wagon for Saul. "You too, Saul?"

She made room for the two newest patients. Pallets were scooted over, the men's in the cell, the women's in the office. The small building was filled to capacity.

Bruce lifted his head off the pillow. "This is getting out of hand. We're going to have to quarantine the town."

"I think you're right." Zoe wrung out a sponge. "We need to do something." She turned to Cade. "Frank Lovell rode to Chesterfield today for more quinine. Even paid for it."

"Frank Lovell? The town skinflint turned humanitarian? Hard to believe," Cade said. "Sawyer, we're going to need a quarantine notice."

Sawyer nodded. "You'll have to write out the sign. Never learned my letterin'."

Zoe pulled two wanted posters out of Pop's desk drawer. On their backs, in bold letters, she wrote, "Quarantined. Stay Out."

By the time the moon came up, the town of Winterborn was closed to all outsiders.

Chapter Twenty-Six

I wonder why none of the children have gotten sick," Zoe said. That evening she and Cade sat outside the jail, leaning against the building's wall. She closed her eyes. "So far, only adults have been affected. Clyde Abbott's son is the youngest, and he's twenty-seven."

"Maybe it isn't the fever. Maybe it's something else."

"Everyone says it's the fever. We'll have to wait until Doc gets back."

He shrugged. "You should go home. There's plenty of help here. Glori-Lee is furnishing the meals. Lilith brought over her soap this morning and checks in every few hours." His gaze went to the open doorway. "And Sawyer is a pain in the neck."

"He's trying to be helpful."

Cade smiled. "Yeah, I guess so. When I was a kid I thought he was strange. But look at him. He's out there keeping everyone away."

His eyes grew distant, and she wondered if he was considering his life on the trail. Having few friends to come to his aid, and even fewer to care about him—what must that feel like? During her own troubles, she had always had Addy and Gracie. And the townspeople. They were beside her through thick and thin. "Do you ever miss Winterborn?" she asked.

"At times."

"But not enough to come back for good."

He tasted his coffee, and Zoe thought he was ignoring her remark. But he wasn't.

"I also used to hate the smell of Lilith's fancy soap," he said, "but it's not so bad anymore."

She was only half listening. Her back was sore from bending over. Other than the Abbots, no new cases had come to light during the night. The patients were stable. Bonnie was better. Zoe wanted to think the worst was over, but her life was in a shambles. Because of the quarantine, no one from the outside could get in to shop at the store. The town trade alone wouldn't pay her bills. The bank wouldn't loan her additional money, and she couldn't take in one more basket of washing and ironing and still help out at the jail.

She opened her eyes, studying the man beside her. Did Cade sense her frustration? He sat calmly drinking coffee, making mundane conversation.

Laying her hand on his arm, she said, "Thank you for helping out. I don't know how I'd have managed without you. I know you didn't expect to stay in town this long."

"I can't go anywhere until I find a place for the kids."

Of course. He certainly wasn't staying around for her sake. "You have a place. You just won't recognize it."

"You're not raising the kids alone."

She stood up, her hands on her hips. "If I were a man, I'd knock some sense into you!"

"If I were a woman, I'd behave like one."

Chapter Twenty-Seven

Get out of my way!" Laticia Wiseman's whip snapped over Harry Miller's head.

He grabbed the horse's collar and held firm. "You can't come in here!" He pointed to the quarantine sign. "Can't you read, woman?"

Sniffing, the woman peered down her long aristocratic nose. "Obviously you can't. The sign's upside down, you fool."

Harry frowned and turned to stare at the sign tacked to the fence post. He turned back. "There's sickness in there. Go back to where you come from."

Raising her whip over her head, she warned him again, "Step aside! I've never been sick a day in my life!"

"Don't doubt it," he grumbled. "Even the fever would run fast from the likes of you."

Laticia handed the whip to her driver. "Lash him, Abraham."

Abraham's eyes filled with uncertainty. "Now, Miz Laticia, I don' think we ort do that."

"Give me that!" she grabbed the whip back and Harry ducked and covered his head with his arms. Giving the horse a smart flick to the rump, she set the buggy in motion. The sudden lurch knocked Harry aside, throwing him into the ditch. A back wheel caught the quarantine sign and dragged it down the road.

Scrambling to his feet, Harry yelled after the departing buggy, "I said you can't go in there!"

Zoe was about to step into the jail when the carriage whipped into town. Jumping out of the way, she gasped when she recognized the children's great-aunt, Laticia.

"Miss Wiseman!" She caught up and ran alongside the buggy. "You're not supposed to be here. We're quarantined!"

"Balderdash! I'll go where I please!"

The elderly black driver tipped his hat to Zoe as the buggy rolled to a stop in front of the merchantile. Grinning, Abraham set the brake. "How'do, Miz Bradshaw."

Sawyer stepped up to intervene, but Zoe waved him away.

Laticia sat straight as a board on the buggy seat, dressed as if she'd come for a funeral. Her plumed black hat was cocked to one side, and a stiffly starched collar, as black as a raven's wing, encased her long neck like a vise. Black bodice, black skirt, black shoes, black gloves, and a black cane with an ivory head completed her depressing attire. The kids were right to hide from her. Zoe had forgotten how scary their aunt was.

As Laticia glared down her long nose at her appearance, Zoe's mind raced with the implications of the unexpected visit. Since Laticia hadn't come for John and Addy's funeral, it was odd that she'd show up now.

"Miss Wiseman, there's sickness here. You have to leave now."

"I'm not afraid of a little thing like sickness. Abraham! Help me off this seat!"

Abraham jumped off the buggy and extended his arm to the elderly matron. "Now, you be careful, Miz Laticia. It's a mite steep getting down."

"Humph. I'm perfectly capable of getting out of a carriage."

Once her feet were on the ground, and she had balanced her weight with the heavy cane, she dismissed Abraham with a sharp nod. "Go on over to the livery and wait for me there. I have business with Mrs. Bradshaw."

"Yes'm." Abraham shuffled off and Laticia turned to Zoe.

She felt herself shrinking under Laticia's scrutiny. The woman had eyes like a vulture's and the children were right. She smelled funny, as if her clothes had been stored in a dank wardrobe. "Is there something I can do for you, Miss Wiseman?"

"I came for the children."

Zoe's spine stiffened. "For whom?"

"My nephew John's children. Where are they?"

"They're playing in the back of the store—"

"Pack their belongings. They're coming with me." The matriarch dabbed a hanky along her jaw. "And get me a cool drink while you're about it."

Zoe struggled to grasp the meaning of her declaration. She was here for the children? She wanted to take them home with her? Surely she wasn't serious.

"You want them to come for a visit?"

Moving the handkerchief to her upper lip, the old woman frowned. "News of my nephew's death reached me only this morning."

"I'm sorry. I sent word."

The woman raised her cane. "I don't fault you. I've been away visiting acquaintances in Wichita, but I'm back now. I will see to the children."

"That's absurd! Their Uncle Cade is here to see to them."

"Piddytash." Laticia glared. "What does that…that bounty hunter know about children?"

Loathing was so apparent in her tone that Zoe's skin crawled. What did Laticia know about Cade? Nothing, she'd wager. Drawing up straighter, she prepared for battle. "Addy left the decision of who would raise the children up to him."

Laticia dismissed the idea with a wave of her cane. "She obviously wasn't thinking rationally before her death. Had she been, she would have left the children in my care." She banged the tip of her cane on the packed dirt road. "Now, off with you! Bring me my great-nieces and nephews! Abraham doesn't like to be out after dark."

"But Miss Wiseman—"

"No buts! Bring those children to me!"

Zoe's cheeks warmed when she realized Laticia's strident words had attracted a crowd. When she saw Cade crossing the street, relief flooded her. She held her breath as she watched the elderly lady's demeanor stiffen as he approached.

"Cade Kolby. The prodigal son returns," Laticia scoffed.

He glanced at Zoe. She shrugged. She didn't know what to say. All she could do was hope Cade could intimidate the grouchy curmudgeon.

"Miss Wiseman," Cade began, "are you aware that the town is—"

"I am not muddled. I know the town is quarantined. I'll leave as soon as you bring the children. Now do it!"

Cade frowned. "What children?"

"John's children."

"Addy's children are staying right here."

Laticia whacked the post above his head. "Don't be impertinent with me, young man."

Zoe turned to locate the sudden sound of cursing. Harry hobbled up, dragging the quarantine sign with him. "Crazy old fool. Knocked the fence down and drug the warning halfway to town!"

Lifting both hands, Zoe called a halt to the fiasco. "Everyone, calm down. Miss Wiseman, come inside, and we'll discuss the matter over a glass of lemonade."

"Stop wasting my time, young lady. Get the children."

"The kids aren't going anywhere." Cade stepped up on the porch, dodging the woman's flailing cane. He seized her arm and ushered her inside the store. Zoe followed. The screen door banged shut behind them.

Brody and Will spotted their aunt, jumped to their feet, and bolted toward the back door, screaming.

Zoe ran ahead and blocked their path. "Stop right there!"

"It's her!" Brody shouted, trying to squirm around Zoe.

"It's the old witch!" Will screamed.

Kneeling, Zoe gathered the boys to her, attempting to calm their fears. "Your father's aunt isn't here to harm you." Zoe never approved of the way John had tormented his children with Laticia's imminent presence.

Addy had always gently reminded her husband that Laticia was family and shouldn't be used as a threat, but there was no denying that John's method of discipline, if not exactly fair, had proved infinitely more effective than a hickory switch. The children regarded their great-aunt as Lucifer—a very unpleasant, musty-smelling evil—and Zoe could see why.

"Boys, say hello to your Great-Aunt Laticia," Zoe prodded. Their mouths fell open, but no sound came out. "Girls," she called. No answer. "Girls! Are you in here?"

Zoe ushered the boys to kitchen chairs. "Sit here while I find your sisters." She poured Laticia a glass of lemonade. "Please sit down, Miss Wiseman. I'm sure you'd like a rest after your trip."

"I'm not here to socialize." The elderly matron wrapped her gnarled fingers around the glass and took a long, noisy gulp. Her lips curled, and Zoe cringed.

"Not enough sugar. Nobody knows how to make lemonade anymore."

"Sit down, Laticia." Cade pulled out a chair for her. "What is this about the children going with you?"

"It's Miss Wiseman to you, young man." She squinted, her eyes pinning him. "Never could figure out how you and Addy were kin. She had a brain."

Cade poured lemonade for Will and Brody. Zoe cleared her throat. "Do you know where the girls are, Cade?"

"I haven't seen them. I've been trying to talk Bonnie out of going home."

Zoe shook her head, scooped up a stack of clean towels from the kitchen counter, and walked into the bedroom to search for the girls. She needed a moment alone. Her gaze centered on a huge lump in her bedspread. Butch! That dog had gotten into her bed again. She set the towels on a shelf and yanked back the spread.

Holly and Missy, heads down, huddled together in the middle of the mattress.

"What are you doing here?" Zoe whispered. "Aunt Laticia has come to see you."

The girls grabbed her around the waist and clung tight. "No, Zoe. Tell her we're sick," Holly pleaded.

"Tell hew we wan away," Missy cried.

She gathered the girls to her. "Girls, there is nothing to be afraid of. She loves you. She's just...she's just..."

"Smelly?" Holly offered.

"I was going to say 'different.' She's different." Actually she was smelly, but Zoe couldn't encourage the description.

She returned to the kitchen with the girls in tow to find Laticia and Cade embroiled in heated debate. Seating Holly and Missy beside their stone-faced brothers, she turned to Laticia. "More lemonade, Miss Wiseman?"

The woman handed Zoe her empty glass. "The children should be with family. The Brightons may be fine people, but they're not family."

"There is another alternative," Zoe offered, glancing at Cade as she poured. "One that I wish you both would seriously consider."

"And what might that be?" Laticia's hostile look gave Zoe chills.

"Let me have them."

"Humph! Haven't you been listening? I said *family* should have them. You're not family." Laticia's stare intensified. "You need to find yourself another husband and have your own babies."

Zoe refused to look at Cade. She didn't want to see that "keep quiet" look on his face. She was sick of everyone telling her to have her own babies. If she could, she would have had a dozen by now.

Cade broke in. "You're absolutely right, Laticia. The kids should be with family. I'm family, and I will keep them."

Zoe lifted unbelieving brows.

Cade squared his shoulders and crossed his arms over his chest. "Until things settle down here."

"And then what?" the woman demanded.

"That's my problem. Have Abraham take you home."

Laticia's cane came down with a whack against the floor, startling all four children a good half foot off their seats.

"I'll stay in this town as long as I want, young man. It'll take more than the likes of you to make me leave." She whirled to look at the children, giving each one a good once-over. "You, there." She pointed to Holly. "Come here and give your auntie a kiss."

Laticia tapped an arthritic finger against her cheek. Zoe nodded for Holly to comply. The girl slowly got up from her chair and walked stiff legged toward the woman. She stayed as far away as she could while still bending to reach her aunt's cheek, where one stray black hair protruded. Zoe's stomach turned over. The children watched, repulsion shining in their eyes.

Springing to their rescue, Zoe suggested, "Children, why don't you take a glass of lemonade over to the livery for Abraham? He's probably very thirsty by now."

"Yeah!" Brody yelled, jumping up from the table. "Mighty thirsty!"

The other three scrambled to see who could get out the door the fastest while Brody quickly grabbed up the pitcher of lemonade.

"Don't stay too long," Zoe called as the screen door slammed behind them. She turned back to Laticia. "Perhaps I can make arrangements with Gracie Willis for you to stay the night in her guest room."

"Gracie who?"

"The mayor's wife."

"Oh, yes. Gracie. The mayor's wife." The spinster ran pointed fingernails through the sides of her gray hair, then rearranged her hairnet. "Yes, I believe I could be comfortable at the mayor's house."

"Well, then. I'll run over and let Gracie know to expect you shortly." Zoe rested her hand on Cade's shoulder for strength. "Would you mind taking Miss Wiseman's things to Gracie's?"

Laticia butted in. "Don't have 'things.' Don't need 'things.' I got what I have on. I don't plan on doing anything to get dirty."

Zoe squelched a fleeting thought. She would love to catch Laticia out of those clothes so she could launder them. Laundry. Heavens! She had patients' sheets to wash tonight!

Chapter Twenty-Eight

Gracie, I'm sorry to ask, but I don't have any room for her to stay with me."

"It's no trouble, dear. One night with Laticia Wiseman won't kill us." Gracie laughed as she set out the coffee service.

"I'm not so sure. She's pretty domineering."

"You left Cade alone with her?"

"Serves him right." Zoe grinned. "Maybe she'll put the fear of the Almighty in him."

Gracie laughed again, and Zoe joined her. "What else can go wrong? From the minute Cade arrived, it's been one disaster after another. I'm barely keeping up with the laundry. Thank heavens you and Glori-Lee are feeding the sick. I don't know if I'd have the time or the food, for that matter. I've run out of produce, but it doesn't make much difference. No one's buying anything." She leaned back in her chair. And each day spent with Cade was another day to mourn what could have been. Cade could have been an upstanding citizen instead of a man who would remain homeless for the rest of his life, however long or short that might be. Only through the grace of God had he not been shot and killed by now.

"Oh, Gracie, what am I going to do? If Miss Wiseman takes those kids, I won't be able to bear it. They're scared to death of her."

Gracie frowned. "I never approved of John's shenanigans. It wasn't right of him to frighten those kids like that."

Zoe sighed, reaching for the creamer. "I'm glad Addy doesn't have to witness this. Do you realize Laticia is the children's only relative other than Cade? If anything were to happen to him—" She couldn't finish the thought. It was too disturbing.

"How'd she get past the quarantine?"

"She made Abraham drive right through. Harry said they tried to run him down."

Gracie laid her head back and laughed heartily. "I'll bet Harry was fit to be tied." Her laughter dwindled to a smile. "Abraham. Is that old black driver of Laticia's still alive? I thought about him just the other day. Wondered what that old woman would do without him."

Zoe took a sip from her cup. "He takes good care of her. I never understood how he stays so pleasant and soft spoken. Over the years, when Laticia visited John and Addy, Abraham was always a gracious gentleman."

Gracie smiled as she stirred her coffee.

"Did you know," Zoe continued, "that Laticia's daddy gave Abraham to her when she was just a girl? Even with slaves being free and all, Abraham went right on waiting on those folks like they were his own kin."

Gracie chuckled.

"Laticia is fortunate to have him," Zoe went on, "but neither one should be raising children at their ages."

"I'll tell you something," said Gracie. "Abraham is wiser than anyone gives him credit for. If you stop and think, he's the only one who knows how to keep 'Miz Laticia' in line."

Zoe lifted a brow. "How so?"

"Ever hear him say, 'Now, Miz Laticia, we ort not do that,' or 'We ort not think that way'?"

Grinning, Zoe nodded. He said it constantly.

"Ever see Laticia do what she said she would after Abraham warned her not to?"

Zoe shook her head.

Gracie slapped her thighs with both hands. "I should say not. He's the only one who knows how to handle her."

"Hmm." Zoe bit into a warm cookie. "Maybe I'll have a little talk with Abraham. Perhaps he can make Laticia see how foolish it would be for her to take the children. Her health won't hold out forever. If she were to get sick, Abraham couldn't take care of all of them."

Gracie patted Zoe's hand. "The way to Laticia is through Abraham. Yes, I'd say a talk with him is in order. And soon."

Chapter Twenty-Nine

On her way back to the store, Zoe stopped by the livery to pick up the children and briefly chat with Abraham.

"Oh, Miz Bradshaw, I don' think Miz Laticia would pay me no mind should I say somethin' about those young'uns. She pretty well set her hat for 'em. Said we need somethin' to look after, fill in the time o' day."

Zoe gently covered the black man's hand with hers. "Abraham, a woman her age has no business raising four young children. What Laticia needs is a pet. Maybe a pretty cat."

Abraham crowed. "Now, that would be a mite easier on me, Miz Bradshaw. A nice quiet cat." His gaze roamed the stable. "Saw one here a minute ago. Right friendly. Black. Reminded me of Miz Laticia."

Zoe hugged the old man affectionately, taking solace in his soft, chocolate-colored eyes. "You're a good man, Abraham."

"Yes'm. You go on home now. Don't be frettin' no mo'."

Zoe's gaze wandered over the rustic stable. "I wish there was a better place for you to sleep."

"I be jist fine, Miz Bradshaw. Jist fine."

After supper, Zoe ironed for an hour and then wandered onto the back porch for a breath of fresh air. It was the first moment she could call her own since early dawn. She held a glass of water to her neck and savored the coolness against her flushed skin. She was wondering how Cade was doing with the patients when he rounded the building.

She sucked in her breath. His unexpected presence made her knees wobbly. She quickly sat down before she fell down.

"What are you doing over here?" She couldn't help noticing how the moonlight heightened his tired features. She wondered if he regretted coming back, if he longed for his old life, a life free of children and family pressures.

"I got the night off. Seth offered to spell me."

Patting the step beside her, she motioned for him to sit. The past few days hadn't been a picnic for him, either.

Sinking down next to her, he removed his hat and then leaned back, his eyes sliding over her with easy familiarity. "You get prettier every day. Anyone ever tell you that?"

"Only men who are in sore need of spectacles."

Resting back on his forearms, he gazed up at the star-studded sky. "You're supposed to say, 'Why, thank you, sir.' Then you flutter your hand in front of your pretty eyes and say, 'How you do go on.'"

She made a face. "Do you ever have a serious thought?"

"Not often. At least, I didn't until lately."

Tree frogs sang near the livery pond. Silvery moonbeams filtered through the branches of the old oak standing in the backyard.

"Do you ever wonder what it would be like to live a normal life, Cade?"

"I wonder, occasionally." Sitting up, he ran his fingers through his hair. "Don't change the subject. You're a beautiful woman. Take the compliment or leave it."

"Put in such romantic terms, how can I refuse?" Her dress was water stained, her flyaway hair a disgrace. She hadn't had time to look in the mirror for, what? Days? She must be a ravishing sight indeed. But then, he'd always thought her pretty. That was still nice to know.

"Have you eaten?" she asked.

"Glori-Lee brought extra food to the jail tonight. I skipped the peach pie and cream."

"Kids weaned you from that, huh?" She shivered. Once the sun went down, the night air cooled quickly.

Slipping to the step above her, Cade gathered her close. Shifting slightly, she sought to escape, but he held her firmly. After a moment, she stopped struggling. There had been a time when she'd considered his intimate gestures as natural as drawing the next breath.

"Better?" he asked.

No, she thought, shaking her head. Worse. His closeness brought back too many unwanted memories.

Leaning closer, he sniffed her hair. His breath, warm against her cheek, sent shivers up her spine. "How do you always manage to smell so good? Like lemon and French soap."

"And what would you know about French soap?"

He nuzzled her neck. "I know I like the smell."

"Cade, please." She tried to move away, but his hold tightened.

"You smell nothing like Laticia. What is that stench on her?"

Zoe grinned in spite of her effort to ignore him. "She always smells like that."

"What is it?"

"Mothballs, maybe? I dare you to ask."

"And get my head knocked off with that weapon she calls a cane? No thanks." His fingers found her funny bone and tickled. Squirming, she giggled, hating herself. *Stop it. Zoe! Get up and go inside. It's insane to sit here, letting him tickle you and responding like a smitten fool!*

Twisting aside, she scooted away to distance herself from him. He grinned, clearly flirting with her now.

"If you're not cold, I am." She sucked in a long-suffering breath and then relaxed in defeat as he scooted closer and drew her back to him. It was insane, but she couldn't say she didn't enjoy his company. If nothing else, they had shared young love and almost a child. She sighed. God did not intend them to be husband and wife, but little changed the fact that they were friends, and she'd have to deal with that. Resting her head on his shoulder, she gazed at the stars. "Admit it," she said. "You're getting attached to the children."

"I've never said I wasn't."

It was true. He might not openly express his affection, but his eyes gave him away. Each time Missy or Holly climbed into his lap, he was theirs for the taking.

"They adore you, you know."

"They're good kids."

I adored you. Once. So much so, I thought I would die when you didn't come back. She blinked back tears, reminding herself the past was the past. Painful though it was, the time had come to bury it. "How are things at the jail tonight?"

"No new cases."

"Still, I worry sick about the kids. They were around John and Addy constantly, even though I tried to keep them away."

He rubbed his hands up and down her arms, warming them. "I think Lilith's soap's causing it."

She sighed. "A fever? Right."

"Bonnie swears it gives her a rash."

His fingers eased to her shoulders, massaging weariness away. Her bones turned to liquid as he gently worked the tension out of her neck.

"Relax, Red."

His low baritone aroused feelings she had considered dormant. She and Jim had had a satisfactory marriage bed, but he had been gone a year. She hadn't realized she missed a man's touch until now.

"You work too hard."

Sensitive understanding mixed with the proper amount of pity. A deadly combination. Did he know what he was doing? How easy it would be to fall prey to his tenderness. His fingers worked magic through her tense muscles. Every bone in her body hurt. She'd like nothing more than to lean into his calm assurance and stay there for the rest of her life.

He lifted the small gold chain around her neck. "Is this the locket I gave you?"

She pushed his hand away. "I wear it out of habit."

His mouth brushed her ear. "I could buy you one made of real gold now."

"I like this one. You gave it to me the night you left."

"And you've kept it all these years?"

"I keep a lot of things, Cade. Don't read anything into it." Changing the subject, she murmured, "I'm sorry you've had to stay so long."

"Don't be. I'm not. I like being an uncle to the kids. Too bad it took Addy's death for me to see that."

She almost felt sorry for him, maybe because she was tired and weak, needing his comfort and support more than she wanted to admit. He'd been thrust headfirst into a chaotic situation, losing his sister, gaining four children, and becoming a nurse and surrogate sheriff until Pop's injury healed all in a matter of days. He was holding up well, considering. "I wouldn't blame you if you walked out and never came back."

"I did that once and regretted it."

His words barely registered. She was bone tired. She would just close her eyes for a moment, and then she'd feel better. As he stroked and kneaded the tension out of her body, events didn't seem nearly as bad as they had an hour ago. The patients were improving, she had only a half bushel of ironing left, and tomorrow...well, tomorrow was a new day...

She felt him draw her against his chest, and she drifted off to sleep, barely aware when he picked her up and carried her into the house.

Chapter Thirty

When Cade opened the jail door the next morning, Zoe was bent over Bonnie, adjusting her pillow. The purpose of his visit deserted him as his gaze focused on her.

An unexplained desire to take her into his arms was so powerful he could taste it. Holding her last night had awakened feelings he didn't need. He'd known from the moment he'd arrived that she wouldn't be easy to walk away from this time. Fifteen years ago he'd been a kid with a head full of fantasy. He was a man now. And his love for her had never dimmed. Had never grown cold, though he'd told himself life was different now.

He and Red were adults now, with a solid chunk of life they no longer shared.

Cade cleared his throat, hoping to clear his mind as well. "Why didn't you wake me?"

She tucked a strand of hair behind her ear. "You were sleeping so soundly, I didn't want to disturb you."

He glanced toward the patients. "Any change?"

"They all ate a good breakfast."

"What about you?"

"I'm fine. Got a good night's sleep." She sighed. "I hope Gracie keeps Laticia occupied for a few hours."

"Laticia's bluffing. She's not going to take those children."

"You can't be sure of that."

"She won't. She may be a blood relative, but no one in his right mind would give her custody of four small children, and she knows it."

"Then what does she hope to gain?"

"The thrill of running her bluff on me."

Zoe looked away, grousing under her breath. "This could all be taken care of by nightfall. If you'd agree to let me have them, Richard Moyer could have adoption papers drawn up in a matter of hours."

"Who's Richard Moyer?"

"Town attorney. He could settle this matter if you'd only be reasonable."

"You forget, Mrs. Bradshaw—'reasonable' isn't my strong suit."

"The longer Laticia stays, the more upset the children will be."

"They're bright kids. They know I'm not going to leave them where they won't be happy."

She straightened to face him. "How could they possibly know that?"

"Because I told them." He softened his tone. "I haven't broken a promise yet, have I? To them," he amended.

Sawyer stopped Cade as he started across the street.

"Hey, hold up there, Kolby!"

Cade turned, wondering if the watchdog ever slept. "Need something?"

The self-appointed town guardian approached, his jaw bulging with his chew. He took off his hat and squared his shoulders. Thin strands of grayish hair poked out around his head in various directions.

"I want a badge." He twisted his hat in his blue-veined hands. Age spots dotted his weathered skin.

"What kind of a badge?"

"One that'll give me some authority. If I'm supposed to keep people outta the jail, I got to have some respect. Laticia don't respect my authority."

"Laticia Wiseman isn't known for her manners."

"It don't matter! She cain't do what she wants and not pay the piper!"

"And you think a badge would lend you credibility?"

Sawyer nodded. "Yes. That's what I want. Some of that credible stuff. Somebody's got to keep the law! The law's the law! No doggone female is above it!"

"All right. Stop by the jail later and I'll make you a badge."

The old man's face beamed in a tobacco-stained grin. He nodded, his hair waving. "Thank ya."

Chapter Thirty-One

A gnat flitted overhead. Cade tipped his chair back, propped his boots on the kitchen table, and rested the stack of wanted posters on his chest. A thick ham sandwich and Zoe's bread-and-butter pickles rested nicely in his stomach.

Clasping his hands behind his neck, he listened to Missy playing with her dolls at the front of the store. A smile touched the corners of his mouth when he heard her say, "Dolly, you sit here, and Bud, you sit there."

As long as she kept the tarantula in its jar, he had no complaints.

Stretching, he yawned, flexing his fingers above his head. The other kids were at the livery with Abraham, and Zoe was at the jail, so the house was unusually quiet. It gave him time to think.

McGill would soon tire of his idle time and come looking for him. And if he came looking, he would discover the kids. Cade was a loner with no family. That's what his enemies thought, so they had nothing to take from him for retribution. If McGill knew he had the kids, the outlaw would go for them. The longer he pushed his luck, the more he was putting the kids in danger. Now this Laticia business, what was he going to do about her? Should he forget the Brightons and talk to that Amish couple near Salina, the ones Pop had heard about? McGill would never find them there. Someday someone would learn about his personal life and they would trace him back to Winterborn. And to Zoe.

Was that the bell over the door? He sat up, listening as the tinkling drifted to him. No, Missy was playing with some sort of toy.

Since the fever outbreak, Zoe's business was down to nothing. Lilith had stopped by earlier for ten cents worth of brown sugar. It took him thirty minutes to get loose from her. Then Pop dropped by to announce that, due to the illness, he was canceling Saturday night's dance until further notice. Cade smiled. *Too bad, Banker Drake. Guess you won't get to dance with Zoe after all.*

Patting his stomach, he dozed. Seconds later, soft snores filled the small kitchen.

"You'we going to weally like Uncle Cade, Bud. He didn't mean to scawe you the othew mowning," Missy whispered through the holes in the jar lid as she crept into the kitchen. "He said he would play with me anytime I want."

She gave the jar a shake. "Awe you awake? Bud?" Peering through the glass, she sighed. "Hope you'we not getting that fevew. Zoe will hate to stick that stuff down youw fwoat." She adjusted the basket of doll dishes and cookies over her arm. "You got a fwoat, Bud?"

As she passed Cade's chair, she paused. "Ooooh, Uncle Cade is sweeping." She quietly set her basket on the table. Stepping closer, she stared at her uncle, leaning real close. He was asweep.

Shrugging her shoulders, she unscrewed the lid, carefully lifted Bud from his bed, and placed him on Cade's chest. "You stay thewe, Bud, while I get things weady fow ouw tea pawty."

She busied herself preparing the table. She spread a napkin to serve as a tablecloth, and then arranged three tiny cups and saucers around the edge. A stack of ginger cookies complemented the tea service. She stepped back to admire her work. Nudging Cade's knee, she whispered, "Uncle Cade?"

Cade stirred. "Hmm?"

Missy tiptoed closer and patted his cheek. "Wake up, Uncle Cade. It's time fow ouw tea pawty."

"Mumphm." Cade brushed the air, smacking his lips.

"Uncle Caaade. Wake uuuup."

Opening an eye, Cade smiled when he saw the intruder. Missy smiled, waving.

Cade's gaze slid down, and his eyes widened. A tarantula sat in the middle of his chest. The spider's hairy front legs flexed.

How come every time he woke up, that spider was on his chest!

Bud started creeping toward his face. Cade jerked his feet off the table, the sudden movement causing the chair legs to fly out from under him. He hit the floor with a jarring crash, certain his back was broken.

Bud scurried across the floor and disappeared around the corner.

Missy stomped her foot. "Uncle Cade! You scawed Bud again."

"Missy, you're going to have to keep that thing in its jar!" Cade swiped the front of his shirt, shuddering. All those years on the trail, and he'd never once woken with a spider on his chest.

Bud rounded the corner, skittering across the plank floor.

Missy ran and scooped him back into his jar. "It's all wight, Bud. Uncle Cade likes you. He's not mean. He won't scawe you again."

"I scared him? Missy, that's a tarantula!"

"Uh-uh." She puffed. "He's my bug."

Cade righted his chair and sank down in it. "I'm sorry, sweetheart. It's just that Bud is—"

"Fuzzy?"

"Yes. Heck yes. That too." He raked his fingers through his hair and leaned back to catch his breath. Missy screwed the lid on Bud's jar.

"He pwobably needs to west a while," she said. "He's tuckewed." She pushed the jar under Cade's nose. "Say you'we sowwy, Uncle Cade."

"Come on, Missy. It's a bug."

Her blue eyes pleaded with him.

"Sorry...Bud." Cade couldn't believe he was apologizing to a tarantula.

Missy climbed up on his lap and put her arms around his neck. "It's all wight, Uncle Cade." She planted a big, noisy kiss on his cheek. "Bud's not mad at you."

Good. He wouldn't lose sleep tonight.

Missy brushed her hand across his cheek. "Awe you weddy for ouw tea pawty?"

He grinned, playing along with her. "A cup of tea would be refreshing, my dear."

"Okay, and aftew we eat, I'll fix youw haiw weal pwetty." Missy scrambled from his lap to perform her hostess's duties. She poured pretend tea into their cups.

He raised his brows. "My hair, dearest? Is there something wrong with my curly locks?"

Missy giggled. "It looks pwetty shameful, Missus Kolby."

"Oh, dash," he trilled. "Then by all means, Miss Wiseman, do something with it. Make me the envy of all Winterborn."

He picked up his teacup, little finger crooked, and took a loud, slurpy sip, soliciting another round of giggles from Missy.

While she busied herself with his head, he thumbed through the wanted posters and resumed reading. Missy stood on a box behind his chair, carefully rearranging his hair.

"If you had long haiw like you did when you fiwst come hewe, I could bwaid it fow you. Zoe showed me how to make a bwaid with stwips of wags she makes wugs with." She combed and combed. "But I can still make it look pwetty."

"Uh-huh, that's nice." Cade focused on one particular poster. Hart McGill.

He glanced up as the bell over the front door jingled. Shelby Moore came into the store and walked back to the kitchen.

"Afternoon, Shelby," Cade greeted.

Shelby's gaze shot straight to the ceiling.

"Hello, Mistew Moowe." Missy wedged her tongue between her lips as she meticulously fashioned Cade's "coif."

"Afternoon, Missy. Where's Zoe?"

"At the jail looking aftew sick people."

"How did you get past the quarantine?" Cade asked.

"What quarantine?"

"The town's quarantined. We have men at each end of town who are supposed to be turning people away."

"I didn't use the road. I took the back fields."

Cade told him about the sickness, and Shelby shook his head. "I'll be statin' my business and leavin' then."

Cade's gaze followed Moore's to the ceiling again, puzzled by his preoccupation with it. Seeing nothing unusual, he asked, "What brings you out in this heat?"

"Lookin' for Pop. Found a dead bull near my place. Think it might belong to Herschel Mallard. Pop needs to come check it before I clear away the carcass."

"I'm taking care of Pop's business for a few days. Guess you heard he broke his leg the other night?"

"Hadn't heard that."

Shelby's eyes darted around the room, refusing to meet his. Cade wondered if he had a wandering eye.

"I'd sooner Pop take care of the matter."

Cade frowned. "I can handle it, Shelby—" He glanced at the ceiling again, wondering what the man found so interesting there.

The farmer lowered his gaze to study his shoes. "Where's Pop?"

"At his place." Cade got up from his seat. "Give me a minute to find someone to look after Missy, and I'll check on that carcass."

Shelby cleared his throat. "Don't mean no disrespect, Kolby, but I druther Pop do it, if he can a'tall." He looked down at his feet, swallowing. "Don't think a man with pink bows in his hair has got any business sheriffin'."

Cade glanced in the mirror, his eyes widening at the sight of five stiff ponytails standing out from his scalp, each tied with a lopsided pink bow. He yanked the bows out of his hair and slapped his hat on his head. "Missy, run over to Gracie's while I ride out with Mr. Moore to see about stolen cattle."

Missy grabbed Bud's jar and held it close to her chest. "No, no, Uncle Cade! We can't go to Gwacie's. Aunt Waticia is thewe!"

Her big, fearful blue eyes tugged at his heart.

"Glori-Lee could probably use someone to help sweep out the restaurant."

Missy's face brightened. "Me and Bud can do that."

"I think Bud would be more comfortable staying here."

"Nooo. Aunt Waticia might come and get him and take him home with hew."

"I don't think so, Sunflower. I can promise Aunt Laticia will not take Bud home."

Missy's bottom lip jutted out and big tears puddled in her eyes. How was he supposed to say no to that? "Okay. You can take him."

Glori-Lee was fanning on her front step when Cade brought Missy, skipping at his side, to the café.

"Bringing you some help, Glori-Lee. Zoe's at the jail and the other kids are at the livery. I have business to attend to."

"I can always use more help," Glori-Lee said, smiling at Missy.

"I shouldn't be too long. I'm going out to Shelby's place to see about a dead bull."

"Take your time. Folks are in too big a hurry nowadays. Need to slow down a mite." Glori-Lee patted the step beside her. "Come up and sit a spell, Missy. I see you got Bud with you. He's lookin' mighty spiffy today."

Missy climbed the steps and sat down, positioning Bud's jar between her and the café owner. As Cade turned to go Missy waved. "Huwwy back, Uncle Cade! Me and Bud will be waiting fow you!"

Chapter Thirty-Two

Shelby, are you sure this is Herschel Mallard's bull?" Cade squatted by the decomposed carcass, his handkerchief covering his nose.

"That's Samson, all right. I'd know him anywhere. See that chip outta his hind hoof? Herschel bragged about it. Thought it made the bull something special."

Cade stood up, dusting dirt off his hands. "Looks like it was shot. If it was someone looking for meat, they'd have butchered it, not left it to rot."

"I 'spect it's that dadburned Nelson gang—same ones who made such a mess at Rider's Pass. I tell you, Kolby, someone needs to string them up by their heels."

"I'll take a look around." It could be the work of a dozen or more penny-ante gangs. Most times they were more troublesome than dangerous, but Cade could see how they were keeping the farmers on edge.

"I'd come with you, but I've got hay to put up before rain moves in."

"Go on with your work, Shelby. I'll look into it."

Shelby nodded, and then he spurred his horse into a gallop.

Giving Maddy her head, Cade picked his way up the road. There was no sign of the criminal. Whoever had shot the bull had covered his tracks.

It was mid-afternoon when he stopped by Herschel's to tell him about the find. He found the farmer walking behind a plow, furrowing a field for winter planting.

"Someone's got to put a stop to this." Herschel took off his sweat-stained hat and mopped his head. "I invested a right good sum in that bull."

"Shelby says he'll dispose of the carcass for you."

"Tell him much obliged."

The sun was low when Cade started back to town. No one in the area had seen or heard anything unusual. Pop would have to follow up on the incident when his leg healed.

Reining in at a stream, Cade dismounted and let the horse drink, and then he leaned down and cupped both hands to fill them with water. A movement on the bank caught the corner of his eye.

The mare reared. Cade grabbed for the reins, but she reared again, knocking him into the shallow water. Springing to his feet, he drew and fired. Pieces of rattler exploded. The headless snake thrashed about on the ground in its death throes. Bolting, the horse galloped off.

Cade put two fingers to his mouth and whistled, but the horse was long gone. Wading out of the water, he kicked the snake carcass into the grass. Maddy hated snakes, and he wasn't overly fond of them himself. He sat down under a tree to wait. She was bound to come back once she calmed down.

An hour passed, and Cade was getting drowsy. A dull ache in the back of his head was becoming annoying. Tipping his hat over his face, he dozed, knowing Maddy would wake him when she returned.

When he next opened his eyes, moonlight shone palely around him. It was well after sundown. The headache at the base of his skull was sharper, and he was chilled to the bone. Sitting up, he scanned the area then ran a hand over the back of his neck, surprised at how hot he felt even though he was shivering. "Maddy?"

Cade whistled again. No familiar whinny came to him. Leaning back against the tree, he studied the rising full moon. He'd left town hours ago. Red had to be worried about him.

He got to his feet and stretched, trying to work out the kinks. He was getting old. Every bone in his body hurt, and it was a good hour-and-a half walk back to town.

Settling his hat lower, he started off. If he got his hands on that horse right now, a snake would be the least of her problems.

Chapter Thirty-Three

Zoe opened the front door for the tenth time that evening. Where was he? It was nearing nine o'clock, and Cade still wasn't home. How long could it take to check on one dead bull?

She was glad Gracie canceled the weekly checker game because of Laticia's visit. Zoe was too worried about Cade to have enjoyed the evening.

"Have you run out on me again?" she whispered tightly. It didn't do any good to tell herself she didn't care. It wasn't just the children who would be disappointed.

"But I don't want to go to bed without kissing Uncle Cade good night," whimpered Missy, sitting at the kitchen table with her brothers and sister and great-aunt.

Hiding her concern, Zoe smiled. "I'll make certain he kisses you the moment he gets here."

"But whewe is he? He's 'posed to be back by now. It's dawk out thewe!"

"He'll be back," Brody promised. He stepped to the back door and looked out. "He probably ate supper with Shelby."

"Yeah, that's it," Will said. "Mr. Moore made Uncle Cade eat supper with him."

"Is that it, Zoe? Is that why Uncle Cade isn't back yet?"

"I'm sure that's it." Missy's face brightened, and Zoe coaxed, "Now, scoot. I'll tuck you into bed."

With a scowl, Laticia poured the last of Zoe's cream into her teacup. "And what makes you so certain that he'll be back?" The plumage on her black hat bobbled as she talked. "Have you ever known him to keep his word?"

Tears rolled down Missy's cheeks.

"Miss Wiseman, it's much cooler on the front porch. Why don't you have your tea there? I'll put Missy to bed, and then we'll visit."

Zoe spoke politely, but she could have throttled Laticia for planting scary thoughts in Missy's head. The child was fretful enough. She had extended Laticia an invitation to eat supper with them, but how was she to know Cade would ride off at noon and fail to return? Ooooh! Where was he?

"It's an hour past my bedtime," Laticia reminded. "Fetch Abraham and have him take me back to the Willises'."

"Brody, go to the livery and tell Abraham to bring the carriage."

The child skipped out to do as he was told.

"Mark my words," Laticia warned. "Even if that Kolby boy comes back, it won't change a thing. I'm taking the children with me in the morning. He's unreliable. And dangerous. He has no business with these children—especially without a wife, but even if anyone were foolish enough to marry him, he would make a miserable father." She stood and walked through the store to the front door, pausing on the threshold to confront Zoe, who had followed her. "You're foolish to think you can ever count on him."

Zoe refused to let the woman upset her. She had no idea what was keeping Cade, but instinct told her he had a reason—a valid reason—for the delay.

Oh, dear Moses, had he met up with one of his enemies? Her knees went weak. Had someone waylaid him on the road? Was he lying somewhere in a ditch right now, bloodied and unable to move?

"I'm sure he'll be here any moment." Zoe took a deep breath, trying to ignore her sudden chill. "It is so like Shelby to insist that Cade stay for supper."

"If it hadn't been for Abraham's queasy stomach, we'd be gone by now,"

Laticia said. "All that rich food you've been feeding us. No one knows how to fix chicken anymore. A body can't eat it without getting sick."

If Laticia had dyspepsia, it wasn't from the chicken, Zoe decided. The killjoy had gorged on five pieces, along with mashed potatoes, gravy, and three ears of corn. She'd barely had room for the cherry cobbler, she'd declared, but she'd managed to put away two servings.

"Are you feeling poorly, Miss Wiseman?"

"Not me." The matron burped. "Never been sick a day in my life. But Abraham now, he's got a delicate constitution."

"Maybe he'd like a little baking soda to settle his stomach."

Laticia held up a bony hand. "I'll see to Abraham's needs. Don't want a fuss made over him."

Zoe smiled inside. Abraham wasn't sick; he was stalling. Bless his dear heart. But poor Lawrence Willis. Zoe wondered if he would ever speak to her again.

Abraham soon arrived with the carriage. After Laticia left and the children were in bed, Zoe picked up her sewing basket and went into the store. She needed something cheerful to drown out the silence. She cranked up the phonograph. The music reminded her of Cade. They had danced to this tune.

She was grateful she didn't have to leave the children. Seth Brighton had to care for his farm and stock during the day, but he wanted to tend to Bonnie at night. He assured Zoe he would fetch her if he needed her.

Zoe sighed as her thoughts came back to Cade. She glanced toward the darkened window. Was Laticia right? Had he ridden off, never to be heard from again? She wished she'd never told him that she wouldn't blame him if he rode away and never came back.

After darning every sock in the basket, she put her sewing aside and changed the cylinder on the phonograph. For the hundredth time, she glanced at the clock. Two in the morning. She walked to the window and pulled the curtain aside. The full moon made it seem almost as bright as day.

The sound of a horse's hooves broke into her thoughts, and she bolted to the back door. "Cade? Is that you?"

A riderless Maddy grazed beneath the old oak. Zoe peered up and down the backyard. There was no one but the mare in sight. *Please, no. Not Cade, not now.* Shelby said he was tracking down the Nelson gang. *Oh, Cade, you fool. Why did you go alone?* A sob caught in her throat and choked her. "Zoe?"

She turned, startled. "Holly? What are you doing up?"

The girl rubbed her eyes while Zoe walked over to her and sat her down. She didn't want her to see Maddy. The child's gaze traveled to the stack of bedclothes in the corner of the room. Cade's.

"Is Uncle Cade sleeping at the jail tonight?"

Zoe didn't want to lie to the child, but neither did she want to concern her any more than she was. "No, Seth is staying tonight, so Cade can be with you. He's still taking care of Pop's business."

Holly's eyes drooped closed. "He'll be here soon?"

Zoe's gaze drifted to the open window. "Soon."

"I can't sleep," Will said, sitting up on his pallet. "It's too noisy."

Zoe patted the opposite seat. "Sit with Holly and me."

Dropping to the chair, Will mumbled, "Brody snores."

"Brody always snores. Why does it bother you tonight?" Holly asked.

Zoe wondered what would happen if Cade didn't come back. Laticia would take them. As much as Zoe loved them, she wasn't their blood kin. *Oh, Cade! How could you do this to me?* She wouldn't let the children go. She'd run away with them before she'd give them up to Laticia Wiseman, run as far and as fast as she could go. Hunt Cade down, and...and...what? What would she do? Nothing. If Cade didn't come back, there wasn't a blessed thing she could do. The children would be lost to her forever.

Brody turned over and then sat up, his hair standing on end. "Is it morning?"

"No. Go back to sleep," Will said.

"I can be up if you can."

"Brody, sit here," Zoe said. "I'll get us some cookies. I think we could use a treat."

Holly lifted her head and peered at her sleepily. "Now? In the middle of the night?"

Brody's eyes brightened. "Honest?"

"Honest." Addy might be rolling over in her grave, but dying from a treat in the middle of the night was better than dying of worry.

Zoe put a plate of cookies on the table as Missy came into the kitchen, clutching the jar housing Bud. "Bud's scawed."

Zoe smiled. "What's Bud got to be scared about?"

"He wants Uncle Cade to pwotect him."

"From what?"

"Aunt Waticia."

Zoe patted her lap, and Missy climbed up. "I think we need to talk about Aunt Laticia." The child settled into place. Holly and Will scooted their chairs closer. "Laticia isn't here to harm you, and she wouldn't harm Bud—most especially not Bud."

"Where's Uncle Cade? I want Uncle Cade."

"Shhh. Here, have a cookie. Let's have a party and think of happy things."

"Uncle Cade makes me happy."

Smiling, Zoe hugged her. He'd better have a good excuse when he did show up, a darn good one. Her gaze drifted toward the darkened window, and she bit her lower lip. *Where are you?*

The clock struck four. Earlier, the children had slipped back to bed. Seated alone at the kitchen table, Zoe glanced at the clock. Exhaustion overcame her, and she was physically sick from worry. Her head ached and her eyes burned. Why had she hoped that Cade had changed? Hadn't she known better than to count on him? Wasn't getting stung once enough?

She slumped on the kitchen chair, cradling her face in her hands. *Drat your hide. Please come back.*

Help. She needed help. From whom? Pop? He wasn't any help with a broken leg. Abraham? Yes. She would have Abraham drive her to where Shelby said he'd seen the dead bull. Where was it? She tried to remember what Glori-Lee had said.

Grabbing her shawl, she left the store and quickly ran to the livery to summon Abraham, then hurried on to Glori-Lee's. Banging on the back door of the café, she called out, "Glori-Lee!" Glori-Lee was always up at this hour to bake biscuits.

The café owner came to the door in her dressing gown, her hair wadded under a brown hairnet. "What in the world?"

"Where did Cade say he was going?"

Glori-Lee thought for a moment. "Why, he didn't say exactly, just somewhere near Shelby's place, then on to Herschel's."

"The kids were up most of the night, so they'll probably sleep late. Can you look in on them for me?"

"You can't go looking for him by yourself at this time of the morning. Get Walt or Ben—"

"No time. Abraham will drive me."

"In Laticia Wiseman's buggy? Are you crazy?"

"I'm hoping to be back before she finds out."

"I'm hoping you will be too. The whole town hopes you will, believe me," Glori-Lee stressed.

Five minutes later, Abraham pulled up alongside the café and Zoe climbed in, pointing in the direction she wanted to go.

"You bring a pistol, Miz Bradshaw, in case o' trouble?" he asked.

"No, Abraham. I'm scared of guns."

"Me too—'specially when I's on the wrong end of one." He pulled a small handgun from his jacket pocket and laid it between them on the buggy seat. Patting it for assurance, he said, "Jist in case o' trouble, Miz Bradshaw. Jist in case."

As they passed Harry at the edge of town, Zoe yelled, "Have you been here all night?"

He straightened and said, "Yes, ma'am."

"Did Cade ride this way when he left yesterday?"

"Shore did. Said something about finding Herschel's bull, dead!"

"Thank you!"

The setting moon cast eerie shadows along the road. The heavy thicket and low underbrush made a perfect cover for outlaws. Zoe found her hand resting on the pistol, "jist in case."

They had gone more than two miles when Zoe grabbed Abraham's arm.

"Slow down!" She pointed up ahead. "Something's there—at the side of the road."

Abraham squinted. "Shore is. Looks ta be...oh, Lordy, looks ta be a body, Miz Bradshaw."

Zoe was out of the buggy before it stopped. She ran so hard, she thought her lungs would burst trying to suck in enough air. Even before she reached him, she recognized Cade. When her heart threatened to explode with grief, she reminded herself that if he'd gotten himself killed, he had no one to blame but himself. She wouldn't care—she wouldn't!

Blindly falling to her knees, she sobbed, "Please, no..." Who was she kidding? She would lay down her life for him. She quickly loosened his shirt collar and felt for a pulse, wilting with relief when a strong, steady beat throbbed against her fingertips. "Abraham, come quickly. He's alive!"

With every ounce of strength she could muster, she lifted him to a sitting position. "Cade, can you hear me?" She patted his cheek. "Cade!"

His eyelids fluttered. "Red? So tired." He leaned against her chest. "Maddy spooked—"

"I know." Zoe brushed his hair back off his forehead and felt the heat. Fear constricted her throat, and she whispered, "Cade, you're burning up." She turned to Abraham as he came running. "Hurry, Abraham, hurry! We've got to get him into the buggy. He's sick."

Chapter Thirty-Four

I can't believe you went out there alone." Zoe gently sponged cool water across Cade's forehead, and then she fussed with his pallet, which she'd laid beside the others in the jail. "Pop's been worried sick about you. I'll tell him you're back."

He cocked an eye open and groaned. "Were you worried?"

"Only because of the children."

"I like it when you worry about me." Cade took hold of her wrist as a spasm crossed his features. "Can you do something about my headache?"

"If I could, I would. Lie still."

"Come on, Zoe. I'm dying."

"There's not much I can do." Heartsick, she knew that he'd come down with the same illness that killed John and Addy. "You're sick, like everybody else." She crossed his hands on his chest and pulled the blanket closer to his neck. "Rest. I don't see how you walked all that way with the fever."

He yanked the blanket over his head. "Don't...tell...anybody."

"What? That the big bounty hunter is human? That's he's flesh and bone just like everybody else? I don't see how I could keep a thing like that quiet." She checked on the others and found them soundly sleeping. She would give all she owned to sleep like that.

She hated her doubts regarding Cade's absence, although she knew the idea of leaving had to be more appealing to him by the day. If she thought about it, she knew he did too. Her gaze fell on him. So sick, so vulnerable—not the big, tough bounty hunter anymore, just a sick, needy man. For the first time in his life he needed her, and as much as the thought irritated her, she welcomed the advantage.

Stepping outside the jail, she found Pop hobbling back and forth, his crutches thumping soundly on the packed ground. Sawyer filled him in on the number of visitors he'd kept from coming into the jail. "Must'a been fifty or more."

Pop frowned. "Sawyer, there ain't fifty people in the whole county. You cain't count."

Sawyer spat and walked away mumbling, "Wasn't fer me, ever' dern woman, child, and dadburned man around would take sick." He hollered over his shoulder. "I got that credible stuff now! People oughta listen t'me!"

"You got what?" Pop called back.

Zoe grinned. "I think he means 'credibility,' Pop. Cade made him a badge."

The sheriff sighed. "That could be a dangerous thing. Sawyer ain't playing with a full deck. He got hit in the head one too many times when he used to box."

"Actually, Sawyer has been a big help, even if he is a little overbearing." Zoe sat down on the new bench the mayor had provided and motioned for Pop to join her. She took a deep breath of the fresh air. "Too bad he didn't have his boxing gloves on when Laticia Wiseman came to town. He had quite a run-in with her."

"Well, who hasn't?" Pop said, lowering himself to the bench and carefully stretching his splinted leg out before him. "That woman might mean well, but she can rankle the best of us."

Leaning her head back, Zoe closed her eyes. "She's going to take the children home with her."

"When?"

"She said this morning, if Abraham's up to it."

Pop leaned forward. "Abraham's sick?"

"No, Cade is. I think Abraham is trying to allow me enough time to settle on a course of action."

"What's Cade have to say about Laticia wanting the kids?"

"He doesn't intend to let her have them, but I can't stop her from taking them."

Pop rubbed his chin. "Laticia's like a dog with a bone."

"I don't know what I'd have done without Abraham this morning. He helped me find Cade."

Pop rose up from the bench and propped the crutches under his arm. "Think I'll go have a visit with Abraham—see if he needs anything."

"He'd like that. He could probably use a break from the children. They're over there pestering him again."

Pop chuckled. "Those kids are too well mannered to pester anybody."

Massaging the back of her neck, she smiled. "Tell them to go to Glori-Lee's for dinner. She said she'd feed them."

Pop waved his crutch and then hobbled away.

Chapter Thirty-Five

Later that day the jail door banged open, startling Zoe. The bowl of broth she was feeding Ida nearly slipped out of her hand, and she grabbed a cloth to wipe up the spills.

"Doc! For heaven's sake, you scared the wits out of me." She rose as he glowered at her, his face puffy, red blotches covering his skin in various patches. "I'm so relieved you're back!"

"Look at me. Look at this rash." He jabbed at his face with his finger. "I got the measles."

"Measles?" Her jaw dropped as the implication slowly sank in. "Measles."

"Measles," he confirmed. "Come down with 'em four days ago. Just felt like riding home."

Relief flooded her, and she dropped to the nearest chair, weak in the knees. Tilting her head back, she began to laugh. "Measles. They've all got the measles, not the fever." That meant that, most likely, Cade had the measles. She was shocked silly by the news.

"I don't find it particularly funny," Doc complained, eyeing her sternly. "Well, maybe it is a little, although measles seems to hit adults real hard."

Bonnie lifted her head off the pillow. "My Jimmy had them a few weeks ago. He wasn't very sick, so I never thought much about it."

Doc collapsed into a nearby seat. "With John and Addy dying of the fever, I thought that's what it was."

Bruce sat up on his pallet, blinking sleepily. "But Ida was out of her head with fever."

Doc nodded. "Like I said, it hits adults hard. Some worse than others." He glanced around the room. "Is that Kolby over there?"

Zoe nodded, grinning. "He came down with the fev—measles this morning. I was about to send for more quinine."

"No need now," Doc said. "It'll run its course."

"But why didn't I get them, or Seth?"

"You both probably had them when you were kids. Makes you immune." Doc looked at Bruce, Ida, Saul, Belle, and Bonnie. "Soon as you all feel strong enough, you might as well go on home to recuperate. I'm sure you'll be more comfortable in your own beds."

"Well, praise the Lord," Bonnie said. She slowly got up to gather her belongings. The others did the same, complaining but visibly relieved.

When Cade tried to roll to his feet, Zoe stopped him. "All but you," she corrected. "You're staying right here until your temperature drops."

Pop walked into the livery and found Abraham keeping the children busy shining the leather on Laticia's buggy.

"You keep this thing looking like new," Pop told him.

"Thank ya, Sheriff Winslow. Miss Laticia's mighty paticlar 'bout her buggy."

"Care if I sit a spell?"

Abraham hurried to pull up a crate. "Here ya are. You jist make yoresef ta home."

Holly helped Pop down as Brody took his crutches, held up one leg, and tried to walk with them. He fell face-first into the hay.

"Not so much fun, is it, son?" Pop asked, chuckling.

Brody sprang to his feet. "How do you do this?"

"Just hope you never have to learn," Pop replied with a grunt.

Taking the crutches from Brody, Holly handed them to Pop. "Better put these up before Brody breaks them. He's bad that way."

Missy hopped on one foot. "Can I twy?"

Pop pulled her onto his lap. "Those sticks are too long for a little'un like you." He retrieved a piece of horehound from his pocket and pretended to pull it out of her ear. "Well, look what I found. This must belong to you."

Will pulled on his ear. "Do I got one too?"

Pop motioned for him to join them. "I'll bet you have." A stick magically appeared from Will's ear, and then Pop flipped Holly and Brody each a piece. "You'd better not eat it until after Glori-Lee feeds you dinner, or we'll all have to answer to Zoe. Go on, now. Glori-Lee's expectin' ya."

The children pocketed the candy and skipped up the road to the café.

Pop turned to Abraham, his demeanor sobering. "Zoe's done good by them."

"Yes'sa. Miz Bradshaw's a fine woman...fine woman."

"She wants to keep them, you know."

"Yes'sa, I knows that." Abraham spit on his rag and rubbed hard on a spot of dirt on the buggy seat.

"I hear Laticia is set on taking them home with her."

"Yes'sa, I knows that too." He slapped the rag against the wheel spokes.

"What do you think about it?"

"Don't reckon I have a say in it, Sheriff."

Pop grinned. "Oh, I reckon you have a lot of say in things, Abraham."

Abraham grinned back, his teeth flashing white in his mahogany face. "Way I sees it, them young'uns need a ma and a pa. Miz Laticia, she's too old ta be lookin' fer a man, but Miz Bradshaw—" He rolled his dark eyes. "She ain't too old a'tall."

"What're you tryin' to say? If Zoe were to marry, Laticia might consider letting her adopt the children?"

"Seems sensible, if'n it was the right man."

Pop's fingers smoothed his mustache thoughtfully. "Hmm—you know, Abraham, you could be right. Perry Drake has an eye for Zoe. Now, he'd make a fine—"

"I sez, if'n it was the right man. Miz Laticia be mighty paticlar 'bout who be a papa to her nephew's chil'un."

"She couldn't find fault with Perry. Why, he's the town banker. They wouldn't want for anything."

"Shore 'nuff, Sheriff, but Mr. Drake be jist one more fish in the pond. He not blood kin."

"Then who? Cade?"

Abraham slowed the rag and wiped in small circles. "Well, now, he ain't jist one more fish, is he."

Pop shook his head. "Laticia would as soon whup him as look at him. She makes no bones about being out of sorts with him. And I don't know that Zoe would have him. She's pretty intent on him cleaning up his ways."

Abraham chuckled. "Yes'sa, jist like married folk."

"She wants the kids…he don't want her to raise 'em alone…" Pop stopped and thought a moment. "'Course, if they were to marry each other, that would solve the matter. But that'd shore take some doin'." He slapped his knee. "Abraham! By doggies, that's it."

Abraham shook the dust from his rag. "I knowed a smart man like you'd think o' somethin'."

Pop grabbed hold of Abraham's arm and pulled himself up. "Hand me my crutches, my good man. I've got to call a town meetin'."

Abraham glanced up. "Right now?"

"Right now," Pop said. "The sooner, the better."

Abraham grinned. "Now, if'n the buggy wheel was to break, it would take me a little while to fix. And it's a might likely to break 'causin' it's old." He paused, scratching his head. "Might take…oh, much as four, five hours to get the job done."

"Broken buggy wheel?" Pop mused. "That'd be a shame. Delayin' Laticia's trip home and all."

"Shore 'nuff, Sheriff. Shore 'nuff."

"Well, now, Abraham, you best go tell Miss Laticia yore shore sorry, but her buggy wheel done broke."

"Yes'sa, I'll do that, Sheriff. Don't 'spect she'll take kindly to it, but it cain't be helped. These things jist happen." He handed Pop his crutches.

Pop winked. "Ain't it the truth?"

Chapter Thirty-Six

Quiet down, now! Let's have some order here!" Pop banged the gavel on the table, shooting Lilith Wilks a warning look. "Lilith, can't you and Margaret exchange those blasted pork chop recipes later?"

"Don't tell me to pipe down! I want to fix pork for supper tomorrow night," Lilith complained.

"Henry ain't gonna die if he don't have pork chops for supper tomorrow night. Everyone, sit down!"

Chair legs scraped noisily against the wooden floor as the citizens of Winterborn took their seats. The town hall was jam packed. Everyone dropped what they were doing to attend.

"This better not be a waste of my time," Frank Lovell complained.

Sam Pritchard took hold of Frank's arm. "Sit down, Frank. You ain't got no place to go. At least you ain't got gout."

"Now then." Pop laid the gavel aside once the room simmered down. "I've got news."

Glori-Lee stood up. "What kind of news?"

"We ain't got the fever. We got the measles."

A stunned silence fell over the crowd as the information sank in.

"Are you certain?" Walt Mews asked.

Pop nodded. "Doc's got 'em, so does Ida, Bruce, Bonnie, Clyde Abbott and his boy, Saul, and Belle. And now Cade."

"Well, I'll be darned." Walt Mews burst out laughing. Others joined in with relief.

"Seems Seth's younger boy had them a few weeks back," Pop said. "He must've started the epidemic."

Lilith stood up. "Seth and Bonnie have always brought the young'uns to the Saturday night dance. Now that I think about it, Jimmy wasn't feeling well a few weeks back. I remember he asked me for four or five cups of punch that night. His eyes were bright as marbles. He must've been runnin' a fever then."

"Well, he's shore enough passed it around," Pop said.

"Would the measles make a body that sick?" Margaret asked.

"Doc said they affect adults harder than children. Fever, runny nose, dry cough, headache, and eye irritation bad enough to fell a grown man." Pop scratched his head. "The patients have gone home, but I'd suggest anyone in here that hasn't had the measles yet to stay clear of the ill for the time being."

"Are we gonna start up the Saturday dances again, now that we know it isn't the fever?" Harry Miller asked.

Pop gave him the evil eye. "We got far more important things to discuss right now, Harry."

"What's that?"

"Laticia Wiseman."

Silence fell over the room. Sawyer stood up. "The woman's a pain in the...neck! All she knows to do is beat folks with her cane and stir up trouble. I'd be more than happy to run the harpy out of town." Sawyer rubbed his shoulder. "I owe her one."

"That won't be necessary," Pop said. "I got a plan." He walked to the back of the room and closed the doors for privacy. When he returned to the podium, he motioned for Abraham. "Come on up here."

Abraham stepped back. "No'sa, Sheriff. I got nothin' ta say."

"You've got plenty to say. Now get on up here. We're wasting time."

Abraham approached the front of the room. All eyes focused on the black man with the snow-white hair. He stood next to the sheriff, nervously twisting his battered straw hat in his hands.

"Tell the people what we discussed in the livery earlier this evening."

"I don't think—"

"Abraham thinks Laticia might back off about takin' the children if Zoe Bradshaw was to marry."

"Marry who?" Woodall Thompson asked, glancing at his watch fob.

Abraham hung his head, whispering under his breath. "Miz Laticia will strip my hide if she hears I'm over here talkin' 'bout her."

"She ain't gonna hear a word about it," Pop promised. "And you ain't talkin' against her. You're doin' her and the town a service."

Abraham nodded. "Yes'sa, I's only thinkin' 'bout Miz Laticia's welfare. She's a good woman."

Shelby Moore stood up near the back. "What's the purpose of this meeting, Pop? Git on with it. I've got to git on home and milk before dark."

"Calm down, Shelby. Here's the problem. We all know what's been going on the last few weeks. Addy and John died and Cade came back."

The back door opened, and Seth Brighton entered the room.

"Sit down, Seth. I was just gettin' ready to mention you," Pop said.

Frowning, Seth took a seat next to Shelby.

"Like I was saying, Cade and Zoe are at each other's throats over who'll take the kids."

Glori-Lee joined in. "Thought Addy left that up to Cade."

"She did," Pop conceded. "But Zoe wants them."

Seth spoke up. "Me and Bonnie are takin' the kids."

"Why would Zoe want them? She's a woman alone," Hank Farnsworth pointed out.

Gracie was on her feet in a flash. "Because she loves those children as if they were her own flesh and blood! Who better to see after them? I don't know why Addy didn't leave them to her in the first place."

"Why should she? Cade is their uncle," Walt called.

"Cade doesn't know the kids," Willa Baker argued. "He never bothered to come back to visit all those years. Why should he be the one to decide their welfare?"

Lawrence Willis waded into the fray. "Because he's the children's blood kin!"

Pop lifted both hands for order. "People, people. This is the problem! We can go on all night about who should or shouldn't have them. No one in this room would dispute that the guardianship of those kids belongs to either Zoe or Cade, but there's a new cog in the wheel."

"What's that?"

"Laticia Wiseman. She wants them."

The women gasped. Beulah Tetherton began to fan herself.

"Isn't that her right?" Perry Drake interceded. "Miss Wiseman is the children's only other living relative. Why shouldn't she assume custody?"

"Laticia is too old to raise four young children!" Gracie declared. "And those kids are scared to death of that woman. I've seen the way they hide from her and shake like a wet dog when she comes near them."

Pop nodded. "Tell her that. She wants to take the kids home with her. If Cade don't take custody, she will."

Roy Baker grunted. "How can Cade take custody of 'em? He's on the road. He can't be a father to four children."

"Wouldn't it be better if family raised them?" Perry insisted. "Laticia can hire proper help. She has the funds."

Seth stood up. "Bonnie and me are takin' the kids. Bonnie's practically over the measles now, and in another week or so I'll have that extra room finished. I don't see what all the fuss is about."

Pop banged the gavel when the room erupted in a noisy debate. "People!" He glanced at Seth. "No one would argue that you and Bonnie would make a good home for Addy's children, Seth, but who among us don't think that Cade and Zoe are the likeliest ones to raise them? Lord knows the kids love those two as much as they did their ma and pa."

Silence cloaked the room. The crowd stared back at Pop. Beulah Tetherton fanned harder. Pop nodded at Abraham. "Abraham?"

Clearing his throat, the old man said softly, "I knows it's none'a my business, but I's agreein' with Pop 'bout there bein' a sensible solution. Now, Miz Laticia ain't gonna back off this matter easily, believe me. She won't stand for Mista Kolby to give away her flesh and blood. No'sa, she won't stand fer that a'tall, but now, the sheriff done come up with a good idea. If'n there was some way we could get Mista Kolby and Miz Bradshaw married, well, then, there'd be no question who'd get them."

The townsfolk stared in awkward silence.

"Course," Abraham said, chuckling, "gettin' those two together ain't gonna be easy."

"This is ludicrous." Perry got to his feet. "Zoe shouldn't be forced into marriage."

Pop waved him down. "Sit, Perry. We all know you're sweet on her, but this town's a family, and circumstances dictate that we lay aside our personal interests and consider what's best for the children."

"Then I'll pursue my intentions. I'll marry Zoe."

Pop groaned and beat his fist on the table. "Are you blood kin to Addy's children?"

Perry frowned. "You know I'm not."

"Then I can't see how that will solve the problem."

Walt Mews cleared his throat. "Getting Cade to marry Zoe seems pretty far fetched. How are we supposed to accomplish such a feat? Those two mix like oil and water. What if they catch on to what we're doing?"

"It's up to us to make sure they don't catch on, leastways until we get 'em married."

"They're sensible adults. How do you think you can pull off something of this enormity?" Perry snapped.

"Yeah, how are you even gonna git them to carry on a civil conversation?" Sawyer grunted.

Lilith rose to her feet. "I would love to see Zoe married. Since Jim died she's had it real hard, trying to run the store and make ends meet. And Cade isn't so bad. He was raised proper. Senda and Mac Kolby were the finest people on earth. But if Cade married Zoe, wouldn't that be inviting all sorts of riffraff into town?"

"It would!" Ken Michael's spoke up. "I don't want to worry about having one of my children killed by a stray bullet from some wanted man's gun."

Voices of dissent swelled through the crowd.

"I don't have anything against Cade. I think he's a fine boy," Roy Baker said. "But Lilith's right. We don't want trouble here in Winterborn."

Complaints rose louder.

"Listen now! Quieten down!" Protests momentarily diminished as Pop took command. "What you're saying are all reasonable concerns. And there are problems you haven't even thought of yet. What about Cade? If we were to trick him into marrying Zoe, what about his safety?"

Expressions in the crowd sobered.

"What about his safety?" Pop repeated. "Cade has enemies, dangerous enemies. We all know he's a good boy. Maybe his occupation isn't to our liking, but Roy? Have you forgotten the time you were about to lose your business, and Cade sent money through Mac to pay it off?"

Roy hung his head.

"And Walt? Have you forgotten the time that storm blew out the front window of the barbershop, and you didn't have the money to replace it? Who was it that sent that twenty-five-dollar wire a month later?"

"Cade," Walt acknowledged. "Addy always kept him informed of the town's doin's."

Pop's gaze moved around the room. "Don't none of us like the way Cade makes his money, but we don't seem to have any objection to how he spends it. Lilith!"

The woman glanced up.

"What about the time your mother broke her hip, and Cade sent the money to pay her doctor bill?"

Ralph Otis chimed in. "Or the time my heifer died during the winter, and my kids didn't have fresh milk. When Cade got wind of it, he had Mac buy another cow and bring it over that same month."

Pop lowered his voice. "That's what I'm saying. Cade is one of our own, and he needs our help. He just don't know it. We all know he loved Addy. He's got to be torn by the decision to stay or go, who to give the kids to, or to keep them himself. I say we're his family. We need to help him out."

"But how?" Lucy Ellen Black asked.

"Well, that's where my plan comes in." He briefly explained what he had in mind, and all but Perry nodded.

"If we go through with this insane plan, we'll have to protect Cade's back," Walt warned.

A few of the men in the crowd seconded the suggestion.

"I'm a pretty good shot, if I do say so myself," Lilith said.

"I can outshoot any man in this room!" Lucy Ellen declared.

"It'll take every last one of us." Pop's face sobered. "And there's no assurance we can pull this off, but if we're going to keep Laticia from taking the children, we'll have to act now. Seth, for the good of Cade and Zoe, you and Bonnie will have to go along with the plan. I know you want the children, but I think you'll agree that Zoe will make them a good ma."

Seth nodded. "Bonnie will be disappointed, but what you say is true. Zoe does a fine job with those kids. Bonnie and I only want what's best for them."

"It's not that Miz Laticia wouldn't treat the chil'un good," Abraham said. "She'd see to 'em real fine, but kiddies need young folk to raise 'em. 'Fraid neither me or Miz Laticia got the energy anymore."

"Then it's settled," Pop declared. "I'll put the plan into action. As soon as the fever breaks, Cade will pop out with the measles. It's not likely he'll make a cheerful groom, but I doubt Zoe will notice." Pop chuckled. "Hate to do it to those two, but who knows, they might take to marriage. There was a time they were sweet on each other."

"The plan is insane," Perry said. "Cade hasn't the fortitude to stick around or be a husband and father. There has to be another way."

"There ain't no other way. Face it, Perry. Those two have been stuck on each other since they were young'uns. We'll be doing them and the town a big favor." Pop banged the gavel. "Meeting over."

Chapter Thirty-Seven

I don't want soup! I want a meal," Cade demanded.

"It's not soup, it's broth!" Zoe took a deep breath, and then she tipped the sheet out from under him. He landed with a bounce on the bare mattress, glaring at her.

"Broth is not soup!" she repeated. "And stop complaining. Since everyone's gone home, you have the bunk now, not some uncomfortable floor pallet."

"Broth is broth. It's runny, flavored water, even worse than soup. At least soup has something in it, like meat and potatoes. A man can't live on runny water or in this miserable jail."

"Runny water is all you have. Eat it or go hungry."

Wearily, Cade sat up on the bunk. He picked up the bowl of broth and stared at it. "I'll eat it and go hungry." He took a sip, frowning. "How do I know this is measles?"

"It only makes sense. You've been around the sick, and you were out at the Brightons' place. Did you have the measles when you were little?"

He shook his head. "I'd remember something this annoying—and I sure don't remember Ma starving me to death."

Zoe plumped a pillow. "You are the worst patient on earth. All you've done is complain."

He shoved the bowl of broth aside and lay back. "I want out of here."

"'Here' meaning the jail? Or 'here' meaning Winterborn?" She knew the answer without asking. He wanted out of Winterborn, away from the measles, from Laticia Wiseman, and from her. He sat up again, reaching for the broth. Tasting another spoonful, he made a face.

"It needs salt."

"It's already too salty."

"You're trying to starve me."

"Starving would be too slow, too humane." She paused. Tapping her fingers on her temple as if devising a sinister plan for his death, she leaned closer to his ear and whispered, "Perhaps I've poisoned the broth—yes—or, even better, perhaps I'll pick some poisonous mushrooms and have Glori-Lee slip them into your food tonight. Poisonous mushrooms. A rather nasty death, but then you're not going anywhere for a few days. You've got time to die slowly, agonizingly slowly. Yes, I must find a mushroom that will cause drooling, foaming at the mouth, maybe nausea, difficulty in swallowing, and bloating. Severe bloating is always a nice touch. Then there's the hope of delirium, hallucinations, eyes bulging, fatigue, fainting—"

Cade grinned as he set the broth aside and lay back. "Tell Glori-Lee that I want a steak. A big, juicy one with potatoes swimming in gravy."

"Don't we all?" Zoe picked up the dirty linen and left the cell.

"Get me another pillow!" he called.

"Get it yourself."

"Come on, Red. My head hurts."

"There's an extra pillow right beside you."

"My water's tepid. I need cool water. My mouth's dry."

"You should have drunk the broth. It's wet."

"For a nurse, you sure are—"

Zoe glanced up as someone entered the jail. Ignoring Cade, she said, "Hi, Pop. How's the leg this morning?"

"Stiff as a poker." Pop limped to the desk and lowered his bulk into the chair. Propping his crutches against the wall, he sat for a moment, catching his breath. "I've missed this place."

"No reason you can't resume your normal duties." She folded a blanket and laid it over a chair. "You've had the measles, haven't you?"

"Had 'em when I was a young'un." He glanced at Cade. "Why you got your face covered with a pillow?"

His reply was muffled. "I feel like that rotten broth."

Pop chuckled. "Sounds like he's gettin' better."

"He must be. He's cranky as an old bear. The pillow over his face is his not-too-subtle way of blocking me out."

Zoe tidied up, stacking blankets in a pile. "Gracie said you called a meeting at the town hall last night. What about?"

"Gracie didn't tell you?"

"Only that you announced the sickness was measles instead of the fever."

"That's what I told them. I thought it'd be easier to get the town together than send someone from house to house."

"I'm sure everyone was relieved at the news." She carried a stack of sheets past the cell and stored them on the shelf.

"They seemed to be."

"Anything else going on?"

"Folks are up in arms about Laticia. Don't want her comin' round to cause trouble. You know how she can be."

Zoe knew exactly how Laticia was. She'd been at the jail twice in the past twenty-four hours, harassing Cade. But Gracie's hospitality and unequaled pot roast had kept Laticia comfortable in her quarters and likely to stay past her welcome.

"Well," said Zoe, "in a few days Cade will be well enough to settle his business with Bonnie and Seth." It wasn't a pleasant thought, but she had to face reality. Without the children, she might sell the store, maybe wait tables for Glori-Lee. She had tried to hold on to Jim's heritage, but she was too tired to fight anymore.

The front door opened, and Seth walked in. Pop smiled. "Morning, Seth. How's Bonnie?"

Seth took off his hat. "She's feelin' much better."

"Stay for a cup of coffee?"

"No, can't socialize. Came to talk to Cade."

Pop nodded toward the bunk. "You'll need to take the pillow off his face so he can hear you."

Seth stepped into the cell. Bending over, he lifted the pillow. "Kolby?"

Cade blinked.

"Got some bad news."

Zoe winced when she heard the gravity in Seth's voice. Was there anything but bad news in Winterborn?

"What?" Cade asked.

"Me and Bonnie can't take the kids. We had a long talk last night, and we decided we want to have a couple more young'uns of our own to fill that extra room I'm building."

Cade swung his feet to the side of the bunk and sat up. "What?"

"I know it's disappointing, but me and the missus don't think we ought to take on Addy's kids."

"But the kids would make you a good family," Cade argued.

"Four more would likely be a strain, Kolby."

Cade got up from the bunk and started to pace. The worry in his eyes broke Zoe's heart. "I was counting on you, Seth."

Zoe swallowed a leap of anticipation when she realized Cade was slowly running out of options. Surely Seth's decision would make him realize he had to give the kids to her. He had no other choice.

Seth reached out to shake hands. "I hope you don't hold it agin me, but I thought you'd want to know now rather than later."

Cade shook hands, nodding. "Sorry it didn't work out."

Seth put his hat on. "Hope you're feelin' better soon. When the rash comes, a little bakin' sody on those spots will help the itchin'."

Seth left the jail, closing the door behind him. Zoe could have heard a pin drop as Cade sank back to the bunk and put his head in his hands.

Pop sat at the desk, running his forefinger and thumb through his mustache. Outside, Seth whistled to his team, and a moment later his buckboard rattled off.

"Well, now." Pop lowered his splintered leg to the floor. "Who wants a cup of coffee?"

"Zoe," Cade called, "get me a steak from Glori-Lee's."

"Glori-Lee is right in the middle of cooking dinner. You'll have to wait."

"I'm not waiting. I'm hungry. I need to get out of here and take care of business. What was the name of that Amish family you mentioned, Pop? The couple over near Salina? I'll ride out there after dinner." He stood up and then swayed before he could take a step.

"You're not riding anywhere," Zoe scolded. "You'd scare a body to death, white as a sheet, shaky legged and wild eyed, talkin' crazy with fever. Get back on that bunk!"

"I've got four kids who need a home. They're not going to get one with me lying around here." Cade reached a trembling arm out for his hat, holding on to the bunk rail for support. "If you won't go after that steak, I will."

Zoe blocked his exit from the cell. "Over my dead body."

Cade towered above her, his features hard. "I'd prefer to do this peaceful, but I am bigger than you."

She lifted her chin. "You're not leaving this cell."

"Step aside, Red."

"No." She crossed her arms and planted her weight. "This could be easily settled if you would only listen to common sense. Bonnie and Seth can't take the children. Everyone else has children, or doesn't want more. That only leaves me—me, who is ready and willing to take them, so you can get on with whatever it is you're in such an all-fired hurry to get on with!"

"Get out of my way, Zoe."

"I have your gun." Her chin motioned to the cabinet. "You're not going anywhere." His dark look didn't shake her.

"You think I'd let you disarm me?"

"I did, didn't I?"

Leaning down, he took a small pistol from one of his boots. The weapon dangled from his forefinger by the trigger guard. "Oops."

His insolence did not deter her, nor did his cocky attitude. "When you're sleeping, I'll get that too."

"I said, step out of my way."

She swallowed, holding him at arm's length when he tried to push past her. "Pop! Help!"

Pop got up from the desk and hobbled to the cell. He paused, his eyes focusing on a corner near the bunk. "Is that Bonnie's ear-bob?"

Zoe's gaze swung to the cell floor. "Where?"

"Right there, beneath the bunk. That sparkly gizbob. She'll be wantin' that, won't she?"

Pushing past Cade, Zoe walked into the cell, dropped to her knees, and peered under the bunk. "Where? I don't see anything."

"Show her, Cade." Pop pointed with one crutch. "It's right there."

Cade knelt beside Zoe. "I don't see anything."

Her head shot up and banged against his when she heard the door of the cell clang shut.

Kolby got to his feet. "What do you think you're doing?"

Pop turned the key in the lock, a big grin on his face. "I'm doing you a favor, son. You two ain't comin' out 'til you decide who's gonna take those kids. You or her. You got the whole dadburned town in a uproar tryin' to figure this thing out! And now Laticia's breathing down our necks. Some of us need relief!"

"Pop! Have you lost your mind?" Zoe ran to the cell door, clasping the bars. "Open this door immediately! The children need—"

"I'll look after the children," Pop said. "You just get your business in order."

"I have ironing sprinkled down, and it'll mildew!"

"That's a mighty good incentive to get this over with as quick as possible, don't you think?"

"Pop, open this door," Cade demanded. "I haven't got time to play games."

Pop hung the key over a hook in the far corner of the room. "Sorry.

I can't hear nothin' but Ben Pointer's hammer hittin' against the anvil."

"Pop!" Zoe and Cade chorused loudly.

The sheriff limped back to the cell. "You two can stay in there 'til you're old and gray, or you can sit down and talk this thing out like sensible adults. It's your choice, but you ain't leavin' 'til you've worked it out. When you come out of that cell, the arguments will be over, and those kids better have a home."

Zoe stared at him.

Pop glared back. "Your pa would whup you for actin' this way."

"This isn't fair. Cade has his mind made up. For his own selfish, impractical, improbable reasons, he won't let me have the children."

Cade's jaw firmed. "She's not getting them."

"See? He'll never consent to give them to me."

"Never," Cade agreed. "So stop wasting our time, Pop."

"That's too bad. You're talkin' like you're going to be in there a long spell. But I have faith in you. If you think about this long and hard enough, the answer will come to you." He leaned closer to the bars. "I'll give you a hint. The answer's right in front of your noses. Has been all along."

Cade rattled the bars. "Why don't you just tell us what you have in mind and spare us the trouble?"

"Nope. That's your job."

Turning, he thumped out the front door and closed it behind him.

"Sawyer!"

Sawyer sprang to his feet. "Yeah, Pop?"

"Still got that credible stuff?"

"Yep."

"Don't let anyone come in 'cept Glori-Lee with the food."

Sawyer grinned, patting his badge. "Yes, sir."

Nodding, Pop hobbled across the street.

Chapter Thirty-Eight

Zoe glanced at the wall clock. Two hours they'd sat in silence. How long could they keep it up?

She glared at Cade. There he lay, hat over his face, ignoring her.

"Cade."

"What?"

"This is insane. If we're ever going to get out of here, we have to talk."

Rolling off the bunk, he stepped to the window to peer through the bars. "We can talk until the rapture, and you won't change my mind. I'm not giving the kids to you."

Measles or no measles, he needed a good throttling, Zoe decided. "Fine, but soon it's going to be out of both our hands."

Cade turned to look at her, his eyes bright with fever. "Pop can lock us up, but the decision is still mine to make."

"Laticia says she's taking the kids home with her. If we're both locked behind bars, she'll do what she wants."

He returned to sit beside her on the floor.

Zoe reached over to feel his forehead. "You'd better lie down. You look sick."

"Isn't that how most starved men look?"

"Stop complaining."

"My head hurts, and it's from not eating."

"You'll be fine in a day or two, as soon as the spots appear."

"That's all I need. Spots."

"Spots are the least of our worries." She sighed, resting her head against the wall. "If I were to get on my knees and beg you, would that convince you to let me have the kids? Wouldn't that make more sense than handing them over to Laticia?"

"Am I mumbling words? No, I said, no." Cade got up and moved to the bunk. Wadding the pillow under his head, he sighed heavily and stretched out.

"Am I so incompetent that you don't trust me with their welfare?"

"I know you'd be a good mother."

Rising, she picked up the other pillow and gently whacked him on the chest. "You stubborn mule!"

He grabbed the pillow out of her hands and pitched it to the floor. "You won't give up, will you?"

"No." She crossed her arms.

Sitting up, he took a long breath and released it slowly. "All right. I didn't want you to know this, but there's someone dead set on killing me before I get him. His name is Hart McGill."

Her hand flew to her throat, and she suddenly felt sick to her stomach. Kill him? That wasn't surprising, not in view of his vocation, but he made it sound as if McGill had made it a personal vendetta. "What does that have to do with me having the kids?"

"McGill's out for revenge. He already killed my best friend. He'll kill anything or anyone connected to me."

"He'd kill children?" She couldn't imagine what kind of animal would kill innocent children.

"He'd pistol-whip a hummingbird if it suited him. When we meet up, only one of us will walk away."

She sat on the bunk beside him, trying to understand. Her hand crept over to cover his and the silence continued. Finally, she said. "Why would he hate you so?"

"I killed his brother."

"Cade. For money?"

"In self-defense. I was taking the man in when he turned on me. It was either me or him, Red. I chose me."

"Does McGill know where you are?"

"I don't know. I spread word around that I was on my way to St. Louis, but he's no fool. I have to get the kids settled and move on before he realizes he's been tricked."

"That's why you're so eager to leave? Because you think you're endangering the children's lives?"

"If I stay, McGill will come to Winterborn." With a finger under her chin, Cade made her look at him. "I won't put the children, or you, in his path."

"I'll move."

"No. I have to place them with someone who has no connection to me. You and I go way back. It would be careless to leave them with you, and I'm not just thinking about the kids. I'm thinking of your safety too. I always have been."

Finding her voice, she said, "You're right, of course." Her words were barely a whisper. "The children must come first." She slid off the bunk and paced the small cell. "But Laticia. Letting her have them isn't the answer. McGill could easily come after her too."

"Not a chance. One look at her, and he'd run like the yellow belly he is."

She smiled, aware that he was trying to lighten the mood. "The kids would be miserable with Laticia. Cade, please. I'll do anything to keep them with me. I'll move, change our names. Anything."

"Red." He reached out to her, and she went to him willingly. Resting against his chest, with his arms wrapped tightly around her, she felt protected from the McGills of the world. "I can't let you move and change your name. This is your home."

She jerked back. He knew nothing about her. Nothing. She'd kept the truth bundled up for so long, she was about to burst. "If those kids are taken away from me, I'll have nothing." The only weapon she had left was the truth, as painful as it was. She didn't want his sympathy, but she wanted Brody, Will, Missy, and Holly badly enough to risk it all. "I'll never have children of my own."

"Of course you will—"

"I can't, Cade. I'm barren."

"Barren?"

"Yes, barren." She watched as his eyes darkened. Pain crossed his features. He gently pulled her back to him. She laid her head against his breastbone, choking back tears.

"Are you certain?"

"Years ago, I—" It was hard. She had kept the awful secret hidden for so long, she couldn't find the words or the heart to bare her soul.

"You could be mistaken. Maybe your husband couldn't—"

"It wasn't Jim's fault."

"Did he talk to Doc Whitney?"

"He didn't have to."

Cade nodded. "Pride. But if he wanted—"

"Jim wanted kids as much as I did. Darn you, Cade!" She sat up, fumbling for his handkerchief. "You owe me Addy's kids!"

"How do you figure?"

She sniffed, dabbing the handkerchief at the corners of her eyes.

"Are you going to tell me why, or are we playing guessing games?"

She sniffed again. "How could you be so blind?" He couldn't know the can of worms he was opening, he couldn't, but maybe it was time he did. It wouldn't change an iota of their lives, but he should know.

"Cade." Her hand caressed his cheek. He was so hot with fever. "I... don't know how to say this. Addy wanted to tell you, but I wouldn't let her. I had such bitterness in my heart." There was no kind way to say it, no way to spare his feelings. "I was carrying your child when you left fifteen years ago."

The words sounded like a cannon shot in the quiet cell.

He stared at her. "What?"

"Shhh—just listen." Dredging up the past reopened the hurt, deep shame, and pain. Sin had a way of demanding its due, though the act, if asked, is completely forgiven. She'd had to work hard on that one. She had lived through long years of feeling as though God had punished her, when in truth he had supplied the grace of forgiveness. Years later, Jim had taught her the beauty of the marriage bed and the joy of God's creation, and the covenant between a man and a woman. She and Cade had given in to a moment of passion, but now they both knew and understood well the consequences of defiance. "At first I was ecstatic. We were going to have a baby. You and I had created a tiny human being. I couldn't wait for you to come back home so I could tell you. I thought we could marry quickly, and your parents and Papa would never know. We wouldn't hurt them with our disobedience to the Word. We'd need only ask God for forgiveness. That was my youthful logic."

He shook his head, disappointment in his eyes. "Why didn't you let me know?"

She bit her lower lip. "When you didn't come home...after a few months I was afraid I couldn't keep the baby a secret...I got scared. At the time Papa was still alive, and I certainly couldn't tell him. I had no one to tell except Addy. I cried constantly. Then the bleeding started. All that blood." She choked on a sob.

He reached for her hand, but she jerked away. "Don't—" She felt driven to confess, to relieve the awful hurt. "Addy found me the night I lost the baby. If it weren't for her, I would have died. She nursed me back to health and never told my secret."

Cade pulled her into his arms and held her tightly. "She never said a word... If I had known. I'm sorry, Zoe."

She sobbed harder. "I'm sorry too. Sorry we never got to see our baby."

"Did Ma know?"

Zoe pushed away, wiping her eyes. "Senda? Goodness, no. If she'd known, she would have come after you and dragged you back by the ear."

"Someone should have."

"I didn't want you to be dragged back. I wanted you to come of your own accord."

He pulled her back, stroking her hair. She felt peace for the first time in years. "I don't hate you, Cade. I thought I did at the time, but that's over now. I learned long ago it's easier not to care than wish for something you'll never have."

"I should have been with you."

She lifted her head to look him in the eye. "What I don't understand is that Addy knew the doctor had told me I could never have children after that, yet she left her children to you, not me, despite how much I love them."

Their gazes clung for a long moment before Cade asked, "Was our baby a boy or a girl?"

"Boy." She looked away. "I was going to name him Cade."

He smiled. "After his pa."

Reaching for a damp cloth, she sighed. "What are we going to do about Laticia?"

"I don't know." He leaned back, closing his eyes as she applied the cloth to his forehead. "She isn't going to rest until the kids are with family."

"Well…" Zoe bit her lip, trying to work up the courage to suggest a plan, a dangerous one, and not without pitfalls. "I have a solution."

"I'm listening."

"We could get married."

"To whom?"

She swatted him. "Each other, Cade."

Cade shifted his weight, and then pulled the cloth off his face. "Didn't you hear a word I said about Hart McGill?"

"Hear me out. It's crazy, but it will work. We marry, the children will be mine. You leave, disappear, and write to them on birthdays and holidays. If you must engage in this ridiculous occupation, you can deal with Hart McGill outside Winterborn. He'll never know about the kids or me. I'll demand nothing from you. I will keep my sacred vow to you, but you would be free to…do as you wish." She couldn't offer any better terms.

"McGill would know. It would never work." He got up and slowly paced the floor.

"I'll do anything to keep the kids. It's the only way it can happen. We have to make Laticia think the marriage is genuine."

"No. I'd be putting not only the kids in jeopardy, but you too. If McGill knew I had a wife and—"

"He won't. You'll be gone. Hart McGill will be tracking you again. Everything will appear normal." She felt surreal, uninhibited. There'd been a time when she would have given her life to be Cade's wife, now she was asking him to quite possibly give his.

He stopped pacing, turning to look at her. "I don't know, Zoe—"

"Call me Red."

He studied her, but the beginning of a smile gave him away.

"Please, Cade. It's the only solution. We'll get Laticia out of everyone's hair. She can't argue that the children aren't with family. You're family, and if you marry me, I'll be family."

"And what happens when I leave? I don't want to disappoint them. They've been hurt enough, and so have you."

How would the children feel when he left? Exactly as she would. Sick. Heartbroken. They would be losing yet another loved one. And the children certainly loved him. But did she? She admitted she had stronger feelings for him than she wanted, but love? So many years had passed. So many hurtful years.

She met his gaze for a long while. "As I said, I'll move. I'll go where McGill can never find us." She would miss Winterborn, but she would have the children. She would find solace in them. Why, then, did she feel the weight of the world on her shoulders when she thought of life without him? "I'll change my name and the children's. Unless…you would change and give up this horrible life you have chosen."

"You think I wouldn't like to?"

"I don't know what to think."

"If it were that simple—to walk away and never look back—I would give it all up in a minute to keep Addy's children and be a pa to them. I'd make my peace with God, and I—"

She reached to touch his hand. "You haven't made your peace with God?"

"A hundred times, Red. But then I went on with my work."

"You believe in a God who forgives."

"I know, but there has to be a turning away, a real effort not to make the same mistake again." Cade rubbed the back of his neck.

"Time is running out. Abraham can't stall Laticia forever. She'll be leaving with the children if we don't do something now."

"I can't get married. I've got the measles."

"There's no law that says a marriage isn't legal just because the groom has measles. Reverend Munson could officiate at the door so he wouldn't be exposed." Zoe warmed to the idea. There was nothing left for her to lose. She'd lost it all fifteen years ago. She walked over to him and lowered her eyes teasingly. "Is the big, bad bounty hunter scared of a little round wedding band?"

Cade snorted. "Real scared." He pulled her to him, his lips a breath away from hers.

"You can't kiss me. You've got the measles," she protested.

"Watch me."

His lips were hot with fever, which only intensified the impact of his embrace. It was not a ravaging kiss, but a tender and gentle one, igniting a yearning deep inside her. She remembered this. Her fingers eased up to cradle his face, the short stubble of unshaven skin tickling her palms. Closing her eyes, she tried to ward off his power over her.

Cade pulled back to study her. "Marriage. To you." His fingers laced through strands of her hair.

"I'll do whatever it takes to keep the children," she said, opening her eyes and looking at him.

"What kind of marriage would it be? Me gone. You and the kids off somewhere. I want what Addy wanted, a good, solid life for them."

Still shaken from his kiss, she made light of the situation. "And I promise you they will have that life. Do you accept my proposal?"

He sank to the bunk, reaching for the pillow. The long wait before he spoke was maddening. "You'll marry Perry."

"I will not. For my part, I'll be married, but you...don't have to feel that way."

"I don't think I've got the strength to make it to the church."

"You don't have to. I'll take care of everything."

"Get the reverend." He laid his head on the pillow and shut his eyes.

Zoe grinned when she saw she'd won. She grabbed a tin cup and dragged it back and forth across the bars. "Pop, bring the preacher! We got it worked out!"

Chapter Thirty-Nine

The jail door closed behind Zoe. Cade got up and left the cell. Pop came in, grinning. Scratching a red spot on his face, Cade peered at his image in the cracked mirror. "I'm going to make a sorry-looking groom."

"You and Red gettin' married? That's shocking."

"Not until I get my steak." Cade sat down and propped his boots on the desk.

Pop chuckled. "I'll tell Glori-Lee to fry you one the size of Kansas."

"Texas," Cade corrected. "Make it the size of Texas, and a potato the size of New York. I'm marrying the redhead. I'll need my strength."

"Maybe I ought to get Zoe one too," Pop said. "We got to keep this marriage on an equal footing."

When he left for the café, Cade sank lower in the chair, tipping his hat over his eyes. A pa. He'd been a pa and didn't know it. Anger rose and then subsided. He could see why she'd never written and told him about the baby. He'd have done the same in her place. Now he and Red were finally getting married. He smiled, and then he quickly sobered. She was right. Marriage was the only way to outfox Laticia. She was hardheaded but not senile. If the kids had a good home, she wouldn't fight him for custody. Red could give them a good home. He'd send money, and she'd have access to everything he had in the banks.

If only there were a way to put my past behind me.

The mental image of her laughing eyes made him smile. "A marriage of convenience." Even spoken aloud, the words disturbed him. He'd once thought that when he married Zoe, it would be for always, but too many years had passed. He didn't blame her. She'd been in his thoughts every day since he'd left, and even more since he'd returned. What he felt for her had grown stronger through the years.

Now that she'd told him about the baby, her feelings toward him began to make more sense. He'd never dreamed she'd been carrying his child. If he'd known, he would have come back. If Addy had sent word, he would have returned immediately and married Zoe. Addy and Zoe thought they knew him so well, but they didn't know him at all. Could Addy's request, that he see to the children's welfare, be her way of making him come home and finish what had started between him and Zoe all those years ago?

The news that he'd lost a child pained him deeply. He might have come home to find a nearly grown son. Would she have lost the child if he'd been here with her? So many questions, so many emotions—how did he sort them out?

The door banged open. He looked up. He could smell his steak a mile away. "It's about time."

Glori-Lee followed Pop inside and set the sizzling meat platter on the desk. "Think this is enough to get you through a wedding?"

"You might want to bring one more. They've tried their best to starve me to death."

"Pop thought I ought to bring one for Zoe." Glori-Lee chuckled as she left the room.

The old sheriff motioned toward the platter. "You don't have much time, boy. Eat up."

Cade looked down at his food. "I guess this ceremony will be a far cry from when Zoe married Jim."

Pop eyed the steak and potato. "Well, a little. How'd you feel when you got the news?"

"A week of being drunk, and a month of resentment later, I swallowed my pride and admitted she had every right to marry another man."

She'd married Jim, but he'd had to work long and hard to even think of another woman. The marriage had been a bitter pill to swallow, even though Cade had known he was being irrational. Why he'd thought she'd wait for him forever, he didn't know.

Putting on a clean shirt, Pop shook his head. "Don't know why you two took so long to see what's right in front of your noses."

Cade pretended to misunderstand. "Yeah, Glori-Lee cooks a mean steak."

"It ain't the steak, Kolby. I'm talking about this marriage bein' the smartest thing you've ever done."

He laughed. "Smart? I gain a wife and four kids and then ride away. You call that smart?"

"Don't you be runnin' down matrimony. You might take to it. Me and my missus, God rest her soul, had a good life, and if you'd give that little woman of yours half a chance, you'd have one too."

"Doris didn't have Red's temper."

"Well, explain that to my horse. I spent my fair share of nights in the barn." Pop jerked his string tie into place. "Seriously, son, I don't want you hurtin' that little gal. She's a good woman, and everybody's fond of her. Your hide won't be worth a plug nickel if you do her wrong."

Cade almost choked on a bite of beef. "I have no intention of hurting her, but you know the reason we're getting married. Zoe doesn't love me."

Picking up Cade's boots, Pop spat on them and polished the toes. "Don't know about that. I figured she had her eye on you since she was a young'un. Wouldn't be surprised if she still did. Now eat up and clean up. You're about to be a husband, Kolby."

Chapter Forty

Zoe hurried across the street with a hundred thoughts racing through her mind. She had to quickly press her good blue silk while Holly helped Will and Missy into their Sunday best. Brody had eaten so many biscuits lately that she hoped he could button his knickers.

She couldn't wait to tell the children about the arrangment. It might not be an ideal solution, but the children would be hers. Hers! Excitement bubbled in her throat. She would be married to Cade, and who knew? Maybe he would like married life so well he would—

Whoa. She paused, drawing a deep breath. This was exactly the sort of irrational thinking she had engaged in fifteen years ago. *Just press your dress and be satisfied. The children are yours.*

"Zoe! Wait a minute. I'd like a word with you."

She turned to see Perry Drake stepping out of the bank. "No time right now, Perry," she called. "I'm in a hurry."

He caught up with her and took her arm to slow her down. "What's the rush? Is there a fire?"

"No, of course not." How did she tell him that she was getting married? They had no ties, but it only seemed proper that she mention it. Still, she knew he would be upset when he heard she was marrying Cade. Drawing a deep breath, she said, "There's no easy way to tell you, Perry. I'm getting married."

His face drained of color. "You mean they talked you into that ridiculous plan?"

"What plan?"

"The town's plan—You don't know?" He shook his head as if the irony was too much.

She frowned. "I don't know what you're talking about."

"Pop came up with the idea to lock you two up together, and the whole town went along with it except me, who had better sense."

She snorted. "I can assure you, this marriage is entirely my idea. I want the children, Perry, and the only way to get them is for Cade and me to marry."

"This is insane. Come to your senses!" He took her arm again, attempting to steer her toward the bank. "Come to my office and let's talk about it. If it's a husband you want—"

Jerking free of his grasp, she stood her ground. "Laticia said that only family could raise the children. If Cade and I marry, I'll be family and there will be nothing she can do about it."

"My dear." She resented the pained sufferance in his tone. "I know you feel obligated to those children because of your close friendship with Addy, but think of the advantages they would have living with Laticia. Advantages you cannot provide them. Their great-aunt is wealthy enough to hire all the help she needs to raise them. They would have the best education available."

"Perry, I love those children and they love me. I know my money is tight, but Cade will find a way to feed and clothe them and love them beyond words."

His eyes turned grave. "I can't believe you're actually going through with this nonsense."

"It's the only solution. Please try to understand."

"If you're intent on this madness, I'll stand by you. I'm aware that this marriage is nothing but a sham. Once Cade leaves, I'll help you have the matter discreetly disposed of."

She couldn't believe his suggestion. She knew the marriage wouldn't be real, not in the physical sense, but he made it sound so sordid, almost cheap. Once, she would have thought the same thing. Vows taken between a man and woman in the sight of God were not to be taken lightly, and Cade would ride away and never come back. But that wouldn't make her devotion to him or the children any less sincere.

She glanced toward the jail. "We'll have to talk about this later. I have to get the children, and—"

As if she hadn't said a word, he went on. "Those children will be grown and gone in a few years. You'll need companionship. It's no secret how I feel about you."

The conversation grated on her nerves. Perry was a confidant and friend, but it was becoming increasingly clear that he only wanted her, not the children.

"There's something you need to understand, Perry. I will *always* have those children. Even when they grow up and marry, they will still be mine. Their children will be my grandchildren."

"Of course, my dear. I didn't mean to imply that you should forget them. I meant that we could have a nice life together once they're grown, just you and me. I've always wanted to travel. We could go back East."

Zoe shook her head and walked away from him briskly, finding the irony of the situation almost laughable. Yesterday she had no prospect of a husband. Today two men were ready to up and marry her. It was almost funny, except there was only one man she wanted. The one she couldn't keep.

"We'll talk later," Perry called as she ran up the front steps to the store entrance.

"Kids!" She hurried past the counter and down the canned goods aisle. "Get cleaned up and into your best clothes." She scanned the kitchen table. Holly, Missy, and Will sat there, long faced. "What's wrong?"

Will's bottom lip jutted out. "Brody's runnin' away and I want to leave too, but he took all the biscuits."

"Running away? What's this all about?"

Holly got up and looped her arms around Zoe's waist, leaning into her. "Brody wrapped Glori-Lee's leftover biscuits in a napkin and said he was running away to California."

Zoe gave Holly a consoling pat. "Where is your big brother?"

Missy pointed to the bedroom. "He's puttin' his clothes in a tow sack."

"Biscuits too," Will added. "He took Glori-Lee's napkin. I told him he'd get in trouble, runnin' away with Glori-Lee's napkin, but he said he didn't have time to listen to a six-year-old whiner." He teared up. "I ain't a whiner. She said he could have the biscuits, nothing about keepin' the napkin."

"Okay, Will, that's enough. I'll wash the napkin, and Brody can return it to Glori-Lee."

Will rose and clung to her opposite hip. "Brody won't let me go with him."

Zoe squeezed the two children tightly against her. "No one is going anywhere."

Missy laid her head down and began to weep. "We don't want to go with Aunt Waticia."

Holly turned dark eyes on Zoe, eyes far more mature than her eight years. "Please don't make us go with her."

"Is that what all the running away is about?" Relief flooded her when all three nodded. "Well, I have good news for you. Your Uncle Cade and I are getting married. That means no one is going anywhere. You're going to live with me."

The spontaneous squealing and leaping was so loud, Zoe had to cover her ears. "Children, please!"

Brody appeared in the bedroom doorway, a sack over his shoulder, munching on a biscuit. "You really going to be our ma?"

Zoe held out her arms, and all four children came to her. "Your ma will always be your ma, but you'll be my very own children now. We'll be a real family." She blinked back tears of joy. "I'll be the best mama I can be."

"Is Uncle Cade ouw pa now?" Missy asked, her innocent blue eyes twinkling up at Zoe.

Zoe nodded. The children looked so happy, she couldn't tell them Cade wouldn't be staying. She wouldn't spoil their day—her day. Her and Cade's wedding day.

"I'm going to call him Uncle Pa," Will announced, his tone serious.

Missy giggled. "Me too."

Zoe laughed. "Get cleaned up while I press my blue dress." She glanced at Brody. "I hope you didn't crumple your Sunday clothes into that bag, Mr. Wiseman. I don't have time to iron them. Your Uncle Pa is waiting for us at the jail."

Missy hopped up and down. "We'we going to get mawwied, we'we going to get mawwied!"

Chapter Forty-One

Sawyer stuffed a chunk of chew into his jaw and called to Susan and Judy, who were trying to peek in the jail window "Go on now. Git. Cade is gettin' married, and Zoe ain't goin' to take kindly to you hangin' 'round gawkin' at him."

The young girls grumbled but stepped off the cement block and melted back into the crowd.

"Make a path, everyone," Sawyer instructed. "The bride-to-be and her brood's comin' through. Did you hear me, Sam? I said step aside."

"Close yore dadburned yap, Sawyer. I'm movin' fast as I can. I got the gout, you know."

Zoe felt proud as a peacock as she and the kids marched into the jail. Lilith handed her a nosegay of black-eyed Susans she had picked from her garden.

Pop had donned a clean shirt for his role as best man, and Zoe had never seen Gracie, her matron of honor, look prettier.

Gracie patted her pale green dress. "I'm as nervous as a June bug in a henhouse."

Zoe flashed her a grin and then quickly wiped Will's nose and straightened Brody's shirt collar. The children were a sight to behold. Her heart beat with anticipation. They would soon belong to her. Her and Cade.

Nearly everyone in town turned out for the event. Zoe noticed for the first time that something wasn't quite right. She didn't think so much about Pop's wearing a gun and holster, but some of the women looked downright strange with a derringer tucked into the waistbands of their skirts. Zoe turned, her gaze scanning the assembled crowd. Half the onlookers were toting weapons. She frowned. Did they think Cade would back out, and they had brought the means to make him change his mind?

"Should the kids be near me?" Cade asked.

She felt his forehead. He was much cooler, and she noticed a couple of red dots on his cheek. "I think the crisis is over. You're breaking out."

Doc stepped over to examine the red marks. "Yep. Should start feeling better now."

The children stood between her and Cade, joining hands. Missy wore a permanent grin on her face and couldn't take her eyes off Uncle Pa. "Awe you glad we'we mawwying you, Uncle Pa?"

Zoe's heart swelled when she saw the love shining in Cade's eyes. He tightened his hold on the little girl's hand and winked at her.

They were family. Even if it was for a short time, they were family. She fussed with the sky blue sash on her dress, aware of the way Cade's eyes lingered on her. Pulling her to one side, he put his mouth close to her ear.

"You look pretty," he whispered, and then he lifted her locket to his lips to press a kiss against the small golden bauble.

"So do you—not pretty," she amended, cheeks warming. "Handsome." She took the locket from his fingers and kissed it too.

Cade patted Zoe's backside as he stepped around her to take his place. She discreetly grabbed his impudent hand and bent his thumb back.

Though she knew the terms of the marriage, she couldn't help her building excitement. Mrs. Cade Kolby, mother to the Wiseman children. Mother. It had a nice ring to it. Ring!

She quickly turned to Cade. "We don't have a ring."

Cade looked blank for a moment, and then he turned to Pop. "No ring."

Pop motioned for Ben Pointer and whispered in his ear. Ben nodded and then hurried out the door. He was back shortly with a token he'd fashioned out of copper. Zoe had never felt so much pride in the townspeople as she did today. Judging by the looks on their faces, they were thrilled to be here. Little did they know that it was nothing more than a marriage of convenience.

But why all the guns? She had never seen Ben Pointer carry a rifle, and his boys had those shotguns over their shoulders. At a wedding, no less!

She watched Brody pull a biscuit from his shirt pocket and hand it to Cade, smiling up at his uncle. Cade grinned, waving the child's offering aside.

Reverend Munson arrived at the jail, and the crowd surrounded him, all smiling and nodding.

"Dearly beloved, we are gathered together in this house of—" he paused, clearing his throat, "—in this place, to witness the joining of Cade Kolby and Zoe Bradshaw in holy matrimony—"

"Git on with it, Preacher," Roy Baker yelled, "before he changes his mind."

Reverend Munson cleared his throat again and then recited the vows.

Reaching for Zoe's hand, Cade gazed deeply into her eyes. She swallowed, her eyes locked with his. Her stomach twisted into knots as he spoke his vows with firm conviction. She was grateful for his compassion. No one would guess by the sincerity in his voice that he was marrying her for any other reason than love.

Her vows were given with the same depth of feeling. Moments later Reverend Munson closed his Bible and pronounced, "You are man and wife."

Everyone expressed their good wishes. All but the measles victims showered kisses on the children and bride, who dutifully returned kiss for kiss.

Cade lifted Zoe's hand and raised it to his lips. "May I kiss the bride?"

Touched by the gesture, she raised his hand to her mouth. "Only if I'm permitted to kiss the groom."

Smiling, he pulled her to him. "You want the measles?"

"You kissed me earlier. I've already been exposed."

"Kiss her, Uncle Pa," Will urged.

Missy giggled, and Holly's face flooded with color.

Brody finished off his last biscuit. "I ain't never gonna kiss a girl," he declared.

Cade grinned at Zoe. "You'll change your mind one of these days, son. Girls can be real nice to kiss."

His tone was soft and persuasive. Zoe instantly leaned into him, welcoming his embrace. Rockets went off in her head. Stars exploded. The day she'd dreamed of most of her life had arrived.

Their lips barely brushed together when a clamor came from outside the jail.

"Step aside! I'm coming through!" The swish of Laticia Wiseman's cane whipping the air caused the townspeople to quickly move back and give her the right-of-way.

Laticia's glare pinned Zoe to the wall. "What do you think you are doing?"

Missy stepped forward, wrinkled her nose, and stepped back. "We got mawwied, Aunt Waticia."

"Married!"

Cade pulled Zoe closer. "Laticia, Zoe and I were just married." He smiled. "She's family now."

"Why wasn't I told of this?"

"It was decided rather quickly..." Zoe ventured.

"Abraham!"

"Yes'm?"

Laticia jabbed the air with her walking stick. "You knew about this?"

"I jist got wind'a it," he said, coming up behind her. "'Bout ta come tell ya, but got a spell with my belly—"

"You and your belly. We're finally going home where we can get something decent to eat." She whirled and poked Cade in the stomach with the tip of her cane. "I don't know what you're up to, but if I hear that these children are living with anyone but you and Zoe, I'll have your hide hung from the tallest hickory. You hear me?"

"Yes, ma'am," Cade said. He glanced at the children and winked. "Better not get too close. Wouldn't want you coming down with the measles."

"Piddleposh. Never been sick a day in my life. Don't intend to start now." She bent to Holly, who shrank back when her aunt came face-to-face with her. "You children ever need anything, you let your Aunt Laticia know."

They nodded, eyes bulging.

"Abraham! Hitch the buggy. We've worn out our welcome."

Chapter Forty-Two

Cade spoke with Pop while Zoe and the children ran home and tidied the living quarters. The children assumed the marriage meant the same intimacies as their ma and pa's, so Zoe knew it was useless to think Cade would sleep on the cot without a powerful lot of excuses.

The thought of their first night together preyed on her mind. She felt like a schoolgirl on her first date.

"Uncle Pa is comin'," Will announced, peering out the kitchen window.

Missy pushed open the screen door and ran out to meet him. Zoe watched her leap up and wrap her legs around his waist, smothering his face with kisses.

"Now that's worth coming home for," he said. He walked in carrying the little girl. He glanced at Zoe. "Next?"

Zoe felt hotness in her cheeks. "Have you seen yourself?"

"No. Why? I shaved an hour ago."

She pushed him to the sink mirror.

Cade sat Missy down, and then he looked into the mirror and groaned. "Do I look like this all over?"

"Do you itch all over?"

"Yes."

"I believe that answers your question." She stifled a giggle. "I'll get the baking soda paste."

"I'll put it on fow you," Missy said.

Cade's eyes met Zoe's. "Thanks, honey, but I think maybe your new ma should do it."

Zoe easily conceded. "I'll bring you the paste."

He wrinkled his nose at Missy. "She sure knows how to take the fun out of measles."

Later that night, Zoe fixed cups of hot tea. Missy was sleeping on a pallet next to Holly, and Cade was stretched out on the bed reading a journal. The sight of him, so comfortable in her surroundings, left her unsettled.

"Feeling better?" she asked softly. She didn't want to wake the girls.

He took a cup from her. "Better, thanks." After taking a sip of tea, he swung his feet to the floor and patted the mattress beside him. "Sit down. I want to talk to you."

She sat down and studied her cup. "We did the right thing, Cade."

"Did we?"

She glanced up. "Don't you think so?"

"I admit I've fallen in love with those kids." He glanced over at his sleeping nieces.

Smiling, she said, "Easy to do." Their eyes searched each other's. "Not so easy to undo, huh?"

"Not so easy, but you know what I have to do. I'll stay long enough to satisfy Laticia the marriage is binding."

"Only if you feel it's advisable. You're free to go any time."

"If I could stay forever, I would. I don't want to go, Red. The kids—you."

Her gaze darted up to meet his. "Me?"

"It's not going to be easy, raising four children on your own."

She smiled. "You've made me very happy. I can't complain."

"Are the children enough for you?"

She thought for a long moment. Was it enough? No, she wanted him. She never thought she would wish this on anyone, but she also wanted Hart McGill dead. "I understand our arrangement."

The mantel clock struck midnight. Zoe knew the awkward moment had arrived. "It's late."

"Do you want me to sleep in the merchantile?"

"No, the children would wonder why we weren't sleeping in the same bed like their ma and pa."

Cade ran his fingers through his hair. "I don't know, Red. I'm not sure I can sleep in the same bed with you."

"Of course you can. I'll make it easy for you." Whether the vows were spoken in earnest or in need, they were no less married. It wouldn't be so hard to lie beside him, to know he was lying next to her, to pretend he would always be there.

"We could—"

"Don't say it." She was having the same irresponsible thoughts, but she was strong. She would not consummate a marriage that held no significance.

She rose and disappeared behind the screen to put on her night-clothes, and then she crawled beneath the covers as though today had been like any other. Cade joined her a few minutes later and lay stiffly beside her.

"Good night, Cade."

"What's good about it?"

She stuffed the corner of the blanket in her mouth to keep from giggling. Eventually she heard his even breathing and relaxed, relieved he wasn't going to make an issue of the marriage bed.

Toward morning, she felt a hand looped around her waist. "Cade!" she warned.

"Huh?" He sat up sleepily. "What's wrong?"

They turned to look at each other, but their view was blocked as a yawning Missy sat up between them and innocently asked, "Is it mowning aweady?"

Chapter Forty-Three

A brisk wind whipped the sheets on the line Saturday morning. Cade rounded the corner of the building and came to a dead stop when he saw his wife. The sight of her trim figure, up to her elbows in fresh laundry, sent blood rushing to his head. She had four or five clothespins stuck in her mouth. Wind buffeted her slight weight as she pinned up a long row of petticoats. The starched muslin snapped briskly in the stiff breeze, tossing her red hair topsy-turvy. It was as if Cade were fourteen again, spying on her at the swimming hole.

Creeping from behind, he reached around her and held the garments to the line so she could maneuver more easily. "Are we running a boarding house?" he asked.

She jumped and then smiled. "No, why?"

His gaze scanned the lengthy stretch of clothes. Overalls, long johns, women's dresses, and children's garments filled the billowing rows. "An orphanage laundry?"

"No."

"Confederate army?"

She pinned up another skirt. "No, silly. We just have a lot of wash."

He shook his head. "No one on earth is this dirty."

"There's a stack of clean blankets in the kitchen. Will you take them to the jail for me?"

"Sure. Can I have a kiss from my wife?"

"Nope. Anything else I can do to help?"

"Baking soda." He scratched an angry-looking blotch. "I'm itching like blue blazes."

She made a sympathetic face. "It must be awful."

The itching couldn't hold a candle to wanting her. Being married in name only was worse than beating himself senseless with a rock. "Where are the kids?"

"Playing at the livery."

"I thought Abraham left."

"He did. They like Ben. He gives them apples."

"I give them apples."

"You spoil them rotten, and you have to stop. They're beginning to expect all the licorice and gum balls you generously dole out from the candy jar."

"A little candy never hurt anyone."

"I mean it, Cade. Stop being so permissive with them. They're crazy about you, and it's only going to make it harder when you leave."

"All right." He handed her a petticoat that looked too big for her. "I'll make it a point to be as mean and cranky as you are—"

She threw the wet petticoat at him. The garment hit him in the face.

Leaning over, he calmly plucked up a pair of bloomers and flung them at her.

A full-blown laundry war erupted, and they fought it out until the last clean sheet lay dirty and trampled underfoot.

His stomach tightened at the sight of her hair falling loose and unfettered over her shoulders, her face flushed with exertion.

Grinning, she scooped up the laundry basket. "I opened a new box of baking soda this morning. It's on the kitchen cabinet." Walking toward the washtub, she called over her shoulder, "Will you be home for supper?"

He shouldn't be. If he was smart, he'd be riding out about now. "What are you having?"

"Rabbit and dumplings."

Rabbit and dumplings. He winked, smiling when she blushed. "Try keeping me away."

He opened the screen door and stepped into the kitchen. It was quiet without the kids' chatter. He wondered what it would be like to be ten years old and have no responsibility other than to keep out of trouble. Moving to the mirror, he made a quick paste of the baking soda and water and dabbed it on his face. A fine-looking groom he made. Measles. At his age. If McGill caught him in this predicament, he'd have a good laugh before he shot him.

Bending closer to the mirror, he frowned. The stubble of beard felt familiar, but it itched as badly as the rest of his body. Rubbing his chin, he did an assessment.

You like this idea of marriage, don't you? Get over it. Don't get comfortable with family life. It's not for you. Not now. The feel of Zoe lying soft and warm against you, drifting off to sleep with the sweet scent of her hair filling your senses. Her soft breathing, so different from the lone coyote call. You like it. You'd give your left arm to keep it this way.

Shoving his thoughts aside, he brushed his hair into place, and then settled his hat on his head.

Crossing the street a few moments later, he dropped the blankets by the jail, and then he headed for the mayor's house. Knocking on the door, he waited until Gracie answered. Her face split in a wide grin when she saw him.

"Mercy, if you don't look a sight."

"Can I come in? I'm not contagious, just ugly."

Gracie opened the door wider. "You looking for Lawrence? He's over at the town hall. He and—"

"Actually, I want to talk to you."

"Oh?" Gracie closed the door and shooed him into the parlor. "I'll make a pot of coffee."

"That's not necessary. I won't take up your time. I wanted to talk to you about a personal matter," he said as they both sat down.

Gracie patted her hair bun, her face reddening. "Well…"

"About Zoe."

"Oh?" She looked puzzled. "Personal?"

"I know you and Zoe are close. That's why I came to you. I'd rather no one else knew about this conversation."

"Certainly." Her features sobered. "It sounds serious, Cade. What's wrong?"

"I'm not sure, but I have a hunch Zoe's having money problems."

"Oh." Gracie folded her hands, seemingly uneasy with the subject.

"She's in trouble, isn't she?"

Her guarded eyes darted about the room, landing on a mussed sofa pillow. She rose to fluff it. "Did Zoe say something to you?"

"No."

Sitting down again, Gracie busied herself picking at a thread on the cuff of her sleeve. "I don't think it's my place—"

"Talk to me about it, Gracie. Is she taking in washing and ironing for extra money?"

"Well...what do you think?"

He thought about the loaded clothesline, not just this morning, but every morning since he'd arrived. "I think no one's that dirty."

Smiling, Gracie looked up. "She'd have my hide if she knew I was telling her problems, but, yes, she's been washing and ironing for other people for some time now. The store has been in financial trouble for years, since before Jim died. He left her a stack of unpaid bills, and the store books carried a lot of credit that somehow never got paid. She's had to take in extra work to make ends meet."

Cade's jaw tightened. "I knew it."

"She's a proud woman, Cade. She doesn't want others knowing her problems. I wouldn't know about them if I wasn't with her every day to see the worry lines around her eyes. She works herself near to death, and now that she has four extra mouths to feed, she's working even harder."

"What debts does she have?"

"She'd never tell me, but I do know the bank payment seems to be the hardest for her to meet. Jim borrowed heavily during the year before he was killed. Lawrence and I have encouraged her to sell the store, but the mercantile has been in the Bradshaw family for years, and she feels she can't let it go."

Cade tamped down feelings of anger. Why hadn't Zoe told him about her situation? He'd offered money for the children's keep, but she refused it. Why? Because it was his money? Blood money? Was pride overriding her common sense? She couldn't lose the store. It was all she had.

He got to his feet. "Thank you, Gracie. I appreciate your honesty."

Gracie sighed. "If Zoe were to find out—"

"She won't." He smiled. "You can trust me on that."

"I do trust you, Cade. You're the best thing that ever happened to her. I hope you stay around a while."

"Me too, Gracie." He slipped on his hat and pulled it low. "Say hello to Lawrence for me."

Perry Drake was bent over a ledger when Cade appeared in his office doorway a few minutes later. Perry frowned. "What are you doing here?"

"We need to talk."

"Sorry. I'm busy." The banker continued with his work.

Cade walked over to the desk and closed the ledger. He met Perry's piqued stare. "You just got unbusy."

"What do you want, Cade?"

"I'm here to pay off Zoe's note."

Perry paused in thought, and then he motioned toward a chair. "Sit down."

Cade removed his hat and took the seat opposite the desk.

"I understand congratulations are in order."

"Yes. Zoe and I were married yesterday."

Perry looked none too happy about the turn of events. Cade knew the man wanted Zoe for himself, but he wasn't there to argue the point.

The banker steepled his fingers. "I'm surprised the town pulled off the ruse so easily."

"What ruse?"

"Tricking Zoe into marrying you."

Cade kept his temper in check. Drake was a sore loser. He expected that. "Zoe wasn't tricked into anything."

Perry pushed back from the desk and crossed his legs. "I understand it's a temporary arrangement. Zoe feels Laticia Wiseman is too old to rear the children. That isn't my thought; it's Zoe's."

Cade lifted a brow. "Who said the marriage is temporary?"

Drake's smile was as cold as a January wind. "Come now, you're not implying a woman like Zoe would actually marry a bounty hunter?"

"I'm not implying anything. What are you trying to imply, Perry?"

"Only that I'll go along with the arrangement…for now."

Cade looked away, fighting the urge to wipe the smirk off Drake's face.

"I'm aware Zoe has a good heart," Perry continued. "She's concerned about your sister's orphans, and her strong sense of responsibility won't permit her to see them go to strangers."

"Really." Cade leaned back and met the pompous banker's eyes. "I get the impression she loves the kids."

Perry opened a walnut box on his desk and took out a cigar. He inclined his head. "Smoke?"

Cade shook his head.

"Pity." He studied the length of the imported cheroot. "I purchase them in Boston. They're very good."

Cade returned to the point of the visit. "How much does Zoe owe the bank?"

Perry held a match to the tip of the cigar, puffing. "Sorry. That's privileged information."

"Not for her husband."

Fanning the match out, Perry grinned. "You're not her husband,

Kolby. You're nothing more than a temporary fix to an impossible situation."

Cade's eyes narrowed. "How much does she owe the bank?"

"I repeat, that's privileged information."

"Not if I'm paying it off."

Perry's feet hit the floor, and he scooted back to the desk. "You can't do that."

"My money isn't good here?"

"Of course it's good. It's just—"

"The note, Drake. I'm paying it off." Cade stood up and confronted the banker. "And you are not to say a word to Zoe about who's done this. Understand?"

Perry pushed back and got up. "We'll see about that. Let's get Zoe in here, and we'll settle this matter immediately."

Cade watched the color drain from Perry's face when he blocked his way. "Not a word, Drake, or you'll not get another cent of my money."

He'd like to think he was intimidating the contemptuous runt, but he knew his limitations. He might have a Colt strapped to his thigh, and a sizable amount in his account, but a man with baking soda smeared on his face carried little authority. Still, Drake ran a bank, and if a man was offering good money, Drake couldn't afford to turn it down.

Straightening, Perry said, "If you'll wait a moment, I'll get the complete file."

Cade sat down and waited for Drake to return. Within a few minutes, he returned, laid a sheaf of papers on the desk, and scanned the long columns. "Are you aware of what you're doing? This is a goodly sum."

"Just tell me how much."

The banker handed him the page with the current balance owed, and Cade read it. "Take it out of my account."

Perry inclined his head. "If that's your decision."

Cade got up to leave. He settled his hat low. The man behind the desk refused to glance up or respond. "I mean it, Drake. I don't want Zoe to know where the money came from."

Perry lifted his gaze. "What am I to tell her? That her fairy godmother came to her rescue?"

Cade winked. "Tell her you paid it off. It'll strengthen your position in my wife's eyes."

Chapter Forty-Four

The front door of the Bradshaw General Store opened the following Sunday, and the Kolby family emerged, dressed in their Sunday best. Cade, Brody, and Will wore suits and ties. The dresses that Zoe, Holly, and Missy wore rivaled the patch of colorful late summer flowers blooming in the porch box.

It was hard for Zoe to believe the weekend had passed so quickly, even harder to believe Cade insisted on attending services as a family. If she didn't let herself think about McGill, she could picture them as a real family. Not one argument had occurred the last couple of days. They were making progress.

Missy paused to preen. Turning in a wide circle, she held out her arms. "Do you like my dwess, Uncle Cade?"

"It's unusually striking, Missy."

The little girl's eyes suddenly clouded. "My ma made it fow me."

Kneeling beside her, Cade pulled her close and held her. "Your ma was a real good seamstress. You must be very proud of such a pretty dress." He drew Holly to his side as well. "And might I say, I'll have to beat the boys away with a club this morning because you two look so fetching."

The tender scene touched Zoe's heart. She hadn't known he had such a soft spot.

"Did you love my ma, Uncle Cade?"

"I loved her a lot, Missy. Your ma was my sister—the way Holly is your sister."

Missy's tears dissolved, and Zoe laughed when the little girl gazed at him slyly, as if he'd said something very amusing but not quite credible.

Cade grinned. "A long time ago your ma and I were little, just like you and Will and Brody and Holly. We played together, ate our meals together, lived in the same house, and got switchings from our ma and pa."

Missy pushed against his chest. "You did not! Ma's too big to get switchings!"

"Missy, stop asking your uncle so many questions." Zoe opened her parasol and studied the sky. "I'm afraid we're in for more rain."

Picking Missy up in his arms, Cade squeezed her affectionately, and then he set her in the buggy he'd gotten from John and Addy's barn. "It won't rain for a while."

"We awe weally going to have fun, Uncle Cade." Missy tightened her hold on Cade's neck. "We'll go to Sunday mowning meeting and thennnn...we'll go on a family picnic."

Cade glanced at Zoe and grinned. "I can't think of anything more fun. Can you?"

Zoe laughed. "Sounds like a great day to me." She straightened her bonnet, nervous about being seen with Cade at church for the first time as newlyweds. The townspeople would look for signs of marital bliss, and all they would see would be signs of more than a week of sleepless nights. It had been a long time since a man had been in her bed. The old saying "two's company, three's a crowd" came to mind. She was relieved that a simple wedding band failed to deter Missy's sleeping preference. She lay between them at night.

Zoe bit back a smile, thinking how nice it would be if the marriage were real. It was torture having Cade so close but so inaccessible.

Cade glanced in her direction. "Something funny?"

"No." She pulled on her gloves and drew a steadying breath. "We'd best hurry or we'll be late for the service."

The steeple bell tolled as the newly formed family arrived. Buggies and carriages filled the field next to the Good Shepherd Church. The Kolby family filed in and came to a sudden stop inside the front door.

Brody glanced at Zoe. "Where do we sit?"

Zoe searched the long rows of wooden benches. The Kolby pew was on the right; the Bradshaw pew, on the left near the front. The Wiseman pew sat closest to the back.

Will polished the toes of his shoes on the back of his pant legs. "Where do we sit now? Are we a Kolby, a Wiseman, or a Bradshaw?"

Zoe glanced at Cade expectantly.

"Yeah, Uncle Cade. What are we?"

Taking Missy's hand, he held Zoe's with his other and led them down the aisle. The children followed. Pausing at an empty row near the front, he ushered the family in.

"Oh," Missy said. "We'we a new family. Just us!"

Cade slid into the seat beside Zoe and pulled Missy onto his lap. "That's right. We're our own family now."

"Oh, goody!"

Zoe settled back in the pew, aware that all eyes were on them. She felt Gracie's beaming consent and Lilith's glowing approval. Though she shouldn't, she felt proud sitting next to her handsome husband. The red splotches on his face were fading and barely noticeable. In her estimation, he was the most handsome man in the room.

Cade shifted in the pew, leaning closer to whisper, "Why is everyone staring?"

Scrunching lower in her seat, Zoe studied the ceiling.

"What's wrong?" Cade's gaze followed hers to the open rafters.

"We're all afraid the roof's going to fall in," she whispered.

His eyes scanned the sturdy beams. "Looks strong enough. Have you been having trouble with it?"

"No, but you're in church this morning."

He gave her a sour look as Lilith got up from her seat and came over to them.

"Hello, dears. My, don't you make a fine-looking family. Addy and John would be so happy."

Zoe tried not to show her bliss. "Thank you, Lilith."

When Reverend Munson took his place at the pulpit, the neighbor slipped back to her pew, and Zoe picked up a hymnal. Cade flipped noisily through the songbook, looking for the right page. Zoe reached over and turned to "What a Friend We Have in Jesus" as Lorraine Munson took her place at the organ and struck a chord.

Cade's deep baritone blended melodiously with Zoe's alto as they sang the first of the morning's hymns. Zoe was taken back years to when they had sung together as children in the same church.

The congregation sat down as the music died away, and Reverend Munson approached the podium with his Bible under his arm.

Turning his benevolent eyes on the newlyweds, he said, "Good morning, friends."

"Good morning, Reverend," the congregation chorused.

"And what a glorious morning it is. I see the Kolby family is with us today." He inclined his head toward Cade and Zoe. "No better place to be than in the house of the Lord."

The minister opened his Bible, and Zoe did a double take when she saw the outline of a six-shooter beneath his suit coat.

Cade leaned close. "Is that a gun?"

She put her finger to her lips and nodded, afraid someone would hear him. Her eyes widened when she noticed the blunderbuss lying across old Bess Harris's lap.

"Reverend Munson carries a gun?" Cade whispered.

She elbowed him to be quiet.

"The Scripture this morning is about love. The Good Book tells us from the beginning of creation, God made them man and woman. For this cause, a man shall leave father and mother, and likewise shall a woman leave her parents, and the two shall become one. Consequently, they are no longer two, but one, flesh." The minister paused, clearing his throat. "Where God has joined two together, let no man come between."

He closed his Bible and grasped the sides of the pulpit, leaning toward the congregation. He paused for a moment as if in deep thought. "Marriage is a covenant between a man and a woman and God."

When Cade squirmed beside her, Zoe pretended she didn't notice. Why Reverend Munson had picked this morning to preach on the sanctity of marriage, she didn't know. Guilt nagged her. A week ago, the children had seemed a viable and sane reason to marry. This morning, the minister's words reminded her that marriage was a sacred union not to be entered into lightly. Her conscience twinged.

What would God have had her do? Turn the children over to Laticia, and watch the fear in their eyes as they went off to be reared by a woman who would make a more appropriate elderly grandmother? Perhaps marriage wasn't the right answer, but it had been the only one at their disposal.

Cade fidgeted in his seat, occasionally glancing at her. Did he feel the pressure, the focused eyes, the consenting nods in the congregation? Zoe suddenly felt too warm.

"A woman should cleave to her husband and he to his wife, forsaking all others," the reverend said. "That's what the Good Book tells us."

Fanning herself with a hanky, Zoe blew a lock of hair off her forehead. He was looking straight at her and Cade. Thirty-five minutes of preaching felt like a month. She hadn't realized she was as rigid as a board until she saw Woodall Thompson checking his pocket watch, signaling that the service was coming to an end.

She fanned harder when the reverend focused on Cade. "This morning I want to close this service in Cade and Zoe Kolby's honor with the message found in First Corinthians."

Zoe bit her lip, trying to control her emotions. The solemnity of the moment silenced all in the room. Not a whisper sounded or a head turned.

The reverend spoke now from memory, choosing words everyone in the room could understand. "If I had the gift of being able to speak in other languages without learning them, and could thus speak in every language there is on both heaven and earth, but I didn't love others, I would be talking only to hear myself talk. If I had the gift of knowing everything that will happen in the future, and knew everything about everything, but didn't love others, what good would it do? Even if I had the gift of faith so that I could speak to a mountain and make it move, I would still be worth nothing at all without love."

The pastor lowered his voice. "Love is patient and kind, never jealous or envious, never boastful or proud, never haughty or selfish or rude. Love does not demand or seek its own way. It is not irritable or touchy, it doesn't hold grudges and will hardly notice when others do it wrong. It is never glad about injustice, but rejoices whenever truth wins out. Love does not rejoice in unrighteousness, but rejoices in the truth. Love bears all things, believes all things. Hopes all things. Endures all things."

Zoe swallowed back tears, wanting to believe. Was everlasting, unselfish love between a man and woman possible? Across the aisle she saw Gracie and Lawrence holding hands. Their union had stood the test for more than forty years.

Edna and Walt sat together, Edna dabbing her eyes with her handkerchief as Walt patted her knee. Thirty-seven years ago, they had started life together.

Everywhere Zoe looked in the church, she saw couples who had taken vows and held them sacred. She had taken vows with a man who didn't intend to keep them. Yet how could she presume to judge Cade when her own life needed a good housecleaning?

Reverend Munson stepped down from the podium. "In closing, the Good Book tells us that faith, hope, and love abide, and the greatest of these is love." He fixed on the congregation. "I hope each and every one of you in this room will remember these words and apply them to your own marriages." His gaze rested on Cade. "For until a man finds his purpose, he will not find happiness."

Chapter Forty-Five

After the service Cade made his way out of the church, pausing to visit with well-wishers. Now that the children were settled and he had recovered from his bout with measles, Zoe knew their days together as a family were over. Reverend Munson's sermon had been poignant, but they had come too far to abandon reason.

Cade promised to make the parting brief and unemotional. He'd tell the children that something came up and he had to leave. He wouldn't mention that he wasn't coming back. In time she would have to find the words to explain why he hadn't returned.

Zoe watched him shake hands, and she knew she'd miss him even more this time. Her newly formed family would never be the same once he was gone. He'd leave a void big enough to throw Herschel Mallard's dead bull through, but that was the bargain they had struck. Endless lonely days and cold nights was the price she must pay for the children.

The crowd started to disperse and Cade took hold of Will's hand. Zoe noticed Missy playing nearby in a mud puddle and sighed. "She'll ruin her dress," she told Cade.

"It'll wash, won't it?"

She called for Missy to come to her, fishing a handkerchief out of her handbag. As Missy ran up, she handed Cade her purse and began to wipe at the muddy stains.

"Missy, you know better than to play in the dirt in your good clothes."

Cade playfully draped Zoe's reticule over his arm and began twirling it primly around his wrist in an attempt to make Missy laugh. She favored him with a toothless grin.

Holly giggled. "Uncle Cade, you're silly."

"And he makes a pitifully homely woman." Zoe teased, joining in the nonsense.

Cade straightened, pretending to take offense. "I beg your pardon?"

Zoe handed him the soiled hanky, and he daintily shook it loosely in the air and executed several graceful pirouettes as the girls' laughter grew louder.

Encouraged by their reaction, he twirled again on one foot, and landed in front of Shelby Moore, who was coming down the church steps.

Moore did a double take of comical disbelief.

The hanky in Cade's hand sagged. "Morning, Shelby."

Shelby pushed past him, muttering something under his breath that sounded like "sissy bounty hunter."

Cade grinned as Shelby stalked off.

Gracie and Lawrence paused to watch Zoe and her family climb into their buggy before turning to speak to Edna, Walt, and Sawyer. Pop joined them, and the six visited for a few minutes.

Gracie's eyes followed Cade and Zoe's buggy as it rattled out of the churchyard. "They make a fine-looking family, don't they?"

Lawrence nodded. "Cade will be leaving soon. It's a shame. They make a fine couple."

Sawyer bit off a wad of chew and stuck it in his jaw. "Yessir, that's a real shame."

"Don't call it rain before you're wet," Pop said. "I have a feelin' those two are gonna make it."

Gracie shook her head. "I don't think theirs is a marriage in the biblical sense."

Lilith frowned. "You mean what I think you mean?"

Gracie nodded.

"Did Zoe tell you that?"

"Of course not. A lady wouldn't tell tales out of school, but…" Gracie hesitated a moment, glancing at the men. "Missy mentioned that she sleeps between them at night."

"Now, that is a shame," Walt said. "Those two need some time alone."

Sawyer spat. "That marriage needs some of that credible stuff."

"It sure does," Pop said. "Anyone in the mood for a shivaree?"

"A shivaree?" Gracie patted her handkerchief to her bosom. "Aren't we a little late? They've been married more than a week."

Pop cackled. "All the better. They won't be expectin' it."

Zoe breezed into the mercantile, pulled off her bonnet, and called over her shoulder, "Get your clothes changed, children, while I make some sandwiches." She walked through the store tying an apron around her waist. There were a dozen and one things she should be doing, but as soon as Cade agreed to a picnic, she'd known she was outnumbered. And besides, he would be leaving early in the week.

"Can I help?" Cade took off his jacket and draped it over the back of a kitchen chair.

"Thanks. Here." She handed him an apron. "Don't get your shirt dirty."

"You mean Jim's shirt."

She looked away. She'd meant to dispose of Jim's clothes, but she hadn't had the heart. Cade's broad shoulders strained the fabric across his back. The arms were tight, and the buttonholes stretched to their limits beneath his larger build.

When she looked back, he was holding up the apron, trying to figure out which end was top and which was bottom. She imagined he wasn't too happy about wearing it.

"How do women get into these contraptions?"

Zoe glanced over her shoulder as she sliced bread. "Need some help?"

He nodded, holding the apron out to her. She slipped the neckpiece over his head, and then reached around his waist to tie the sash.

"Thanks."

"You're welcome." She continued to slice bread, feeling warm beneath his perusal as he watched her perform the mundane task. "Something wrong?"

"I was just wondering what hit me."

"What do you mean?"

"How did I get into this predicament? Not that long ago I had only myself to worry about. Now I'm in an apron about to have a picnic with my wife and four kids."

Smiling, she ignored the rush of sentiment his confession provoked. "And?"

"It's not a fair fight." His voice dropped to a husky timbre. "Five against one."

"Are you going to help or not?"

"What do you want me to do?"

Be a husband and a father. Love me, stay with me. If you loved us, you'd find a way to make it work.

"Get the picnic basket from the back porch and pack a jar of relish. Oh, and wrap up a few cookies, but not too many. Brody will eat them until they're gone."

Cade absently filled the basket.

"Cade!" She put her hands on her hips. "You put a jar of tomatoes in the basket. I said relish. And please pack the chicken."

"Sorry," he murmured.

"We can't take our clothes off in front of the boys," Holly complained as the children emerged from the bedroom. "Brody said he has to go in his long johns 'cause he can't find his everyday britches."

"Oh, pooh," Missy said, wrinkling her nose. "Bwody has a hole in the seat of his long johns."

Zoe untied her apron and laid it on the back of a chair. "No one is going to a picnic in his underwear. Cade, if you'll finish packing dinner, I'll find the elusive britches. Hurry along, girls, and change your clothes." She left the room.

"Anybody here?"

Cade glanced up to see Shelby Moore standing at the screen door. "Come on in, Shelby."

"Hate to bother you on Sunday, but—" Shelby eyed Cade. "Pop still laid up?"

"Yeah. What can I do for you? Found any more dead bulls?"

"It's my chickens this time, but it can wait. I see you're busy."

Cade looked down and then jerked off the apron. "Getting ready for a picnic."

"I think I'll wait for Pop to get back to sheriffin'."

"I can take care of it, Shelby."

"No disrespect, Kolby, but Pop can handle it later."

Shelby left as Cade absently reached up and scratched an itch on his chin.

In the late afternoon, the children swam in the cool water. With a full belly, and the kids occupied, Cade lay on the blanket beside Zoe, who dozed. He rolled to his side and gazed at her. She deserved the well-earned rest. He'd never known a woman who worked as hard as Red did. He lifted a lock of her hair and let it slide between his fingers. The silken tress smelled of soap and sunshine. Snapping off a blade of grass, he ran it lightly under her nose.

Murmuring, she brushed her chin.

He lowered the blade, tickling along her jaw line, and then he moved it along her forehead in soft, fluttery strokes.

Her hand grazed her nose and she squirmed, opening her eyes.

Tenderly he brushed hair from her cheek. He caught her hand and held it against his face. Her gaze softened, her skin, warm. The scent of wildflowers wafted on the air, reminding him of earlier times.

"Stop it."

"Why don't you make me?" He scooted closer. They were nose to nose. Her breathing quickened, confirming she wasn't as immune to his advances as she claimed.

"Cade, the children will see us."

"So? They know we're married." He caught the tip of her ear in his between his lips and playfully tugged.

Shoving him aside, she sat up. "Behave yourself."

"When you're around, I can think of only one thing." He watched a blush brighten her cheeks. She was beautiful, and he wanted her with a passion he'd never known was possible, a passion that had grown over the years, smoldering and intensifying like a fire in his soul.

"You're impossible."

"Do you know I used to think about you every night before I went to sleep?"

"You did not."

"I did, Red." He tilted her chin with his finger and admitted in a low voice, "Every night I imagined your smile and the way your left cheek dimples when you laugh." His finger lightly moved across her lips. "Want to know what else I imagined?"

"No."

"Coward." What would it take to convince her that he loved her? It wasn't fair to love her and then to leave her, but he couldn't help himself. He wanted this woman more than life itself, yet it was her life he had to protect.

"You're terrible, you know it?" She rolled to her side.

"Give me an opportunity to redeem myself." He slipped his arm around her waist and pulled her back to face him. She looked as young as she had the day he'd left. The same beautiful smile, the same fiery red hair, the same tiny waist—but she wasn't the young girl he'd left behind. She was a woman now. A lovely, desirable woman.

Her gaze softened. He twisted a lock of her hair around his finger. He'd be a happy man if she always looked at him the way she was doing at this moment. "What did I do to put the twinkle back in those lovely eyes?"

"You gave me the children."

That wasn't the answer he'd hoped for, but it was a start. He lowered his head to kiss her and she didn't pull away. His lips closed over her warm, familiar sweetness. She tasted so very good, responding to his kiss like a woman awakened. When they parted, she whispered, "I'll be forever grateful, Cade." She touched his cheek. "I'll be the best mother to our children that I know how to be."

"Our children, Red? They're yours now."

"No." Her fingers traced his nose, his eyebrows, his cheeks. "No matter what happens, they're ours." She threaded her fingers through his hair and sighed. "I'll write you often, and the children will write too. Maybe someday, when they're older, you can come visit."

Her eyes filled with pain, and he squeezed her hand. This was the exact thing he didn't want to put her through, the hurt he didn't want to face. "No letters, no visits. It has to be that way, Red."

"You don't want a letter from me? Or from the children?"

The anguish in her voice tore at his heart. It wasn't what he wanted, but he had no choice. "No. If they found one of your letters they'd come after you. I can't risk that."

"Then don't leave."

"Do you want me to stay?"

Silence hung between them like a heavy, dark shroud. Zoe sighed. "Would you stay if I asked?"

A cloudburst opened above them and the children squealed.

Zoe grabbed up the basket and gathered the corners of the blanket as the first drops fell.

Taking her hand, Cade called the children out of the water. "Run for the buggy!"

The kids scrambled onto the bank. "Can we play in the rain?"

Brody asked, holding his face toward the sky with his mouth open to catch the drops.

"Can we?" Will yelled, mimicking his brother's action. The boys danced and jumped around, snatching water from the air.

Cade laughed. "Why not? Don't drown yourselves!"

"Thanks, Uncle Pa." Will raced in exuberant circles.

The girls picked up big globs of mud and flung them at their brothers.

"Uncle Pa," Cade repeated as he and Zoe made a dash for the buggy. "Do I look like an Uncle Pa?"

"You look like every Uncle Pa I've ever seen."

They fell onto the buggy seat in a fit of laughter. With a couple of yanks, and Zoe's help, Cade raised the leather top into place.

"We might as well have played in the rain with the kids," Zoe said, collapsing breathlessly against the back of the seat. "We're just as wet."

Shivering, she snuggled up against him. Rain pattered against the top of the buggy. They were alone in a very small, very damp cocoon. With the tip of his finger, he turned her chin toward him. "Hello, Mrs. Kolby."

"Hello, Mr. Kolby."

He lifted his hand and brushed a lock of wet hair from her forehead. "I've missed you."

She shouldn't permit this, but when he nuzzled her ear she couldn't stop him. Didn't want to stop him. "The trail is a lonely place. It gives a man a lot of time to think. Of what he's had and what he's lost." His lips found her earlobe, and he nibbled. "I never knew how lonely I was until now."

"Zoe?" Brody yelled.

At the sound of his voice, she sighed and sat up straighter.

"Can I have another piece of chicken?" Brody called.

"In the food hamper." She slid out of the carriage into a light drizzle. God did not mean for this union to exist.

Chapter Forty-Six

Who was beating a drum? After handing Brody a chicken leg, Zoe wiped her hands on a cloth, seeking the source of commotion.

Children squealed. Cowbells clanged and shotguns blustered. "Is it a circus?" Zoe asked. Cade sprung out of the buggy, reaching for his gun.

Zoe's hands flew to her cheeks when she caught sight of a strange procession coming into the clearing. "Wait! Don't shoot! It's Walt and Lawrence…firing in the air."

Sawyer approached the buggy, ringing a cowbell. Lilith banged on a kettle with a wooden spoon, while Margaret burst into a zealous rendition of "Oh, My Darling Clementine," substituting Zoe's name for Clementine's.

The children, wet and muddy, joined in the gleeful melee. They clasped hands and skipped around in a circle, singing along at the top of their lungs.

Cade turned accusing eyes on Zoe.

She shook her head, feeling color drain from her face. "I think it's a shivaree."

He shook his head. "Tell me it's not."

She took hold of his arm for support. "Play along…they mean well." It was the town's way of playing a trick on the new bride and groom.

Usually such shenanigans were held on the wedding night, but Cade had been so sick…

"Zoe. A shivaree?"

Gracie and Lilith swooped in and grabbed Zoe by both arms. "Stop this," Zoe protested, trying to break free as they pulled her along to a waiting carriage. Cade reached out to save her but was stopped by Walt and Lawrence.

"Hold him, men!" Sawyer shouted.

Squirming, Zoe caught sight of Pop cackling on the sidelines, jabbing a crutch in the air. "By doggies!" he said. "Surprised ya, didn't we?"

"Surprised" was putting it mildly. The women hustled Zoe into a buggy. "Gracie, have you lost your mind?"

"Far from it, my dear. Just relax. You're in for the time of your life."

Lilith picked up the reins and slapped them against the horse's rump.

"Where are you taking me?" Zoe yelled above the commotion.

"Can't tell you," the women shouted back. "It's a surprise!"

"What about the children?" Concern overwhelmed the bride as she looked back. Walt and Lawrence were on either side of Cade, holding tight.

Gracie patted her hand. "Don't worry about your young'uns. I'm taking them home with me for the night."

Zoe knew that her friend's intentions were well meant but disastrous. "Gracie, I'll not stand for this."

"Just set back and enjoy the party!"

Glori-Lee waited in front of the café. "Pull up to the side entrance. I got my best room waiting!"

Gracie and Lilith got out and brought Zoe with them. All the balking in the world failed to match the strength of the two older women. Zoe finally gave in, jerked her dress into place, and climbed the side staircase in lieu of being bodily dragged.

Their footsteps sounded on the plank floor as they marched toward a bedroom, the scent of gardenias drifting in the air. Pausing before a closed door, she waited with pained tolerance as Gracie opened it. When the door swung wide, she gasped. Heavy green drapes covered the windows. The room was lit with flickering candles, and the bed had more ruffles on the ecru canopy and spread than Zoe had ever seen. Puffy, colorful pillows lay across the bed and around the floor. Two glasses and a bottle of something sat on the bedside table. Pale green silk scarves garlanded the backs of a chair and matching settee. Why…it looked like a sheik's den of iniquity!

Zoe's gaze came to rest on the tub in the middle of the room, filled with sudsy water. The familiar scent of Lilith's gardenia soap rose from the hot water. Her hand shot out to stop Glori-Lee's when the woman began to unbutton her dress. "What do you think you're—"

"This won't hurt a bit," Glori-Lee said, a big grin splitting her face. "You just get in that tub and soak a spell in Lilith's perfumy bubbles. Once you're all pink and pretty, you can slip into this lovely soft nightie."

Gracie held up a flimsy, pale blue, off-the-shoulder satin gown for Zoe's inspection. A white ribbon laced through the tatting around the neckline and tied in a bow and then trailed down to the hemline. The gown was beautiful, and under other circumstances Zoe would have been delighted to wear it for Cade.

"Girls, I know you mean well, but I can't, I won't—"

"Shush." Gracie pushed her toward the tub, where Lilith stripped Zoe's camisole and pantaloons off before helping her into the bath. Then Lilith scooped up a small pail of water and poured it over Zoe's head.

"You're drowning me!" she protested, covering her bareness with her arms.

The older woman rubbed a bar of sweet-smelling soap over her hair, working up a mountain of lavish suds, while Glori-Lee lifted one of her legs, then the other, running a washcloth back and forth. Zoe had to admit the attention felt good. She slid deeper into the hot water as Gracie reached for an arm to lather.

"That's it. Don't fight it, dear. We have to get you pretty and smelling sweet for your man."

Chapter Forty-Seven

"Now, son," Pop said, "if you hadn't put up such a fuss, we wouldn't have had to tie your hands."

Cade sat in a tub at Walt's bathhouse, trussed up like a Christmas turkey. "Pop, when I get loose—"

Pop chuckled. "You'll be too occupied to retaliate."

"Never saw anyone who hated a bath like you do," Walt said, adding a kettle of hot water to the tub.

"Owwww! Watch where you're pouring that!"

"Yeah, take it easy," Pop said. "You don't want to scald the groom."

Sawyer doubled over with laughter. "Wouldn't want that now, would ya, Cade?"

Cade struggled to climb out of the tub, but Pop pushed him back down with the tip of his crutch. Walt dunked his head under the water. He came up, sputtering.

"The only part of my body I intend to use tonight is my foot, to kick all of you from here to kingdom come!"

"Now, now, calm down," Walt said. "Cain't start a marriage without a shivaree. Don't 'spect you and Zoe have had much time alone with all those young'uns around."

Lawrence lifted Cade's foot out of the water and scrubbed it hard with a brush. Cade jerked it back under the suds.

"Ticklish?" Lawrence asked. "Never would have thought it."

"Don't do that."

Lawrence snickered, trying to grab his other foot. Cade snatched it away.

"You are ticklish!"

"I'm not ticklish. I'm just particular about who washes my feet."

"No time to be bashful." Pop sat on a keg, propped his splinted leg on a box, and watched the antics. "Think of it as ministry. We wash your feet, you wash ours."

Cade lifted his bound wrists and slapped them hard on the water, soaking the onlookers.

"Now look what ya did," Lawrence said, pointing to the front of his drenched trousers. "The wife'll skin me."

"Let me out of this tub!"

"Pipe down. They can hear you in the next county." Lawrence rubbed a towel over Cade's head. "Okay, Walt, he's all yours. Get his hair combed up real pretty-like. We want him to look real special for his missus."

Sawyer held up Cade's clothes. "I'll just take these home with me."

"Don't you lay a hand on those clothes!" Cade's demand fell on a closed door. He turned to Pop. "Get me out of here."

Pop shook his head. "They got their hearts set on a shivaree. Best just ride it out, son."

Walt finished combing Cade's hair. "Now comes the tricky part." He pulled out a straight razor. "I can shave you with you sitting real still, or you can wriggle like you've been doing and take your chances."

Cade froze in place as Walt slid the sharp instrument over the lower part of his face in several swipes until his skin was smooth. The sting of lotion slapped on his cheeks brought him to life. He put his elbows on the sides of the tub and lifted himself up.

Pop stepped back, away from the splash. "Now the missus is gonna be real pleased."

Cade glared at him. "Winslow, you're a dead man."

Laughing, Pop and Walt slapped each other on the backs.

"Get my clothes!"

Pop chuckled again and held up a white cotton garment and matching hat with a tassel. "Oops. Ain't got nothin' but this here nightshirt. Guess it'll have to do."

"I am not wearing a nightshirt," Cade warned through clenched teeth. He stepped out of the tub, and Walt began to towel him dry while Cade tried to smack his hands away.

"Suit yourself," Pop said, tossing the garment aside. "But," he added, giving Cade the once-over, "can't say Zoe will be too thrilled when you show up in your birthday suit. She might take offense."

Walt folded the towel and laid it on the counter. "From the looks of this place, you'd think we gave a polecat a bath. More water on the floor than in the tub."

"Serves you right. Now get my clothes."

"Put the nightshirt on, son. You're not getting your clothes 'til mornin'." Pop snickered. "Come on, Walt, let's get this ornery polecat over to Glori-Lee's."

Walt looked Cade straight in the eye. "What'll it be? We untie you so you can put on the nightshirt, or you stay tied and walk naked as a jaybird through town?"

Chapter Forty-Eight

Scrubbed, rinsed, and buffed, Zoe felt like a baby as Gracie and Lilith rubbed her down with a large fluffy towel. When the women finished, Glori-Lee held up the satin nightgown. "It'll be big on you, but I figure the size won't matter."

Zoe reached for her clothes, but they had mysteriously disappeared. She quickly tucked the towel around her closer. "Now that you've had your fun, ladies, I have to go home. The children—"

"Oh, no, you don't." Gracie held her back. "The fun has only begun."

Lilith opened her pin watch. "You'd best put on that gown. You should be getting a visitor—" a loud knock sounded on the door, "—about now."

Gracie reached to open the door, and Zoe quickly jerked the gown out of Glori-Lee's hands and over her head. She stood frozen in place as Lilith tied her hair back with a blue silk ribbon.

Pop shoved Cade into the room, and she bit her lip to keep from laughing. He was wearing a ridiculous nightshirt and a cap with a fuzzy tassel that hung just below his left ear. The nightshirt struck him midway between his ankles and knees. Barefoot and hairy-legged, he looked about as humiliated as she felt.

The sheriff turned his head as the older women filed out. "Sleep tight," he said, and then he closed the door.

A moment later it opened again, and a pair of boxing gloves sailed into the room. "Little gift from Sawyer. He thought they might come in handy with you two."

The lock clicked into place.

Zoe's mind flittered with guilt. Jim, God rest his soul, had been a good and honorable man. He'd given her his love and support, but even Jim had known that Cade was in her heart, and he'd accepted it. Now Jim was gone. She was married to Cade.

"I hope you know how to pick locks," she murmured.

He stepped to the door and rattled the handle. It refused to budge. "I think Pop is getting senile."

"I think the entire town is out of its mind." Exhausted, she climbed under the covers, and lay back. Gracie sure knew how to fashion a comfortable bed. "We'll just have to make the best of it until morning."

"No."

"Does the big, fierce bounty hunter not like the idea that he's at someone else's mercy?" Zoe couldn't help but laugh at the disgruntled expression on his face. "You're pretty bossy for a man wearing nothing but a silly-looking nightshirt."

"It's not funny, Red."

"Really?" She smothered a yawn. "I think you look quite charming, and those boxing gloves. What an appropriate gift. We'll have to thank Sawyer." When his eyes darkened to a challenging hue, she shrank deeper under the covers.

He lifted a sardonic brow. "Want to fight?"

She knew better than to taunt him when he was in this mood. In her most innocuous voice, she answered, "No. Why would you think that?"

He walked over to her and jerked back the covers. Scrambling to the opposite side of the bed, she glared at him, conscious that she'd gone too far. "Don't you touch me!"

"You've had a burr under your saddle since the day I rode into Winterborn. When you came out of the store, you were mad enough to shoot me." He reached for the boxing gloves and pitched them at her. "Put 'em on, Red. You want a fight. I'll give you a fight."

She threw the gloves back. He caught them against his chest and chuckled.

Pulling the covers over her face, she screamed her frustration into the mattress. The man was so infuriating!

No sooner had the scream ended than she felt a rush of cool air. He yanked the covers off again. His hands found her waist, and she felt herself being lifted from the bed.

"Put me down!"

"No. It's time we settled this."

Her face flamed beneath his arrogant perusal of her bare shoulders as he set her on her feet. "Stop looking at me. Have you no shame?"

"I have nothing to be ashamed of," he said. "I'm looking at my wife. There's no law against that."

"I'm not your wife, and you know it."

"That must mean the good reverend doesn't have the power to marry folk." He chuckled. "What will people say when they learn every married couple in the county is living in sin?"

"You know what I mean."

"No, I don't." He was a breath away from her now. "Admit it, Red. You're still in love with me."

She pushed him back, full of frustration. Nothing she did intimidated him. He stood with a grin on his face as if he considered this situation little more than juvenile amusement.

"I don't love you."

"You don't."

"I don't.

"All right," he said, picking up the boxing gloves, "let's fight." He grabbed her right wrist and shoved a glove on her hand.

"Stop this," she said, trying to shield her left hand. He reached behind her, tugged her hand to the front, and pushed the other glove on. After tying both laces, he took a step back to assess her with a grin. She watched in trepidation as he reached out with his left fist and tapped her on the chin.

"Come on, Red. Fight." He grinned, grazing her chin again. "That's what we do best. Fight."

With a flourish, she rested the gloves on her hips. "Cade, you're acting like a child. Do you know how ridiculous you look in that gown and nightcap?"

"Yes. Let's fight."

"I don't want to fight. Our agreement was to marry for the kids' sake, and you know it."

"I don't make deals. I agreed to marry the woman I care about so she could have what she wanted. Addy's children."

She drew a deep breath. "Care about? I'm not a fool, Cade. You married me because Seth and Bonnie changed their minds and Laticia pushed you into a corner."

"That's it, get mad. Let it all out, Red. Let me have it." He stepped closer, pointing to his chin. "What are you waiting for? Come on, hit me!"

"Don't be absurd."

He tapped her on the jaw. "Cat got your tongue? Since when have you been reluctant to tell me what you think?"

She shook her head, refusing to appease him.

He reached out and boxed her shoulder. "Let's duke this out, man-to-man."

"No!"

"You'd like nothing better than to get rid of all that anger that's been eating at you for years. Here's your chance. I'm offering you a way out. We're not going to settle anything between us until you make me pay for walking out on you."

Zoe crossed her arms, refusing to rise to his bait.

"We're locked in here until morning. We can make it either pleasant or nasty. It's your choice."

The challenge in his voice said he was dead serious, and the look in his eyes meant business. She squealed when he lightly boxed her jaw with his bare knuckle. "Stop it!"

He tapped her again. "Come on, fight me."

"Leave me alone!"

Cade jabbed at her shoulder, forcing her to take a step back. The man had lost his mind! He was nothing more than an overgrown child, taunting her into this madness.

"Come on, fight me!" With the flat of his hand, he pushed her shoulder. "Get rid of the resentment, Red. I was a thoughtless cad—say it."

"Why? So you can feel better?" If he wanted absolution, he'd come to the wrong place.

"No, so you can. Brrrkkk, brrrkkk."

Zoe's eyes widened as she watched him tuck his thumbs into his armpits and flap his elbows. He strutted around the room like a chicken, making obnoxious clucking sounds. If she hadn't known better, she'd have sworn he'd been drinking. "Stop it!"

"You can't tell a cad from a chicken?"

"Ooooh!" She hauled back and landed a center punch to his stomach. He stepped back and put both hands where she'd made contact. Then she socked him in the jaw, smiling when she heard a groan. "Is that what you want?"

"Maybe not that hard, but you got the idea." He cocked a brow. "Give me another shot."

"Leave me alone, Cade. I don't get mad like I used to." She swallowed hard, trying to control her temper. "You can continue this childish taunting, but I'm going to sleep."

She threw herself onto the bed, landing stomach down on the overstuffed boxing gloves, silently berating them, the lock on the door, Pop, and Gracie, but most of all Cade—the one who'd hurt her, the one who wanted to fight, the one who would leave her again. Tears burned her lids as years of frustration screamed for release.

Getting up, she walked to him and unleashed everything she had in one blow after another until he finally fell backward on the bed.

"That's more like it." His eyes fixed with hers.

"You snake!" She rushed at him with a flurry of punches.

"Hey, I thought you didn't get mad anymore." He pinned her arms to her sides.

She crumbled, sobbing. "At first, I wondered what happened to you, wondered if you were dead or alive. I thought I'd lost you and the baby." She broke free and punched him soundly in the midsection.

He grunted. "I didn't know about the baby. I was wrong, I admit it. But you were wrong for not telling me."

She flailed at his chest. "Why didn't you come back? Why didn't you love me enough?"

"I was young and foolish." He blocked a direct hit to his nose. "I'm sorry. I never meant to hurt you."

"Really? I suppose you thought leaving me here, alone, would make me happy?" She punched his arm. "I loved you, and all I got in return was a few short letters, a box of smashed chocolates, and a broken doll!" Tears rolled down her cheeks, and she shivered as he pulled her to him and kissed them away.

He gently lifted the locket around her neck and rested it across his fingers. "It makes me proud that you've continued to wear this." He thumbed another tear from her cheek.

She bowed her head, unable to meet his gaze. There was so much he'd never know or understand. She surrendered the gloves. "I'm finished now."

Cade untied the strings and pulled the gloves from her hands. "Are you sure you're finished?"

"I'm finished. You win."

He threaded his fingers through her hair. "No one wins unless you're ready to forgive me."

"Perhaps I could, if I knew why you didn't come back." She felt tears well and blinked them back.

"For a million reasons, none of them good enough." He pulled her to his chest. "One day turned into a week, then a few months, then years. Then Addy wrote that you had married Jim. For some crazy reason that cut me to the bone. I felt betrayed. After a while, I realized you were better off without me."

She pushed back, but he stopped her.

"Let go," she said.

"I did that once. I have no intention of letting go now."

She eased toward him again, tired of fighting. "You'll be leaving, and I have no intention of putting myself through the same agony."

"I love you, Red. No matter what's happened in the past, I love you."

"Loving you was never the problem." She studied his intense, questioning look. "Forgetting is what's difficult."

"You never forgot me."

Tears rolled. She'd never forgotten him for a moment. "You've been with me every night of my life since you rode out."

His gaze met hers. "Tonight is ours. Let's not waste it this time."

She hesitated for a moment. Maybe she would never forget, but she knew it was time to forgive and let go of the pain she had been carrying for fifteen years.

She put her arms around his neck and whispered, "You are my husband, Cade, and I...I am ready to spend this night with you as your wife."

A look of tender hope and love crossed his face. Feeling lighter than she had in years, she smiled as she drew his head to hers and kissed him.

Chapter Forty-Nine

Late Monday night Zoe left Cade in the kitchen and went to answer the door. Their honeymoon had been short, but it really had been very thoughtful of the town. The memory would see Zoe through many a long, lonely night. Gracie handed her a note. "Perry just brought this by. I thought you might like to have it."

"Perry?" Zoe opened the white envelope and her smile gradually receded as she read the legal document. Refolding it, she put it in her pocket.

"Well?" Gracie said. "What is it?"

"The note to the store."

"The note...to your store?"

"Paid in full."

"Oh, my. I knew Perry thought that you and he—but now that you and Cade are actually man and wife..." Gracie swelled with indignation. "Why do you suppose he'd do a thing like that?"

"I don't know. Of course I can't accept it."

"Appears to me that it's already done. That man had a lot of gall."

"I can't let Perry pay off my debts."

"Well, the man certainly knows how to give a wedding present. You gotta hand it to him. One other thing you should know. Roy had business in Suffox County yesterday. While he was there, he told Lawrence that he heard several men talking about Hart McGill."

At the mention of McGill, Zoe went cold. "McGill's in Suffox County?"

Gracie nodded.

"Is Roy sure?"

"He says McGill is bragging how he's coming after—well, just bragging. You know how men are."

"Thank you, Gracie." Zoe shut the door and returned to the kitchen, where she found Cade ironing. Glancing up from the board, he grinned and gestured toward an overflowing basket. "There was such a pile, I thought I'd help."

She wanted to cry when he held up Brody's best Sunday shirt with a scorched iron imprint on the side. Guilt flashed across his face. "I'm not very good at this—"

She was so overcome with gratitude, with love, that it took a moment before she found her voice. "This is the worst day of my life!" She burst into tears.

"Hey—I'm ironing, not printing money—"

"Gracie just told me that Lawrence said that Roy heard McGill is in Suffox County."

The silence was deafening. Stepping to the window, Cade pulled the curtain aside and looked out. "Is he sure?"

She nodded, choking on a sob. "McGill's...here." A moment later she felt his arms slide around her waist and pull her against him.

He buried his face in her hair, his warm breath brushing her temples. "We knew this was possible."

"No," she whispered. "It's too soon."

He held her tightly and let her cry it out. When her sobs subsided, he helped her wipe her eyes.

"Better?" he asked.

She shook her head. She would never be better, not as long as McGill threatened him. "And as if that weren't enough, Perry's lost his mind."

"Really?" Cade wiped his hands on a cloth. "How so?"

"He paid off my bank debt.'"

Cade crossed his arms and leaned back against the table. "He paid off the loan?"

"Apparently."

"Why would he do that?"

Was that jealousy in his voice? Her heart thumped at the thought. "Naturally, I can't accept it."

"Why not?"

Zoe took the cloth from him and wiped jelly off the kitchen table. "Would you want me to accept a gift of that magnitude from Perry Drake?"

"Why not? What difference does it make who paid the bill? You're out of debt, aren't you?"

"Yes, but that isn't the point. I don't think Perry can comfortably afford this, and I frankly don't want to feel obligated to him when—" She paused.

"When what?"

She took a deep breath. "When you're gone. I don't want him to think I would—"

"Marry him?"

She turned, eyeing him sourly. "This is not funny."

He leaned over and whispered, "You're too much woman for Perry Drake. Don't look a gift horse in the mouth. Take the windfall and run."

"I wouldn't think of it. I don't have feelings for Perry Drake. I never have, and I never will." She rinsed a cup. "What are we going to do about McGill?"

"Forget McGill. I'm leaving at first light. He won't find me, and Pop will tell him that his information is stale."

"But he—"

He caught her by the waist and kissed her. Hard. "I said, forget McGill. Now pack some clothes for you and the kids. You're leaving when I do."

Hope sprang alive. "You're taking us with you?"

"I said when I do. Not with me."

Chapter Fifty

A rooster strutted through the barn, lifted his beak, and crowed at the rising sun that shone through cracks in the door. Cade looped the girth under Maddy, kneeing her sharply when the horse puffed her belly. "Don't give me any trouble, girl. I've got enough woman problems." Cinching the strap tight, he then stepped back and smacked the horse on its flanks. "Just because you got a pretty face, don't think you can work me."

Zoe entered the barn holding a cup of steaming hot coffee. She'd helped herself to a pound from the store. Standing on tiptoe, she kissed Cade good morning.

"A kiss for me," he teased.

"A kiss for Cade." Their eyes held for a moment.

"I love you, Red. Don't ever forget it." He glanced up as Pop tottered into the barn.

"There you are, Cade—oh, mornin', Zoe. You're out and about early today."

Cade draped his arm around Zoe's waist. "I'll be in to say goodbye in a few minutes."

She nodded and kissed him again before slipping around Pop and out the door.

Grabbing Maddy's reins, he led the animal out of the barn. Pop trailed behind him.

"Guess you heard the news?" Pop asked.

"How long have you known McGill was getting close?"

"Not long."

A muscle in Cade's jaw worked. "Why didn't you tell me?"

Pop caught up, latching onto his shirtsleeve. "Hold up. We need to talk."

Shrugging Pop's hand away, Cade grabbed Maddy's bridle and swung aboard. "Too late for talk."

Pop hurried to keep pace on his crutches. "No use getting bent out of shape, Cade. I didn't tell ya because I knew the town had ya covered."

Cade reined up. "The town what?"

Pop paused to catch his breath. "I said, the town has ya covered. No one's gonna let McGill get ya."

Cade's features hardened. "I take care of my own back."

"That might be, but now you got a little help."

Dismounting, Cade looped the reins around the hitching post, and then he lifted his hat and settled it low on his forehead.

Pop met his even gaze "You haven't noticed the guns the townspeople been totin'?"

"I've noticed. I guess they have a right to carry guns if they want."

"They're protectin' ya!"

"Me?"

Pop nodded. "We took a vote, and it was unanimous in your favor."

"Why in the world would the town think they'd need to protect me?"

"Because..." The elderly man paused, glancing toward the store entrance. "We figure it was the least we could do, seeing as how we forced you to marry Zoe."

Shaking his head, Cade smiled. "No one's forced me to do anything. I'm not a fool. Go over to Glori-Lee's and get your breakfast. She'll be taking biscuits out of the oven about now."

"Okay, bury your head in the sand like a dadburned ostrich, but it's the truth!" Pop shook a crutch at him. "If it weren't for the town, you wouldn't be ridin' outta here today, confident your nieces and nephews have a good home."

Pausing on the lower step, Cade braced his hand on one of the porch posts. "All right. What's this all about?"

"You ready to listen?"

"Depends on what you have to say."

"When we, the town, realized that you and Zoe couldn't do anything except butt heads, we decided to take matters into our own hands. John and Addy's kids were likely to suffer if we didn't do something, so we called a town meeting and decided we had to get you and Zoe together or the kids would go to Laticia."

"The kids are my responsibility."

"A responsibility you weren't living up to."

"Pop, you're talking crazy. You, or the town, didn't have a thing to do with me marrying Red. I've loved that woman most of my life."

"You think not? Who locked you in the jail?"

"Zoe came up with the marriage idea."

Pop shook his head, his tongue pushing out his lower lip. "She—"

"Suggested it," Pop interrupted, "like we knew she would. Or like we hoped you would, if you two ever stopped hagglin' long enough."

Cade shook his head. "Did Zoe know anything about this so-called plan?"

"Not a thing. She'd have never gone along with it if she had."

Slapping the post, Cade stepped up onto the mercantile porch.

"No use doing something foolish," Pop warned. "What's done is done. The kids are where they belong, and there's no reason you can't stay around and be a husband to Zoe and a pa to those children. Let McGill come after you. Bring this thing to a head and get it over with. The town's willing to stand and fight beside you. What more could you want?"

"I'm leaving, Pop. I'm saying goodbye to the kids and Red, and I'm going."

"Don't be a fool. There's nothing out there for you." Pop limped up the steps, trying to block Cade's path to the inside. The old man's faded blue eyes pinned him with a long, silent scrutiny. "Listen to me. You're like my own boy. Give it up, son. The good Lord's provided everything you ever wanted right here. Reach out and take it. Take what you've wanted ever since you rode out of here fifteen years ago. Are you blind? Your sister's giving you another chance. Don't be a fool and let it pass."

Cade reached for the door handle. Pop rapped his hand with a crutch.

"Listen to me. Stay here and fight McGill. When it's over, you'll have Zoe and the kids. You ain't lived no life that cain't be changed with a little effort."

Cade's shoulders slumped as the weight of Pop's words washed over him. "I wish it was that easy, Pop."

"It is that easy. You're the one making it hard, you stubborn fool. Is it the money?"

"Not solely."

"Then stay. Until a man finds his purpose, he's never goin' to be happy. Isn't that what Reverend Munson says? You've found your purpose; now stay with it."

Cade nudged him aside and reached for the door handle.

"Listen to me, knucklehead! If you was my boy, I'd turn you over my knee, no matter how big you are. Maybe you've found your purpose, and you're just not man enough to recognize it!"

Cade entered the store and slammed the screen door behind him.

Zoe peeked from the kitchen when the noise made her drop a skillet. "Cade?"

"Get the kids up."

"What? What's the—"

"Get the kids up, Red. I haven't got time to argue. I want to tell them goodbye."

The look in her eyes cut him to the bone. His one regret was that she would never forgive him.

"God forgive me," he mumbled as he grabbed a handful of jerky and tossed it into a knapsack. He walked through the store, stuffing other dried and nonperishable food into the bag.

He glanced up a moment later to find four tousled-haired children watching him pack.

Missy's lower lip jutted out. "What's wong, Uncle Cade? Are you mad 'bout something?"

"I'm not mad, Sunflower. Something's come up and I have to leave." The little girl's eyes followed him as he moved about the store.

Zoe reached out and drew Brody close. Cade refused to look at them. He'd never thought leaving them would be this hard. *Sure, Pop. Stick around, raise the kids, be a husband. Easy to say, hard to do after the life I've lived.*

Stay, and McGill would always hold the winning hand. Even if he outdrew the thug, there were more brothers, more kin, looking to settle the score. Pop accused him of not being man enough to stay, but he was man enough to walk out and give Red and the kids a chance at a normal life.

"Don't go away, Uncle Cade." Brody's lower lip trembled. "You ain't taught me how to shoot a pistol yet."

"Sorry, son." Cade turned his back. "Things don't always work out the way we want them to."

Missy started to cry, holding on to Zoe's skirt. Holly reached over and took her sister's hand. "Don't cry, Missy."

"Uncle Cade is leaving," she sobbed. "I don't want him to leave." Missy's tear-rimmed eyes implored Zoe. "Make him stay, Zoe. Make him stay!"

Zoe drew the child closer, quietly soothing her.

"Are you tired of being a pa already?" Will asked. His grave eyes fixed on Cade. "We could be better."

Cade closed his eyes. The boy's words tore at his heart as badly as Zoe's silence. Leaving was the most difficult, painful thing he'd ever done.

Zoe left the children and came to be by his side. "You'll need sugar and coffee." She reached for the items, helping him sack them. Their eyes met and darted away. As she edged past him, she laid her hand on his shoulder and squeezed. "You'll need warm clothing. It'll be getting cold soon. I'll pack a few of Jim's things."

The knot in his throat tightened. "I don't want your husband's clothes."

"Don't be foolish, Cade. It's good, warm clothing. Jim would want you to have them." She disappeared into the back rooms. The children hadn't moved from the doorway.

"You're really going." Brody stared at him.

"Yes, son." Cade wanted to take the boy in his arms and tell him the truth. Ten was old enough to understand that life didn't necessarily deal from the top of the deck, and there were worse things than being a coward. A coward could be tempted to stay and subject his family to his enemies, but a man ran hard and fast to protect the ones he loved.

"It ain't fair!"

"Brody, don't raise your voice to your Uncle Pa," Cade warned.

"I hate you! You shoulda never come back. Ma said you'd stay. She said once you got here, you'd love us enough to stay and keep us. She said you'd marry Zoe 'cause you was always sweet on her, but Ma lied! You ain't gonna stay. You're gonna run away and never come back, just like you always do!"

Brody's words cut deep. Addy promised innocent children that he'd come back for good? Why would she do that? Why? He knew why. She could read him like a book. Pop was right. She was giving him a way back, but she'd failed to take his life into consideration. He wasn't the callow youth who'd ridden out of here looking for adventure. He'd found a bushel basket of it, enough to sicken him. He'd gone at life like a kid eating too many green apples because no one was there to stop him. Now he was paying the price.

Oh, Addy. Why did you promise something I can't give? Don't you think I would stay if I could? Don't you think I know you loved me enough to give Red back to me? Don't you know how it hurts?

The front door slammed shut, and he glanced up to see that Brody was gone. "Brody!"

"I'm going with my brother!" Will shouted. "We don't want to live here anymore! You're mean!" He raced out the door before Cade could get around the counter.

Missy dashed after them. He reached out and snagged the hem of her nightgown. "Zoe!"

Zoe appeared in the doorway. "What's wrong?"

"The kids are running off."

"Maybe I'll go with them."

He glanced at Missy, who was kicking and squirming on the floor. "What are you doing?"

"I'm having a big ol' fit so you won't go!"

Leaving the girls to Zoe, he walked to the door and jerked it open. "I'm going after Brody and Will."

"Cade," Zoe called, running after him. "You have to go now. I'll go after the boys." She paused in the doorway, her eyes begging him. "Go on. I'll go after them."

He reached out, touching her lips with his finger. "I can't go knowing there's a couple of little boys out there crying their hearts out, thinking I don't give a darn about them."

Her eyes pleaded with him. "Hart McGill is a county away. I thought we agreed the children's safety came first."

"That was before I knew what an Uncle Pa was."

She caught him close. "I can't keep up this facade. It's tearing me apart to let you go," she whispered.

Drawing her to him tightly, he rocked her in his arms. "Say it," he whispered harshly.

"I can't—"

"Say it, Red."

"I love you." She wrapped her arms around his neck and buried her face in his shoulder. "I love you."

Kissing her roughly, he then set her aside. "Fix breakfast. I'm going after our boys."

Chapter Fifty-One

Cade crouched beside the trunk of a hickory, watching the boys. Overhead, a songbird trilled to its nearby mate.

Brody and Will were on their knees at their parents' graveside. Dirty tear-streaks smudged their faces and, as usual, Will's nose needed wiping.

Rising, Cade walked over and handed the boy a handkerchief. "Blow hard."

Will jerked away, swiping his sleeve across his nose. "Don't have to do nothin' you say. You don't care 'bout us anymore."

Cade knelt between the two boys. Brody jumped up and ran to his grandparents' tombstone. "Look," Cade said, "I don't want you to think I don't care about you. I do. A lot. Now come on. Let's go back home. Zoe's worried."

Brody kicked a clump of dirt. "Why should we do what you say? You're not our pa. Our pa is there." He pointed to the fresh mound of dirt that held his father's remains.

Will sat back on his haunches. "We come to say goodbye to Ma and Pa. Then me and Brody's gonna be bounty hunters. We're going to shoot people, just like you."

Cade looked away. Bounty hunters. When had he ever encouraged that? "And where do you plan to do this bounty-hunting?"

"Wherever you do," Will answered.

"And how do you plan on getting to where I go? On foot?"

"Brody knows the way. He knows lots of stuff."

Cade glanced at Brody, who was staring at his bare feet. "That right, Brody? You going with Will? In your nightshirt?"

Brody refused to look at him. "What do you care?"

"Well, you may not believe it, but I do care. I can see why you'd be mad at me, but why Zoe? Do you want to hurt her?"

"You did," Brody spat out. "Ma said you hurt her real bad once."

"Yeah," Will agreed. "But she said the good in you would come through someday, and you'd come back and make it up to her."

Cade picked up a rock and threw it. Addy again. He was at a loss to explain why she'd filled their heads with empty dreams.

Brody smacked his hand against a tombstone. "You ain't got no good in you. You came back just to hurt everyone again."

"I think it's time we had a talk." Cade motioned for the boys to sit down. "You're both old enough to know the truth."

"I don't want to know any ol' truth," Brody said.

"That's too bad, because you're going to hear it. Sit down."

Brody kicked the dirt a couple more times before he dragged himself over to where Will sat. Cade pointed to a spot beside Will. Brody plopped down, propping his chin on his hands.

Sorting his thoughts, Cade took a moment. "First of all, being a bounty hunter is not what you want to do."

"You're one," Brody said.

"And if I had it to do over again, I'd have made a wiser choice."

"Like what?" Will peered up at him.

"Like farming or running a livery—or a thousand and one other jobs that would be a better way to make a living."

He sat down between them, putting his arms around their shoulders. "I'd like to be your pa. I just can't."

"Why not?" Will asked. "Don't no one tell you what to do. I hear you tell Zoe that all the time."

"This is different."

"Uncle Pa." Will's eyes pinned him. "If you didn't have to chase that bad guy, would you stay here and be our pa?"

"I would, Will. I'd like that."

"Then stay."

"There's this man…his name is Hart McGill. He's looking for me."

Will leaned into Cade's embrace. "You can hide under Zoe's bed. That's where I hide from Holly when—"

"You don't understand, son. McGill is one of the bad guys. He wants to kill me." Cade wasn't sure if the boys understood. "I can't put you and your sisters and Zoe in danger. I have to go far away from Winterborn so McGill will never know about my family."

Will squirmed. "He might shoot you dead?"

Cade nodded. "That's what he'd like to do."

Brody leaned back on his elbows. "I could shoot him dead, I'll betcha."

"Yeah," Will seconded. "Brody says he's gonna learn how to shoot."

Cade shook his head. "Guns aren't the answer, boys. A man doesn't learn to shoot so he can kill another person. He respects a gun and the harm it can do. You shoot a shotgun so you can hunt rabbits. You fire a rifle to kill deer to put meat on the table. The only time you shoot another person is to protect those you love or good people trying to live by the law."

"Is that why you like shootin' bad guys?" Will asked. "To protect people?"

Cade ruffled the boy's hair. "I don't like shooting anyone, but I wouldn't stand by and let an outlaw run roughshod over innocent people. That's why I hunt the bad guy and turn him over to the law."

"Or shoot him," Brody reminded.

"Occasionally I shoot, but not unless he forces me to."

Brody stood and walked around the gravesite. "If you showed me how to shoot a pistol, I could scare McGill so bad he'd run away and never come back."

Cade laughed. "I guess you could, but you're not going to."

"I could try!"

Will threw his arms around Cade's neck and hung on for dear life. "I don't want you to be dead. Please, Uncle Pa, don't let that bad guy shoot you. Brody and I will help you put him in jail."

Cade stood, lifting Will with him. The boy wrapped his legs around Cade's waist and held on tight as Cade extended his hand to Brody. "Come on. We'll do a little target-shooting before I leave." He should be riding out right now, but when he looked at their faces, he knew he couldn't go, not yet.

He drew a steadying breath, cupping the back of Brody's head with his hand and pulled him tightly against him. "Brody, you're the man now. When I leave, I want to know I can count on you to see to the household. Keep Zoe and your brother and sisters safe."

Brody solemnly nodded. "You teach me to shoot a gun, and I'll protect 'em."

"That means you won't be able to leave to be a bounty hunter."

Brody stuck his chest out. "No, sir. I'll take real good care of your family, Uncle Pa."

Will yanked on Cade's sleeve. "Does that mean he's my boss now?"

"Red's the boss, but Brody's your big brother. He'll watch your back. That right, Brody?"

"You mean if somebody at school wants to beat up Will, I can sock 'em in the nose?"

Cade chuckled. "I'd try talking it out first." He paused, and then conceded, "but if reason fails, sock them in the nose."

The three males walked back to town in silence, except for an occasional sniff from Will to staunch his runny nose. Cade offered his handkerchief again. This time, Will took it. After using it, the boy handed it back, and then he fell into step with Cade, trying to match his stride. Cade smiled, realizing there had never been anyone who'd wanted to be like him. He'd have to be blind not to see how the boys looked up to him. He walked beside their short bodies, watching them kick dirt. He'd like to be around to see them grow to manhood. And the girls, he'd give an eyetooth to be there when suitors came courting, to make sure they were worthy of such treasure.

He shook away the thought. For someone who knew nothing about kids, he was taking his role as Uncle Pa awfully seriously.

"Hey, Ben!" he called as they approached the livery.

The blacksmith glanced up from his anvil. "Hey!"

"Me and the boys are going to do a little target-shooting behind the building."

Later the three turned to see Pop, on his crutches, round the corner of the livery. Will ran to meet him. "Uncle Pa showed me and Brody how to shoot! I shot a bottle a hunnert miles in the air!"

Pop let out a belly laugh. "A hunnert miles? That's a long way, boy. How'd you do that?"

Will shaped his hand in the form of a gun, his finger pointing toward a bale of hay. "Ka-pow! Ka-pow!"

"That'd do it," Pop said, then raised his eyebrows to Cade. "Thought you were gone."

"I am. I had this one last thing to do for the boys."

Pop looked at the youngsters. "How'd you do, Brody? Your bottle go two hunnert miles?"

Brody beamed. "Almost. Look how many times I shot." He proudly displayed the redness on his right hand, which was beginning to swell. "We can have rabbit a lot this winter."

They turned as a carriage pulled up beside the livery. Cade hurriedly reloaded the Colt, relieved when he saw who climbed out of the buggy.

"Abraham!" Will squealed. "I shooted a bottle!"

A big smile split the old man's face "A bottle? Now ain't that somethin'."

Brody ran to meet him. "I shot a bunch of 'em."

"I see a bottle ain't safe in this town no mo'."

Pop hopped over to the buggy. "What're you doin' back in town?"

Abraham wrapped the reins around the brake and got down. "Miz Laticia wanted me to bring this here big box o' clothes for the young'uns. Said no kin o' hers was goin' round lookin' like ragamuffins."

"Sounds like Laticia," Pop said, his gaze running over the big wooden box. "She musta bought out half a store. This crate's big enough to bury one of Mallard's bulls in. Sturdy as they come."

"She sure 'nuff bought out half the mercantile," Abraham said, "jist afore she come down sick as a dog. Now she's got them red spots."

Cade slipped the Colt back into his holster. "Laticia has the measles?"

Abraham grinned. "Doctor says she be laid up a few days, then she be her ol' sef agin."

Pop slapped the black man on the back. "And you thought you'd get outta town before she's her old self again."

Grinning, Abraham shook his head. "Now, Sheriff. I ain't sayin' nuthin' bad 'bout Miz Laticia."

"You never do, Abraham," Pop agreed. "She's a lucky woman to have you to look after her."

"No'sa. I's the lucky one. Owes a lot to Miz Laticia. Taught me how ta read 'n' write when she jist a young girl. Back then, wern't looked on too favorable for a black man ta read." He let out a hearty laugh. "Miz Laticia paid no mind ta what others said. Said she wern't gonna have some ignernt soul drivin' her round. So ever'day she drummed them numbers and letters inta my head 'til I learned 'em."

Cade glanced at the boys. "Help Abraham get the box of clothes unloaded, and make sure you send a proper thank-you to Aunt Laticia."

The boys jumped up into the buggy, pulled open the box, and rifled through the contents. Brody wrinkled his nose when he held up a boy's blue velvet coat. "Sissy clothes."

Will pulled out a pair of shoes his size with silver buckles. His cheeks puffed, holding them up for Cade's inspection. "Do I have ta?"

"Miz Laticia don't know much 'bout what young'uns likes ta wear," Abraham apologized.

"The clothes are much appreciated," Cade said. "Zoe can alter whatever needs to be fixed. She's handy with a needle and thread."

"You ain't goin' to try to haul that box, are ya?" Pop asked, glancing at Cade.

"Not me. The three of us can't move that crate. We'll have to empty it and carry the clothes to the store. Abraham can keep the box."

"Don't know what'd I'd do with such a big ol' box." Abraham scratched his head.

Pop smacked a crutch across the top of the container. "We'll keep it. Someone might have need of it."

Chapter Fifty-Two

Grim faces confronted Zoe when the Kolby family sat down for a last breakfast together. Feeling plenty glum herself, she avoided Cade's gaze as she took a pan of biscuits from the oven. The scent of rain hung in the air as Missy dished up fried potatoes and Holly poured Cade's coffee. Thunder rolled in the distance.

Cade glanced at Missy and Holly and smiled. "Thank you, girls."

Despite the girls' red eyes and the slight quiver in their chins, Zoe thought they had accepted Cade's decision to leave.

Latching onto Missy's skirt, he tugged playfully. "Cat got your tongue this morning?"

Zoe shook her head warningly when Missy started to tear up.

He quickly changed the subject. "Sounds like rain's moving in."

"We can always use rain," Zoe said, taking her seat at the table. She reached for Holly's hand, and the family formed a circle. "Brody, will you bless the food, please?" She bowed her head as Brody said grace. When the amen was pronounced, she forced her mind to go blank. If she allowed herself to think, she would start crying, and that's the last thing Cade needed.

He picked up a knife and buttered a biscuit for Missy, and then he glanced at Brody. "Haven't you got something you want to tell Zoe?"

"Cade taught me how to shoot a pistol!"

"Me too," Will said.

Zoe picked up a bowl of gravy and started it around.

Cade smiled, his glance bouncing back and forth between her and the boys.

"Is that so?" she responded.

He reached under the table and gave her thigh a reassuring squeeze. "A boy needs to know these things. Doesn't mean he'll be a bounty hunter."

Her lips drew into a tight smile. "I suppose that spending your last hours with the children taking a nice walk would have been much too ordinary."

"That's how we saw it, wasn't it, men?"

The boys nodded, stuffing scrambled eggs into their mouths. "It was okay," Will said. "I hit a bottle a hunnert miles in the air!"

"I hit mine two hunnert," Brody said.

Cade took a bite, winking at Holly. "I thought the girls could help me tie my bedroll to the back of Maddy's saddle. What do you say, Holly? Would you do that?"

Holly nodded halfheartedly.

Zoe passed the butter. "Eat your breakfast, Missy."

"I'm not hungwy."

"Of course you're hungry." Cade lifted her fork and tempted her with a bite of eggs. "Come on, sweetheart, it's good."

Shaking her head, the little girl looked at Zoe, her eyes brimming with tears.

"It's all right if you want to leave the table. I'll keep your food warm in the oven."

Missy got up and ran into the bedroom. The family ate in silence except for the occasional ping of a fork scraping a plate, a noisy swallow of milk, or the clunk of a glass being set down.

Zoe choked down her food as the clock chimed eight, sounding like a dirge.

When somebody banged on the back screen door, she jumped as if she'd been shot. Relieved, she noted it was one of Brody's playmates. "Brody is eating his breakfast, Freddy. You'll have to come back later."

"Pop said come and get Cade quick," the ten-year-old blurted out. "Cade is eating—"

"Hart McGill just rode in town." Freddy Henderson jumped on one foot, then the other. "Pop said Cade's got to come *right now*."

The mouthful Zoe just swallowed soured in her stomach. "No," she whispered.

Brody scraped his chair back from the table, tipping over his glass of milk.

Zoe's heart pounded so loudly she was sure Cade could hear it. Nausea coursed through her in violent waves. She closed her eyes, taking deep breaths.

Cade slowly laid his fork aside and got up.

Her hand came out to stop him. "No…" The plea was a pitiful cry, that of a wounded animal in need of help.

He squeezed her hand before reaching for his gun belt and fastening it around his hips. Tying the leather strap to his right thigh, he faced Brody. "You remember what we talked about this morning?"

Brody nodded, his face as white as the stream of milk running off the table.

"You take the others and keep them in the bedroom until someone tells you to come out."

Brody's eyes widened.

"It's all right, son. You're the man of the house now."

"You gotta mind me, Will." Brody herded Will, Holly, and Zoe toward the bedroom. Zoe turned and looked at Cade, praying this was a nightmare and she would wake up soon.

"Go on," he said. "The kids need you."

"I can't let you leave, not like this…" She felt light-headed, powerless. The room spun, and she lifted her hand to her forehead, trying to orient herself. She couldn't fall to pieces now. She must put the children's needs above hers. Squaring her shoulders, she took a deep breath. "All right…all right. The children will be fine…I'll be fine. Do what you have to do." The words tasted bitter in her throat.

Cade pushed back and came to her, his firm shoulder supporting her. His familiar scent filled her senses, and she reeled with fear.

"Listen to me, Red." He gripped her arm. "If anything happens to me, you and the kids leave Winterborn. Do you understand what I'm saying? McGill will come after you."

She nodded, swallowing. "Yes…I'll leave with the children, but I have no place to go…"

"Pop will help you."

Cade moved her toward the bedroom where she could hear Missy's hysterical crying. She had to calm the child. *Please, God, give me the strength to do this for Cade.* She patted Cade's hand. "I'll be fine, I'll be fine…I just need a minute." Her knees buckled, and she fell against him for one blissful moment. Her arms wound around his neck, and she buried her face in his shoulder, and then she kissed his cheeks, his eyes, anywhere she could blindly touch. He matched her kisses, nearly crushing her in his hold.

"My prayers go with you," she whispered, knowing the need in her voice for him to run, and not look back, belied her outward calm.

"Listen to me, Red." His expression was so tender it nearly took her breath away. "Because of you and the children, I didn't leave. I couldn't. Now my past has caught up with me. McGill is here. I can't run anymore." He wiped a tear from her cheek. "Can you understand?"

"Oh, Cade, I couldn't bear it if…."

"Shhh." He laid his fingertips across her lips.

"Do you remember why I gave you the name Red?"

"Because of my hair." She touched his whisker-roughened cheek, needing to absorb his every essence.

"That's what I told you, but it was because you had the temper and strength of a man, and I admired that." He smiled. "Find that strength, sweetheart. Be the woman I know you are. Be brave for the children."

She started to laugh and didn't know why. "It wasn't my hair?" Her laughter turned to quiet sobs, wracking her body as he kissed her before he turned to leave.

"Go into the bedroom, Red."

Quickly, she released the clasp on her locket and put the chain around his neck. "I want a part of me to be with you out there."

He pulled her to him again and kissed her so hard she could barely breathe. Then he left.

Brody emerged from the bedroom and took her gently by the hand. "It's all right, Zoe. I'll take care of you."

The boy led her into the bedroom. Outside the window, the faint sounds of men's shouts came to her. It sounded as if Main Street were being cleared of horses and buggies. Lifting her head, she heard the children crying, their young voices full of fear. She took a handkerchief and wiped Will's runny nose as she heard another yell. Her heart raced.

Gathering the children to her, she searched for words to allay their fear. The apprehension in their eyes made her want to cry harder, but instead she dried her eyes. "Shall we say a prayer for Uncle Pa?"

They nodded.

"Dear God…" The words ceased, and Zoe broke down. Holly picked up the thread.

"Dear God. We are scared for Uncle Pa. We love him a lot. The preacher says that you love us so we know what love feels like. Please keep Uncle Pa safe. Amen."

Zoe wiped her eyes, smiling at Brody. "Have I ever told you the story about Cade and Pop going coon-hunting when Cade was just about your age?"

Brody shook his head, his face pale with worry.

"My," she said, "were those two ever a sight. They took off for the woods, guns over their shoulders, ol' Blue on the trail of something. The other dogs joined in all that baying, having not the slightest idea what they were howling about…"

Her eyes moved to the window. The commotion outside was getting louder. Lifting her voice, she spoke over the noise. "Pop said they were just all imitating ol' Blue, but that old dog sure knew how to hunt…"

Chapter Fifty-Three

Waving a crutch in the air, Pop yelled at the women gathered on the corner. "Git off the street!" When the flock didn't move, he yelled louder. "Go on home, now, there's gonna be a shoot-out!" Hobbling across the road, he motioned for horses to be untied and buggies moved. "Get these animals out of here!"

Men released horses and sent them galloping with a brisk swat to the hindquarters. Buckboards and buggies rattled toward the livery.

At the north end of town, Hart McGill's silhouette loomed as storm clouds moved in. A sharp crack of thunder split the dark morning sky. Cade rounded the corner of the general store and Pop hobbled to meet him.

Main Street cleared. Onlookers ducked into nearby businesses and jerked the shades down.

Cade lifted his hat, ran his fingers through his hair, and then settled it low. Glancing to the north end of town, he said, "Looks like I stayed a day too long."

Pop's weathered face looked older than Cade had ever seen it. "You don't have to do this, son. Let me run the no-good out of town, tell him to move on."

Cade studied McGill's outline. The image of Owen Cantrell's widow was seared in his mind. Owen had been shot down in the prime of his life by this coldhearted outlaw. Twenty other men had lost their lives to this animal. "I can't do that."

"Then jest concentrate on what you're doin', son."

"Get out of here, Pop. This is my fight."

"It's my town."

Cade took a money clip out of his pocket and handed it to Pop. "If this doesn't turn out good, see that Red gets this. If I lose, McGill will come after her and the kids next. Tell her to buy a place out of state, somewhere far away, where she and the kids will be safe."

Pop waved the money aside. "Don't need that. I got a piece of land in Missouri so remote, mosquitoes cain't find it. I'll take care of your family if anything happens."

"Thanks, Pop."

"The only thanks I want is for you to come out of this alive." He put his hand on Cade's shoulder. "You keep a steady hand. You can take him. There ain't a better gun around than Cade Kolby's."

Cade smiled. "Tell my family I was thinking of them."

Pop nodded. "You need to tell 'em, not me. It's not over 'til it's over. Now, git out there and do what you gotta do." He limped across the street.

Dark clouds hovered overhead, turning daylight into dark. Thunder rolled as the storm moved in. Settling his hat lower, Cade stepped into the middle of Main Street, his mind cleared of all thoughts but one. McGill. His hand rested loosely at his side, his gaze focused on the man who stood at the other end of town.

Cade took his stance, one he'd taken more times than he cared to think about, but it felt awkward and unnatural today. Main Street was empty, except for a lone mutt who ambled along in front of the bank.

Dust swirled off the rooftops as he stared McGill down. Gusts of wind whipped at his clothing, and bits of debris stung his face. He blinked against the growing gale.

The bearded outlaw spit to one side. "Finally showed your cowardly face, huh, Kolby?"

Cade's hand hovered over his holster. "You must be getting old, McGill. What took you so long?"

McGill advanced, his sinister eyes glaring at Cade through the swirling dust. "You shoulda knowed better than to try to hide from a McGill. You're a dead man, Kolby."

"We all have to go one time or the other."

"And this is your day." McGill's fingers flexed loosely at his sides.

They each took a step closer, then two. Lightning crackled. Rain poured from the heavens.

Cade saw Pop out the corner of his eye, leaning against the side of the jailhouse, hand on his gun. Ahead of him, Cade recognized faces of various Winterborn citizens beginning to appear behind store columns and peeking around the corners of buildings. The barrel of a gun protruded from the partially open door of Walt's barbershop.

Cade took another step, then another. McGill's eyes narrowed. "Heard you took yourself a right purty wife. Too bad she's gonna be widowed again. Twice couldn't be much fun, but don't you worry none. Ol' Hart will see to the little woman's needs." He laughed. "Got me a hankerin' for those redheaded women. They got a lot of fire, if you know what I mean."

Pop's whispered words reached him. "Don't let him rile ya, son."

"Steady as it goes, boy," he heard Walt whisper.

Cade's eyes never left McGill's right hand. He took a deep breath, blinking against the rain starting to pepper down.

"Yep, heard wifey is real purty. 'Spect she'll be real lonely after yore dead." McGill's hand flew to his gun.

Cade dropped to one knee and fired. The Colt exploded with a deafening roar at the same time McGill's Buntline Special blasted, the gunfire overpowering a clap of thunder.

Hot lead grazed Cade's left arm. Blood seeped through his shirt, crimson against the blue, rain-soaked fabric. He fell to the ground.

"You filthy piece of dog meat!" yelled McGill. The Peacemaker had caught the desperado in the leg above his knee, dropping him. McGill sat up, gripping his thigh and moaning in agony as he got off another round. The slug seared a hole through Cade's hat, knocking it several feet in the air.

Taking slow and deliberate aim, Cade rose on one elbow and fired again, then fell back as a volley of bullets sent Hart McGill to his just reward. When Cade looked up, McGill lay in the dirt, staring sightlessly into the whistling wind. Rain pelted onto the road, splattering mud across the outlaw's face.

The men of Winterborn calmly blew the smoke from their gun barrels and shifted back into the shadows.

Rolling to his side, Cade yanked loose his bandanna and tied it around his bleeding arm.

Pop quickly hobbled over and shoved him back to the ground. "Oh, merciful heavens, Cade's dead!" he bellowed.

Cade rolled to his side to get up. "I'm not dead."

Pop planted a boot in the center of Cade's chest. "Oh, yes, you are. Stay!" he ordered.

Cade rolled onto his back and clamped his eyes shut, gritting his teeth against the fire in his left arm.

"Don't move a muscle," Pop repeated, and then he turned and hobbled over to where McGill lay sprawled. He counted the holes in the outlaw's chest and he whistled under his breath. "Nine. Shoulda been ten. Walt Mews can't hit the side of a barn." He hurried back to Cade. "You okay, son?"

"Okay. Just grazed. What's going on? Who told those men to get involved? This was my fight."

"Not necessarily. The town likes to protect its interests, and keeping you alive happens to be one of our main interests right now." Pop glanced around. "We gotta act fast."

Townspeople poured out of doors and alleyways. Lawrence, Roy, Walt, Ben, and Woodall passed Gracie, Margaret, and Lilith on the run. Frank Lovell hurried along beside Bess Harris. Doc came running with his black bag. He leaned down and put his ear to Cade's chest. "He's dead."

Motioning for the crowd to gather near, Pop bent low. "Now listen to me. We ain't got time for chitchat. No telling who's watching these goings-on. We got to unite and put on the act of our lives."

"Tell us what to do," Roy Baker whispered.

Lilith covered her face with a hanky.

Pop kept his voice low. "We don't want no other vengeful outlaws comin' around here, so here's what we're gonna do. We're gonna have a funeral the likes of which this town ain't never seen, and we're gonna have it this afternoon."

Cade gritted his teeth. "If you can pull this off, Pop, I'll never forget it."

Pop smiled. "You're dead. Hush up."

The crowd turned to stare at Cade, who still lay in the middle of the street.

Pop straightened and motioned for Roy and Ben to step forward. "We need two good strong men to carry the deceased to their restin' places."

"Carry McGill to his grave? I wouldn't waste the time or the effort," Ben declared.

Pop shot him a peeved look. "Listen to me, you knuckleheads. Hear what I'm sayin'. Pretend you got some learnin! Two men were killed in a gunfight here today. Two. Cade Kolby and Hart McGill. Get it?"

One by one, heads began to nod in the crowd.

"Kolby's dead," Walt said. "Bit the dust, a goner."

Cade groaned. "It won't work."

Pop glanced down the street. "Darned if it won't. Don't move a muscle. You're dead, boy. Dead as a doornail."

"How is this going to help anything?" Cade asked. "I can't come back to Winterborn."

"Kolby cain't come back, but now, his cousin in the Arizona Territory, who looks an awful lot like him, could ride in here any day and pay his respects, couldn't he?"

Blank faces confronted the sheriff.

"Couldn't he?" Pop prompted. "Think about it, people."

Lilith glanced at Cade. "You ain't got no cousin in the Arizona Territory."

Gracie punched her, and Lilith's expression turned peevish. "Well, he ain't. I'd know a thing like that. Senda never said a thing about a cousin—"

"Lilith, you're turning senile," Gracie patiently explained. "Don't you remember? Cade and…and…Tray…Williams, Senda Kolby's sister's boy, looked so much alike when they were young'uns, Senda said she and her sister could hardly tell them apart. Why, I'll bet Tray so strongly resembles Cade that if, say, Cade had been able to grow a beard and put on a few pounds before he died, why, it'd be hard for anyone to tell Cade and Tray apart. Don't you suppose?"

"Cade hasn't—oh." Lilith stopped short. "Oh." She grinned. "Well, yes, seems I do recall Senda saying how much those two babies favored each other. Goodness, someone needs to wire Tray immediately that his cousin Cade has been shot and killed in his line of work. Tray needs to come and see to his cousin's widow's needs."

"Why, Tray might have his own family," someone argued.

Gracie intervened. "He don't."

"It will never work," Cade predicted in low undertones.

Agreement went up. Everyone recalled cousin Tray. Walt winked at Cade. "Nice fellow. Not as wild as Cade, as I recollect."

Roy scratched his head. "Yes. More settled. Always told the wife that Cade's cousin Tray would be more likely to take a shine to family life than him. Tray would be a great comfort to Zoe and those children."

Lawrence grinned. "Why, no telling. Zoe could end up marrying Cade's cousin, and the two of them could live right here in Winterborn and raise Addy's kids. Tray might have a strong head for business, might even get the general store back on solid footing."

Sawyer spit. "For the life of me, I cain't remember that boy. Senda's nephew, you say?"

"Take our word, Sawyer. Someone notify the deceased's family right away." Ben grinned. "Who wants to help me get the bodies into the stable?"

Chapter Fifty-Four

When a rap sounded at the back door, Zoe felt faint. She willed her legs to move. Taking a deep breath, she opened the back door and saw Pop. The grim look on his face confirmed that her worst fear had been realized.

"No," she whispered.

"No," Pop repeated. "He's alive, Zoe."

Her knees buckled, and Pop reached out to catch her.

"Come on, girl, don't give out on me now." He hobbled with her to a chair and sat her down.

"Where's Cade?" She met Pop's gaze, tears running down her cheeks.

"Fit as a fiddle, with the exception of a little nick in his left arm. Doc will see to that after the funeral. Cade's about to get laid out. You up to attendin'?"

Zoe was so busy laughing through her tears that she was aware of only one thing. Cade was alive. Then she sobered. "What?"

Pop quickly explained the town's plan. Zoe's eyes widened in disbelief. And gratitude.

"Now," Pop continued, "I want you to leave this house with a long face and wearin' widow's weeds, you hear? No matter how relieved you are, if we're gonna keep your man around, you're gonna have to act like you've got the weight of the world on your shoulders."

Zoe threw her arms around Pop, enveloping him in an exuberant hug. "Thank you, Pop. Thank you!"

The children heard the commotion and came running out of the bedroom.

"Cade's alive," Zoe announced.

"Oh, boy!" Missy danced around the floor, latching onto Holly. "Oh, boy, oh, boy!"

Brody and Will beamed.

"Honest?" Brody asked.

"Honest," Pop said. "But we're all gonna have to playact for a little while." He explained what happened, described the hastily devised plan, and outlined the roles they had to assume to pull it off. "Can I trust you kids to act real sad?"

"I can act real sad," Brody said.

"Me too." Will nodded.

"I can cwy anytime you want," Missy offered. "Weal, weeeal loud."

Pop gathered the family to him and smiled as he patted Zoe, who was still sniffling, on the back. "Well now, ain't this nice. Family helpin' family." He nodded. "Now that's how it should be."

"You in here, Abraham?" A breathless Pop entered the dimly lit livery a few minutes later. Maddy whinnied in her stall.

"I's here, Sheriff."

"Did you do what I told ya?"

"Yes'sa. I's got the buryin' box ready."

"We gotta work quick. You think a body will fit in there?"

"Don'cha worry. That box big enough to hold five men. You was right, Sheriff. Laticia's clothes box done shore come in handy."

"Fill it with rocks and nail the lid shut real tight, Abraham. Then take a rock and scratch 'Cade Kolby' 'cross the top."

"Yes'sa." Abraham grinned. "Miz Laticia be real proud ta know I's usin' my learnin' ta write. Might make up for her having them red spots. Oh, lordy, Sheriff. The wrath o' the devil hisself descended on the house when she come down wid da fever. Blamin' that 'no-good Cade Kolby.'" Abraham chuckled and hammered the last nail into the makeshift coffin. "Yes'sa, that 'no good Cade Kolby.' May he rest in peace."

Pop put his hat on. "We'll bury McGill in a whiskey barrel. He ought ta like that. And Abraham? This is between me and you and the town. As far as anyone knows, Cade Kolby and Hart McGill killed each other in a shoot-out."

"Yes'sa. This ol' black man don't know nuthin' 'bout nuthin'."

Pop adjusted his crutches under his arm. "Things should settle down around here now for a spell. I got a wire this mornin' from the sheriff of Wizard County. Seems the Nelson gang is behind bars. They won't be causing no more trouble and McGill's dead." Pop took a deep breath. "All in all, I'd say it's been a right good day."

Chapter Fifty-Five

The rain cleared by late afternoon. Reverend Munson stood before an open grave. "It is, indeed, a sad occasion that brings us together."

Zoe wept beneath an umbrella, holding the kids close beside her as she surreptitiously searched the crowd. Where was Cade? She wouldn't be surprised to see him standing nearby, witnessing his own funeral. Her body convulsed with happiness and she swallowed, trying to maintain a somber demeanor. When she saw him, she was going to kill him herself, with love.

She lifted her eyes and stared straight ahead. The whole town was present, weeping, crying, carrying on. Her gaze suddenly focused on a tall figure standing near the back, dressed in a black poncho, hat pulled low over his face.

The man crossed his eyes and stuck out his tongue at her.

Her mouth dropped open, and she quickly looked away. Cade! He was here. The man who'd never arrived in time for a funeral in his whole life!

The makeshift coffin stood beside the open grave as the reverend read from the Bible, intoning, "Ashes to ashes, dust to dust."

Gracie and Lilith fell upon each other's shoulders, sobbing.

"Gracie, did you eat onions for dinner?" Lilith hissed.

"Quiet down, Lilith. I wasn't sure I could cry on cue, so I got an onion hidden in my hanky." Gracie raised her hankerchief to her face until fresh tears welled.

"I'd do anything for Zoe, even attend a funeral service for a man who isn't dead, but I can cry on my own, thank you very much, and I have no intention of smelling like a stew pot!"

Reverend Munson closed his Bible and Missy stepped forward, holding Bud's jar close to the wooden box. "Bud wants to say good-bye, Uncle Cade." She laid her baby face against the coffin. "Bet you wish Bud could stay with you, huh, Uncle Cade?" She flashed a missing tooth grin.

Several hours later, a knock sounded at Zoe's back door. She raced to answer it and threw herself into Cade's arms. "I was so worried about you."

"Shoot. I'm fine. Exceptionally fine for a dead man." He shrugged out of the poncho and kicked the door shut with his boot, and then he kissed her long and hard and with the assurance that nothing would separate them again.

"Where have you been?"

"Lying low on the outskirts of town. I sneaked in the back way so I wouldn't be seen."

"Oh, Cade, do you think what the town is trying to do will work?"

He pulled back just enough to look at her. "At first I didn't, but I'm willing to try anything, Red, in order for us to be together. I'll have to stay out of sight for a few weeks. Then my so-called cousin will arrive from the Arizona Territory to help my grieving widow and my kids. He'll fall in love with you, a given, and we should be able to live a normal life."

She had to laugh at the absurdity. "Are you willing to give up so much for me and the children, even to the point of becoming someone else?"

His features sobered. "I'd give up anything for you and the kids, even though it won't be easy. It's not easy now, faking my own death."

"Tell me what you'd give up for me?"

"I'd give up my life for you. My reputation. Bounty-hunting, for sure. My identity. Good grief, woman, you've brought me to my knees."

"Repeat the part about bringing you to your knees. That idea makes me very happy."

His eyes shone with such love, the sight stole her breath away. "You win. Is that what you want to hear?"

"It was never a game between us. But yes, that's what I wanted to hear."

"I thought so." He kissed her again. And again. "I suppose you also want a decent proposal?"

"That would be nice."

His eyes softened. "You know I've never stopped loving you."

"I prayed that you didn't. Lord forgive me, even when I was married to Jim. He was such a good man, and I loved him for that goodness, but it was always you in my heart."

He drew her closer. "Will you marry me?"

"Who's speaking?"

"Shoot." He thought for a minute. "Tray somebody."

She cocked her head with a warning look. "I need you to be a little more specific."

"Okay. Tray Williams. Picture me twenty pounds heavier, with a beard."

Her fingers lightly brushed his cheeks. "I think you would look very handsome in a beard."

"You didn't the day I rode in."

She grinned. "You weren't Tray Williams the day you rode in."

He caught her hand, stilling it. Looking deep into her eyes, he whispered, "Red, will you marry me and make me the happiest man on earth?"

Touching her mouth lightly to his, she luxuriated in the warmth of his love. "Of course I'll marry you. What took you so long to ask?"

"Reverend Munson doesn't need to be here to make it official first, does he?"

"I don't think so. We've taken vows once, whatever your name is."

Gazing into her eyes, he whispered, "I, Tray Williams, take you, Zoe Kolby, to be my lawfully wedded wife. To have and to hold, in my arms and in my heart for as long as I live. I promise to love you more each day, and I promise never to leave you, or God, again."

Zoe laughed and wiped tears with her sleeve. "I, Zoe Kolby, take you, Tray Williams, to be my lawfully wedded husband. I promise to let you hold me in your arms and in your heart from this day forward, 'til the day I die."

He smiled. "There's one more thing."

She knew what she'd left out, what she hadn't told him, what was in her heart.

"If you don't say the words, I'll make you."

She grinned. "How? By kissing me to death?"

His hold tightened. "If that's what it takes."

The passion in his gaze made her weak in the knees. "All right. My love will be only for you and our children."

"Not quite there, but closer." He grinned. "I don't want Perry Drake hanging around, trying to…"

"Pay my debts?" She eyed him knowingly. "You paid off that note, didn't you?"

"Me? Why would you think that?"

"Wipe that grin off your face. I put two and two together last night. If Perry was inclined to do such a thing, he would have told me up front. You, on the other hand, are sneaky, conniving, underhanded—"

He touched her lips with his finger. "Say it."

"I said it just before you left to face McGill."

"I want to hear it again." His eyes darkened. "Now that I'm not so rushed."

"All right. All right! I love you. I've always loved you, and I always—"

His kiss stopped her, and she was lost in a sea of delight. Nothing had ever felt more right, more welcome. For the first time, she found security in his embrace.

Gently, sweetly he ended the kiss. Her head swam with a million things she wanted to say, questions she wanted to ask, prayers, deep grateful prayers she wanted to say, but for the time being, resting in his love was enough.

Then he put an arm beneath her knees and picked her up like the bride she was.

"Cade! Your wound—"

"Forget the wound. The pain is worth holding you in my arms."

He turned toward the bedroom, but she stopped him, saying, "Wait. First we need to wake the children and let them see you."

"They're sound asleep. We'll tell them in the morning. What's our name again?"

"Williams," she said, resting her head on his chest.

"Uncle Cade!" Missy suddenly latched onto Cade's thigh. "You'we home!"

He lowered Zoe's feet to the floor, but he caught her arm and pulled her close as though she might get away.

Brody shoved his way in front of Will. "I cried real hard at your funeral, Uncle Cade. I pinched my arm so I could make real tears."

"He pinched my arm too," Will said, sulking. "Made me cry out loud. Then Holly thumped me on the head."

"You were making a scene," Holly said primly.

Cade smiled and drew the family into his embrace. "You all did well. Even I was convinced I was in that big box." He bent and kissed each one. "You kids listen to me. We're family now, and we always will be, but Cade Kolby is dead and buried. I'm Tray Williams, and when I come back in a few weeks, we'll all get married again. We'll be the Williams family."

Missy ran from the room and returned in seconds, thrusting Bud's jar in Cade's face. "Bud, this is Tway. He looks like Uncle Cade, but his name is Tway Williams. He's going to be youw daddy."

Zoe laughed out loud.

"Tway Williams, tell Bud you love him."

Cade stared into the jar. Beady eyes stared back. He cleared his throat and shifted, turning to Zoe for help. She nodded his compliance. Taking a deep breath, he muttered, "I...I love you, Bud."

Zoe said, "I think it's time everyone kissed Tray good night. He's had a very trying day."

After smothering Cade with enthusiastic hugs and kisses, the children scampered to their beds. Cade pulled Zoe into the store, shut the connecting door, and then took her in his arms. In the dark quiet he said, "I can't believe I just told a tarantula that I loved him."

"I thought it was very touching. Cade would have never been so sentimental, but Tray...I think I'm really going to like that man."

His mouth found hers, gentle but possessive. The future lay before them, uncertain, exciting, with the promise of God, family, and love. As his lips wandered to nuzzle her neck, Zoe tilted her head back, gazed upward, and whispered, "Thank you, Addy."

It could have been her imagination, but she could have sworn she heard Addy say, "You're welcome. What are friends for?"

About the Author

Lori Copeland is the author of more than 90 titles, both historical and contemporary fiction. With more than 3 million copies of her books in print, she has developed a loyal following among her rapidly growing fans in the inspirational market. She has been honored with the Romantic Times Reviewer's Choice Award, The Holt Medallion, and Walden Books' Best Seller Award. In 2000, Lori was inducted into the Missouri Writers Hall of Fame.

Lori lives in the beautiful Ozarks with her husband, Lance, their three children, and five grandchildren.

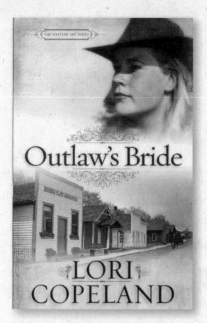

Outlaw's Bride

LORI COPELAND

What are you going to do, McAllister? Put your life on hold forever and let a woman like Ragan slip through your fingers so you can pursue scum like Bledso?

Johnny knew Bledso wasn't worth a hair on Ragan's head. Why couldn't he let it go and just get on with his life?

Convicted of a bank robbery he didn't commit, drifter Johnny McAllister is sentenced to do time in a rehabilitation program in the home of Judge Proctor McMann, a gentle, wise soul who believes in second chances.

Johnny's aim is to be a model prisoner. He hopes to be released early to return to his life's mission: to find and kill Dirk Bledso, the man who wiped out his family 16 years before. Johnny has planned for everything...except his encounter with Ragan Ramsey, the judge's beautiful and kind housekeeper, and his involvement with the generous folks of Barren Flats.

Can this would-be outlaw let go of his hate and anger and embrace something better— something he can't yet see?

A tender romance that shows how even the hard law of the West doesn't stand a chance when God's mercy, warm friendship, and true love come to reside in a lonely man's heart.

To learn more about books by Lori Copeland
or to read sample chapters, log on to our website:

www.harvesthousepublishers.com

HARVEST HOUSE PUBLISHERS

EUGENE, OREGON